# Dreams of a Random Capitalist

"I dreamed of a kindly capitalism, nurturing everyone: the world showed me that kindly capitalism only exists in dreams."
- RC

I0621607

## Book Summary

A Military Drone kills a Billionaire Humanitarian: an American Journalist investigating the accident discovers it was an assassination.

Following the money and interviewing several people, the Journalist uncovers the true story of the murder victim as a complex person with an intriguing past who was generous, kind, and a humane capitalist.

An impossible story, written by a failed journalist, interested in solving a mystery: who killed R.C.?

# Dreams of a Random Capitalist
## Second Edition

Print Book ~ ISBN-13: 978-0-692-24112-7
Print Book ~ ISBN-10:   0692241124
eBook ~ ISBN-13:   978-0-692-24113-4
eBook ~ ISBN-10:   0692241132

Published by Y57N^Media LLC
United States of America
June 2014

# Legal Disclaimers

This book was written with the best intentions of creating a peaceful and benevolent work of fiction, written for the purpose of creating lawful entertainment. Everything in it is entirely fictional, including but not limited to; the characters, names, places, events, transactions, descriptions, explanations, thoughts, feelings, ideas, and philosophical perspectives of the characters. Nothing contained in this book should be interpreted as having any connection to the real-world or to real persons or to real events. This work of fiction is not intended to be, and it should not be interpreted as, any form of guidance, suggestions or advice to anyone on any subject matter whatsoever. It should not be interpreted as an allegorical message of any kind, and it is not meant to be a religious, political, legal or social movement document. It is neither a call to action of any kind, nor is it a political critique of anyone alive or deceased. It is neither an autobiography nor is it a biography. Its contents have no real-world connection to the industries, interests or activities of: governments, non-governmental organizations, economics, marketing, journalism, military contracting, finance, law, accounting, taxation, investment, healthcare, aviation, manufacturing, bio-technology, software, science, technology, morality, ethics, philosophy, Religion, politics, education, literature, motion pictures, music, or the arts. The author does not have any access to, or possession of, any governmental or any military information of any kind: the Military equipment capabilities mentioned in this book are described solely on the basis of the author's fictional imagination.

# Trademark Notice

Trademarks owned by Y57N^Media LLC, are listed below as book-titles-in-the-series: **Dreams of a Random Capitalist** ™

Dreams of a Random Capitalist ™ - *Prengalthibarr Mokxshama Vienteubbii*
Dreams of a Random Capitalist ™ - *Quattrini Extraho Hilarito*
Dreams of a Random Capitalist ™ - *The Sacred Spreadsheet*
Dreams of a Random Capitalist ™ - *Social Semiconductor*
Dreams of a Random Capitalist ™ - *The Clan of Taking*

## Honorable Mention of other intellectual property

Any other products, services, business companies, musical songs, public persons, and/or any other intellectual properties honorably mentioned in this book, are the exclusive intellectual property of their respective owners. A list of honorable mention of intellectual properties that are mentioned in this work of fiction is provided at the end of this book.

# Dedication

This book is dedicated to loved ones near and far; here and gone; past, present and future...

# Table of Contents

# Introduction

## Falling to Earth:
*A billion dollar Drone kills a billionaire humanitarian-accident or assassination?*

*"An impossible story, written by a failed journalist, and a very Merry Christmas to you"* was his final voicemail message for me. His story and message were presents too heavy for me to shoulder: what was I supposed to do with all of it? Yes ... Merry Christmas.

Delivering presents to one of his families in Canada, he saw his children now as grown adults enjoying their own lives: everyone was happy, safe and financially secure. All things seemed to be going well for them. A warm sense of loving pride filled his heart and soul. Smiling broadly to his children and grand-children and waving goodbye just before sunset, it was time to get home to Seattle and prepare for a business meeting the next day. Driving to his private airport, he looked hopefully to the future: in a few days from now he could meet his new wife in Seattle.

At his private Canadian airport, his jet was ready and waiting for him. Although born a poor orphan, his hard work had made him now a wealthy man, allowing him to travel at supersonic speeds in his own favorite customized YF-35 jet. A high-speed takeoff made him smile from the rush of adrenaline. Feeling exuberant, he sped the jet to its maximum, causing the engine to light an afterburner effect of orange flames. A high speed take off with afterburners flaring was a signal to his five escort chase jets, that he was hurrying to get airborne before the sunset light faded; before the night could steal away his beloved scenery during a nineteen-minute flight home.

The Selkirk Mountains below him were covered in snow, glowing pinkish-orange from the sunset light. To get a bird's eye view of the mountains he turned his jet upside down and decreased speed. He looked down at the beautiful snowy mountains and the sunset light fading over the horizon, certain that this flight would be one of his few and precious solitary moments. He looked back behind him: jet exhaust left a faintly pinkish-white crystalline condensation trail spiraling back towards a family he loved.

The smiling pilot maneuvered his jet into a circular holding pattern easily visible to radar before crossing South over the U.S. Border. He radioed to Canadian and American Air Traffic Control Authorities requesting permission to enter U.S. Airspace and land in Seattle. Patiently waiting for a few seconds before a radio reply, he felt a bit melancholy: getting back to business was sometimes a sad event for him; the working parts of life were too busy, too full of transactions and too many demands upon him. Looking out the fragile glass canopy of his jet, he switched on his favorite music, listening to the song "Tom Sawyer" by the band Rush. As the music softened his melancholy feelings, he reflected that it felt like a timeless moment: all of the silent sunset orange sky and faintly flickering stars seemed to be his. He felt the sensation of floating effortlessly in air several miles above the ground like a mythical angel.

Seventeen miles away from him an airborne U.S. Government Drone flew its first test mission near the U.S. border. Rushed into production at the last moment, its outer skin was colored a mottled pastel gray like ashen fireplace-soot. Its integrated software was 77% complete, yet it was approved by a committee to be installed anyway since it was considered acceptable for a test flight. Several hi-technology systems within the Drone were also nearly finished but not quite, too many parts and electronic systems were less than fully baked before it was served up for testing. This flight was supposed be a test of its integrated systems including automated guidance, telematics and virtual electronics for targeting multiple hostile threats. As the Drone sliced through the cold air at a speed of over Mach 2.7 the Drone's human pilot sat comfortably still in a temperature controlled bunker in Nevada. For good luck the remote Drone pilot had a superstitious custom of playing his favorite song, "Spacegrass" the original demo-version by the band Clutch, into his head-phones during liftoff of the Drone. As the song finished, he switched off his music and made the last few human flight control inputs to guide the Drone to the south east edge of the airspace dedicated exclusively to its test flight pattern. Once the Drone was positioned at its cruising speed flying supersonic at Mach 3.2 and flying steady at an altitude of 63,000 feet, its remote human pilot activated the Drone's electronically controlled autopilot. Within thirty-eight seconds of being on autopilot, the not so fully-baked Drone detected and locked onto an atypical radar contact North of the Canadian Border heading inbound toward the United States.

Back in Nevada the atypical radar blip also appeared on the remote human pilot's video monitoring screen mirroring exactly what the Drone saw with its electronic eyes. The remote Drone pilot assumed the atypical radar blip was part of the testing exercise, merely an electronic ghost-blip; something that the engineering test crew had projected into thin air by radio waves in order to challenge the Drone's automated detection systems. "I wish they would realize this test would go perfect if I could be running the show my way and controlling the Drone ... this automated stuff and testing on auto-pilot just puts me to sleep: now is an awesomely righteous time for a coffee break." From the Drone's perspective the new radar contact was a new task to evaluate as friend or foe. The blip was initially categorized as a potential problem: it was not traceable to a known airport in Canada. It was heading directly for the United States. The Drone was pre-programmed with defensive attack protocols, including counter-offensive first-strike and pre-emptive strike rules-of-engagement attack routines, all requiring that every flight pattern of any aircraft determined to have hostile intent should be treated immediately as a potential hostile target. The Drone followed its next programmed step in the hostile threat response by efficiently churning through each line of software code, concluding that to defend the boundaries of the test flight area it must immediately switch from a test flight autopilot subroutine into real-world mission ready kill-or-be-killed mode. Of the several weapons already onboard the Drone, it chose a set of two missiles. That selection was the result of a software optimized algorithm designed for maximum destruction of targets.

From its high altitude high speed course, the Drone slowed its speed, turned abruptly North toward Canada and dropped its nose down toward the target jet on a path to intercept the real-world jet represented by the mysterious radar blip. The Drone's human controller was away from his video control console so the alarms and Drone movements were not seen by human eyes. The Drone dutifully signaled to its home base that it was now in electronic kill-mode. The next programmed steps were that if the remote human pilot did not intervene and take over manual control within ten seconds of that notification of kill-mode, then the Drone's target acquisition software would pursue at high speed an attack in order to fulfill its mission. No human intervention occurred within ten seconds, so at eleven seconds, the Drone accelerated toward the target. At twelve seconds it received and recorded in its onboard computerized flight database a radio signal that successfully breached and passed through its several firewalls of 'scrambled-scatter-down-encryption' protection, instructing the Drone to activate its onboard missiles to be ready in 'weapons hot' status. The Drone's entire systems worked together in parallel with the Drone's radar and infrared sensory equipment, feeding real-time data to the weapons targeting computers. A kill-shot algorithm specifically instructed the Drone, with devilish precision, to feed the target co-ordinates to the missile weapons and start a rapid launch sequence while it one last time simultaneously searched for a match of all known flight plans of peaceful aircraft on file electronically with the Aerospace Defense Command Authorities of both countries. If, on this last step of target verification, the Drone found a match between the suspicious target radar blip and any flight plans on file with Air Traffic Control, then it would abort the missile attack. After comparing all available flight plans to the unpredictable jet's electronic blip and flight movements the Drone could not find a match. The target blip was unverified and therefore classified as an imminent hostile threat. The collective intelligence of the Drone's software program finished evaluating the target jet within fifty-seven milliseconds. Three seconds after concluding that a threat was inbound to the U.S., the Drone locked its radar guided missiles onto the immediate hostile threat. With no apparent human intervention (obviously having no freewill itself) the Drone faithfully executed its war-fighting programming by launching a missile at the target jet.

The missile's speed did not allow time enough for the targeted pilot to eject. The Drone's infrared and video cameras recorded high-resolution images of the launched missile's impact on the civilian jet's tail section. The video showed one-hundred frames per second of high definition color imagery of the blinding flash from the explosion followed by two seconds of brilliantly colored orange flames. Fragments of the civilian jet showered down from the starry skies onto the frozen snowy ground, pulverizing into smaller fragments upon impact. Perhaps it sounded like a million pieces of shattered shards of glass falling onto a frozen metal floor.

The Drone turned south, accelerated up to high altitude and high speed and sent an immediate radio confirmation signal to its remote human controller that it had efficiently executed a kill-shot: target vaporized and completely gone. Without emotion, the war machines continued with electro-mechanical indifference to what had transpired, and within the next millisecond, the radio signal that had taken over the Drone stopped transmitting, placing the Drone into re-set and re-boot mode; the Drone then turned itself back onto electronic auto-pilot, following again its originally programmed autopilot flight path toward home base in Nevada. Picking up where it left off, the Drone was now flying along its pre-set course, as if nothing had happened.

Nineteen seconds after the explosion and eight hundred miles away, the Drone's remote controller human pilot returned to his computer monitor after an unauthorized break for coffee. The computer monitors were signaling several alarms, which triggered a base-wide alarm: "Oh no! No way could that have happened!" The Drone's remote human pilot picked up a red emergency phone connected to the Drone project headquarters phone and spoke solemnly, with a trembling vocal tone, "Sir we have a major problem here." One minute after that call, the White House Situation Room was notified, and the President's Press Secretary and the Chief of the Department of Defense appeared together on CNN within the hour, trying to keep consistently phrased between the two of them, their official story drafted hastily with a purpose to reassure the news media and the civilian population that the Drone strike was a training mission and that no one in the U.S. or Canada should be worried about any weapon systems being out of control. While that press conference was happening, the U.S. President ordered a full investigation into the accident, requesting that the Department of Homeland Security be involved to assess whether terrorism may have been a factor.

The pilot from the blown up jet lay dead in pieces on the ground: he left behind a few children, one widow, six ex-wives, some relatives and several people who had business dealings with him.

I would like to think that there were Deities of some kind watching over those events and that some mercy was granted to the dead civilian pilot. Perhaps the missile explosion finished him off instantly so that he did not suffer any pain before dying. The official certificate of death for the pilot listed time of death as eleven minutes after sunset on Christmas Day.

All seven of the former wives of the dead pilot banded together and filed a class action lawsuit of wrongful death against the U.S. Government, the U.S. Air Force, the U.S. Department of Defense and the Drone's Engineering Contractors and Software Vendors. They seek 46

Billion U.S. Dollars in combined punitive and compensatory damages. The case is still making its way through the U.S. Courts.

I knew the dead pilot. He was an American. The story of his life is a challenging one for me to tell. The story of his death is a nightmare. His world was full of ethical business dealings, unorthodox creativity in the development of technology: yet most of his life was full of humane generosity, enjoyment of the great outdoors, a cherished appreciation of warm golden sunlight, aesthetic admiration of both beautiful women and the exquisite beauty of nature, frequent hikes to any available alpine paradise, loving care of family and genuine concern for friends. The media in both America and Canada, had over the years, publicly mocked him by calling him the "Renegade Random Capitalist." Most people I talked to, after his death, called him "RC" instead of saying the condescending euphemism 'Random Capitalist.' Hardly anyone admitted to me that they knew of his brain tumor, or the timeline of it being diagnosed eleven years before his death. RC's brain tumor had, for several years, provided a challenge to him and provoked unanticipated new thought processes that allowed him to function in the real-world quite nimbly: he daily navigated a complex multi-step approach to business transactions that most of his family and friends say was a skill he was much better at than anyone else on Earth. Those he made economically independent loved RC. People and organizations that opposed capitalism hated RC. He was criticized unfairly for doing business under the guiding principles and punctilio of "emotionally sensitive economics" or "the benevolent, cooperative and humane form of capitalism." As a journalist, my interpretation of his approach to business, was that he really meant it when he placed property rights and material goods as things that should never be pursued at the cost of, or as more important than, humans and human rights. He helped many people live a better and more meaningful life.

Where have my manners gone? I should introduce myself. I am an award winning independent investigative journalist who interviewed that dead pilot a year before his death. Pursuing the truth behind his story, figuring out the interesting points of his life and more importantly the causes of his death, is making me lose my mind. This story is the toughest thing I have dealt with in my life: it is even tougher than the experience of being downsized and made redundant, when my newspaper employer did away with the journalist department five years ago. That unemployment has damaged my ego and when combined with the negatively lonely feeling like I have no place in the economy ... and combined with the near impossibility of additionally trying to survive the tough economy ... all of that seems now nothing at all, when compared to my internal struggle over this story. There is much of his story I do know and that I can share with you. I knew RC better than some of his acquaintances.

He was a public figure, controversial for the contradictory nature of his benevolence and also his extremely successful form of profitable capitalism that was more humanistic than others who favored a more competitive or harshly profit driven style of business activity. The public reaction to RC's accidental death was unsurprising to me. RC had forewarned me about the controversy he provoked everywhere he went, in our interviews before he died. People said things and maintained their rhetoric consistently towards him both before and after his death. Environmentalists from both countries were furious at the military: "they could have killed the only herd of Endangered Woodland Caribou in the lower 48 United States." The military claimed national security reasons for not disclosing any information. There were a few eyewitnesses. The local village mayor had a terse comment about the need to get the military of all countries to immediately quit flying risky equipment over populated areas. The local police were silent: "we have no official comment." The tourism business associations in the area met to try and figure out how to advertise the public relations exploitation opportunity and gain the notoriety of the situation by extolling tourism related benefits of the area without being moribund regarding the accident. Stories from the Canadian and American newspapers near the border cited interviews with eyewitnesses. Most stories I read were brief, speculative and falsely dramatic. Lazy journalists in both countries often imitate each other's work, directly stealing written content, in order to meet their deadlines. If you take the time to read all the relevant stories, as I already have, the most regurgitated snippet of news about the incident rehashed how a U.S. Citizen with a murky businessman's past died under the color of unusual circumstances. For me, the most disquietingly offensive newspaper line is "American Blood spilled when a tourist flying his jet above the snowy ground of British Columbia Canada was hit by a missile launched from a rogue U.S. air surveillance Drone." News media, of which I supposedly was still a part of at that time, collectively characterized his death as an accident. Repulsive to me as ever was the composition style of the story: any student in a fifth grade writing class could have written more interesting news articles! Other residents of the area, who knew RC, were disgusted that several organizations and people riding the wave of buzzing news didn't seem to worry about self-censoring their news lines out of respect for the dead guy's family. Knowing RC's view of life and what mattered to him personally, he would have been upset that no one seemed to write about how the family might have felt about reading the whole thing in the newspapers. The only thing that bugged most everyone else who was a member of the media was that while alive, RC was too aloof and mystically allegorical in the content of his communications with the news media. What bugged RC about the press was that they really didn't get what he was trying to do and they did not understand that he was trying to be a good man in what from his perspective was a viciously greedy modern world.

RC had served his country. Way back in the day when the Persian Gulf War was in full swing, RC's official cover story for the work he did was dutifully and expertly performing the inane job of flying large amounts of cash around to military bases on payday, delivering huge sums of money to paymasters. That was his cover official job of record; however no one seems to know what he really did for the U.S. Government. Speculation among colleagues included computer hacking within the shadowy secret world of electronic-intelligence operations. However the official record shows that during that time, his small cargo jet, which he flew alone, suffered engine failure from fuel that was contaminated with water. Miraculously he was able somehow to bail out of the plane with the duffle bags of money strapped over his elbows. His parachute opened barely in time, he hit the rocky ground hard, breaking his left ankle. The jet crashed over a mile away from him and caught fire. Both the jet and his portable radio were destroyed before he could call a mayday request for help. Fighter pilots nearby saw the crashed jet in flames on the ground and radioed it in as a crash report. Because his jet flew off course into enemy territory over the Zagros Mountains and because of the huge fireball seen by pilots flying over the Persian Gulf, RC was reported as crashed and presumed killed-in-action. The military leadership had given up on him too quickly. After he gained consciousness from the hard parachute landing, he started navigating by using an old magnetic compass to make his way out, all on his own, lugging the cash to fulfill his job duties. Within a day he made it to a small creek, following it downstream until it turned into a river. He traveled at night and forced himself to press on without sleep until he eventually got out alive, back to civilization, with the cash. When he finally encountered friendly forces near the Gulf waters' shoreline, RC borrowed a radio and reported into his contractor's commanding officer. When they sent a rescue chopper no one believed it was really RC until he hobbled on base with his broken ankle, yet he returned with all of the cash. After the war, he spent the next decade fighting in Court to get his legal status cleaned up to expunge the official record of mistaken information. His Lawyers were exasperated with the military system. They continually proved that he was not "killed-in-action," and further that he was not a super spooky spy working for any branch of the government. RC quickly grew so disgusted with the military bureaucracy and their blind and mindless conformity to higher authority that he turned immediately to becoming a private businessman, sometimes over the years trying mercifully to deal positively with new governmental leadership by risking to contract with the government for technology development, but often he quit out of disgust and disillusionment since the same military leadership remained in power over the contracting portion of secret operations.

That accidental crash was a beginning point to an active life and it also was the biggest gap of missing information for me in trying to connect the dots of his life by using only partial information. My research conclusions seem incomplete: the gaps are the parts that are clouded, murky, silent and unfathomable. I tried to follow the trajectory of his life: that painstakingly detailed effort has apparently gotten me nowhere.

In the present day when I read again the newspaper stories of his death I still feel stunned. How he died seemed shockingly cruel and brutal: it was altogether accidental and therefore an inappropriate end to a fruitful and benevolent humanist's life. While alive, why had he survived already through so many near misses with death only to be killed in that manner? I thought of calculating the odds of RC being accidentally killed. For some reason I went back to my interview notes and searched for his most significant experience of cheating death. Reading through several different newspapers' obituaries of RC, I learned some facts and several rumors that RC never mentioned during our interviews before his death.

Personally, I remember RC as borderline enigmatic and definitely contradictory: he was the most unusual person I have ever met. To say that there were a few unresolved contradictions about the facts of his life was a colossal understatement and misunderstanding of the complexity of everything about him. Those who knew him as an acquaintance did not know his country of origin. All knew that he was an orphan and although RC shared that he knew he was of mostly Caucasian ethnicity, he wanted to

**14**

find out more about his heritage since he also did appear to be Eurasian in his facial features. Graduating from an orphanage, RC was raised by adoptive Asian parents in Canada. People I interviewed described his parents as a generous and humble couple who spent most of their life helping people settling into society after being held in internment camps during World War II. They moved to Seattle and RC grew up mostly in America. RC's linguistic skills were quite accomplished, language to him seemed sacred, he enunciated with great care and with perfect clarity, fluent speech among seven different languages. His IQ was high. I always got the sense he was far ahead of me each moment during our interviews, thinking way ahead of whatever I was saying as we visited in the coffee shop. However after our first tense interview, he grew more kindly and patient enough to slow down the pace of our spoken ideas and opinions with enough pace-setting, to let me catch up to his points and conclusions. His sense of humor and wit and what things in the world actually made him laugh, can only be described as being a predominantly British sense of humor, with a sharpness of irreverence. Rarely though, from time to time, he was also a contrary fellow, especially acerbic in the presence of people who were pretentious, vain, arrogant, or indifferent to humane considerations.

The only journalistic effort of my distinguished career that has seemingly defeated me was getting to the true meaning of RC's life and death and his accomplishments along the way. The failure is a fact of my career that has really perturbed me. I have not been able to answer the questions of RC's motivations: why would he expend super-human efforts to make vast amounts of money, then consistently be so generous and give it away? Was it secular humanism motivated by guilt from someone who lost their Religion? Was it benevolence from an atheist for the good of social evolution? Did RC have his own brand of a Pascal's wager, fearing some unknown Deity that would judge him upon his death based upon generosity? All stories I have worked on thus far in my journalist's life have been solvable, until this one. I viewed what he left behind as a web of economic and social complexity that is too far beyond me to fully understand. I don't like that situation. If RC were still alive to read any of this, his response would most likely be laughter as a reaction to my naïveté, followed by an off-the-cuff remark along the lines of: "the Goddess of Chaos and Entropy disrespects all egos, ambitions and emotions: but today, she is a goddess that is massively focused on disrespecting especially your molecules. You should strongly consider keeping your day job: that is likely the only way you will ever be able to feed yourself on real bread and water. Realistically, I do not expect you will make <u>any</u> money from your writing."

After his death, during my many nightmares, I am interviewing RC's ghost. I am constantly interrupted by his ghost laughing at me as if I am a naïve idiot. From such a nightmare, I wake up highly upset, wishing and wondering if it is more realistic that RC had engineered an elaborately faked death for some dark purpose of his own design. To force myself forward into the real-world far away from the dream-world I question myself and push my mind to find the answers to why RC died. All of that questioning leads nowhere. I am going in circles, with no resolution and no way to get off of that merry-go-around. I cannot fathom what the goal of such a faked death and such an elaborate deception would be. RC seemed to me to be the one in seven-billion type of person who could anticipate many things in advance of events that would happen in the real-world. Knowing what most likely would be ahead of him in life, he would have several escape plans ready to go to deal with and survive any eventuality. But no one who is real can live through that type of incident. A mid-air exploding missile took him out. The confirmed facts are that he is dead: that is reality. I have to accept it.

He is dead and long gone and so many people are still grieving. What a loss. I can almost hear his voice saying something to me philosophically and ethereal like: "The free market economy failed humanity long before I died in that jet crash, yet I feel like I failed humanity because I didn't live longer ... I was trying to help ... unfortunately I ran out of time." Memories of him haunt me perpetually.

Realizing that I knew RC only briefly, I interviewed his family and friends in order to capture their stories too: the combined information is a story that is also a collective memory of his humanity, identifying it as so rare in the modern world that it is well worth recording for all to read. Knowing his vast financial resources, sensitive humanity and mysteriously creative and prolifically productive intellect, there are times when I wish there was enough evidence to doubt whether the man is truly dead. What I mean is: imagine the unlikely odds. A super-secret surveillance Drone goes haywire, shooting missiles into a private jet that was peacefully flying inbound to the U.S.A. from Canada resulting in the innocent civilian pilot being killed. That isn't a good spy novel story line: it is not a plausible story ... Drones are designed to never make mistakes. Automated Drone technology is supposed to be used on enemies, not friends, and not to kill a dreamer... *right?* Why use a drone?  Isn't that *overkilling a dreamer?*

Please excuse me while I get another cup of coffee: after that I will share the stories I have researched about him based on my interviews with RC before his death and my interviews of his family and friends after the funeral.  I have a few flashbacks to share first.  It will lay the backdrop and the beginning to what I knew of him.

## Chapter 1

## Public Funeral Speeches and Private Interviews:
*Worshipful praise fueled by anguished grief...*

Driving to attend RC's funeral, while stopping for a few minutes at every intersection stop-light in downtown Seattle, I reminisced about my interviews with RC before his death.  It is more accurate to confess that I experienced involuntary flashbacks.

My first flashback carried me to the time over five years ago when I first met RC in a Seattle area coffee shop.  It was a completely unplanned and random encounter.  I had just finished ordering my favorite drink: a special blend latte' containing syrup flavors of Chai Tea, Hazelnut and Mint, with an underlying base of four shots of espresso, ultimately topped with a slathering of whip cream and finally the absolutely necessary chocolate sprinkles; it was a work of art, or as I affectionately referred to it "my liquefied heart-attack."  To keep secret my artful latte' recipe, I bribed the baristas behind the counter with five dollar tips, dropped into the tip jar ... I received a quizzical facial expression from the girl who was already at age 21, a tattooed, pierced and veteran latte' lady ... she seemed worried that the extra money dropped in the tip jar signaled my intent to be interested in asking her out on a date.  That was not my intent!  Instead, my hope was of relaxing at a quiet coffee location and I was only trying to give hush money so that they should keep my latte' recipe secret.  I probably should have patented the drink recipe, because on subsequent visits there ordering the same drink, they jokingly titled my drink the "Journalist's Dragon."  Painfully clear to me on my first visit to that coffee shop, I had made a mistake in stopping here: this place was obviously too noisy and too bohemian to be the quiet sanctuary I was looking for.  Yet what made me linger there a bit was the palpable mirth and energy in the air: it was as if the air was full of laughter from fun and funny people...breathing in this atmosphere would surely cheer me up.

RC walked in the door quietly and stood patiently at the end of a long line of people.  It was an autumn morning, moments after 6:00am.  I remember the time because I looked up from reading my New York Times newspaper when the room full of human voices murmuring as background noise abruptly fell silent. I looked up, curious to see what was happening. It was RC's presence that changed everything in the room. Willfully ignoring so many people, or oblivious to his effect on the crowd, he seemed to mind his own business by quietly keeping to himself as he gazed out the large glass windows facing east, smiling toward the approaching sun. He must have been admiring the beauty of the sunrise sky: the sunlight was like silver-yellow and orange fingers of the Gods that gently grasped the clouds, quietly pushing away the gray Seattle skyline to show a beautiful blue arc of Heaven. RC seemed happy to see the sun. RC was dressed for a hike in the mountains. His clothes were clean, but not fashionable. Trying unsuccessfully to remain inconspicuous, it was noticeable to me that there were several bodyguards around him: perhaps that would explain why the people in the room fell silent. If he showed up at one of my parties dressed like that, the ladies who enjoyed running with the bad boys would have gravitated to him instantly. He was alpha-male for sure, yet also appearing to be both intellectual and athletic. The spoken words to his bodyguards that I could overhear seemed to show a highly intelligent mind at work: that was totally unexpected and therefore made me curious; what an unusual combination, since in my experience those are mutually exclusive qualities ... and further, when those qualities were combined with the personal appearance of that heavily guarded man, it still struck me that it was strange when the normally boisterous coffee shop full of a variety of people immediately fell silent.

With a spirit of curiosity fueled entirely by caffeine from my latte' I boldly walked over to introduce myself to the strangely cool apparently too important guy with bodyguards. The bodyguards intercepted me twelve feet from the protected dignified man. Moving my head to one side to make eye contact with the important person, I said loud enough for him to hear me: "Hi, I am a journalist. I would like to please interview you for a book I am writing about why Seattle people go to coffee shops at 6:00 am in the morning." As one of the guards produced a Taser-weapon and was poised to zap me, RC turned toward me, walked through his bodyguards, smiled in a bemused manner and shook my hand firmly: his eyes were silver, not albino, but silver and his face resembled a farmer's weather-worn and sunbaked tough and serious looking face resulting from the experience of a life of hard work and hardship encountered outdoors. The guard seemed slightly disappointed that he would not get a chance to zap me, sighing as he put away his weapon. "Good morning. My name is RC and I usually don't give interviews, however, in this case, my press secretary will visit with you now: she will get you what you need." I thanked him, smiled and offered my business card as a gesture of bona-fide appreciation. He warily, yet professionally took my business card then motioned with his muscular and large left hand toward a group of a dozen or so people dressed in business suits – they all looked like they were Secret Service clones, except I noticed that their faces represented a variety of several nationalities. My best guesses about the bodyguards were that of the ones in suits, two were former Mossad Special Forces agents, one was likely from the Japanese Secret Service, another two were probably former K.G.B. agents and the other three were from some Central Asian Country. The bodyguards were heavily armed, with Uzi machine gun pistols casually displayed at the edge of the open lapels of their loose fitting trench coats. All guards had on conspicuous earphones for real-time radio coordination. There were four Chevrolet Suburban vehicles parked directly out front of the coffee shop, all colored black with darkly tinted windows and each of those vehicles had three guards at the front, back and passenger side doors. I also heard a helicopter overhead that seemed to be circling in a regular flight path revolving around the coffee shop. Escape cars, a helicopter and bodyguards ... how ironic ... it was apparent to anyone within sight of RC that he alone looked muscular enough and his posture showed a military bearing that altogether signaled to the crowd that he could take out with a single kick anyone stupid enough to assault him. So, why did he need bodyguards? I looked around again to see if there were hidden cameras for a reality television show. The sense of that scene unfolding in front of me being surreal was an understatement. His glowering bodyguards were watching me intently: when RC gestured for them, they immediately moved to form a protective semi-circle around him. They hustled him about twelve feet away from me: after the 'breach of security' by this journalist, no one else was going to get access to that guy. The overprotective posture of his posse was a hilarious response of overcompensation to a perceived risk. My first impression was that this guy was either someone important to the government or a rich and vain paranoid psycho who worried about being targeted for assassination while traveling anywhere out in public.

From the middle of the semi-circle of bodyguards, a female press secretary walked toward me slowly. Under the watchfully worried eyes of the protective cocoon of guards, she smiled and as she got closer to me I noticed she appeared to be Tibetan. While speaking in perfect English, with a slight accent, the press secretary explained a few ground rules to me. I hated people who tried to tell me the rules, so I instantly thought less of her. "RC is his name. He is an extremely private person. His name is really an acronym of his true birth name, as it was jokingly yet respectfully given to him during his college days – his friends could not pronounce his Celtic name, which rhymes with "Prengalthibarrrr" so instead, they referred to him by his initials. First it was the initials RRC for Renegade Random Capitalist, but to save time it devolved into the cryptic term "RC." Officially, he is a businessman, a private citizen of the United States and he does not give interviews except in special circumstances. Please take my business card, there is my contact information: please email me your questions. I will inquire as to whether he is willing to respond, or not. I would not get my expectations too high as his over-booked schedule does not allow time for anyone or anything not already pre-planned at least two-years in advance."

Trying to hide my sinking feeling from losing hope of getting an interview, I pretended to smile and attempted to thank her with a professional tone of voice that did not betray my despondent feelings. As a momentary diversion, I let my mind use free-association of what I observed, and my very first silent thoughts I had to keep from blurting out were; 'funny thing, he does not appear Celtic to me: instead he appears to be much more Caucasian in appearance with a handsome blend of Central Asian facial features ... this from my journalistic interviewing experience ... he appeared to have features similar to people I have interviewed from Kyrgyzstan.' Such obtuse observations from the realms of geo-politics and human anthropology were clear signs that my conscious self was taking over my internal dialogue and that emotionally it was impossible to hide that I felt like I had just been passed over for the last ticket to attend a media event at the White House with the President. My feelings of despondency were soon left behind with what happened next.

Emerging from the protection of the guards, RC sent two of the similarly-suit-dressed-clones to get RC's coffee for him, while the remaining guards were cautiously yet submissively urging him toward the main exit door. Halfway across the room, RC stopped in his tracks when an older Asian couple entered the doorway: he must have recognized them. RC bowed toward the couple, slowly reaching out his arms gesturing slowly toward and almost touching their feet: he simultaneously and with a hushed voice said something directly to them in a foreign language that I could not quite identify. Whatever RC said to the couple, the older Asian man laughed hilariously. Smiling, RC motioned for his body guards to make a path open through the crowd and for them to help the old couple to pass by up to the counter for service without anyone in their path. When they passed him RC dug in his pocket for cash, sending ahead one of his errand girls to order for and pay for coffee and scones for the older couple to enjoy. The Asian couple graciously smiled back at him and said in perfect English: "Thank you young man. We give you our blessings. Our prayers will be that the Gods will forever grant you infinite peace, prosperity and happiness." RC bowed reverentially one more time, clasping his hands in a prayer posture and then without showing his back to the older couple he slowly exited the building, smiling at them. As the last one out of the coffee shop, following the entourage, the press secretary I spoke with already, looked back at me from the doorway threshold and when I made eye contact with her, she shook her head at me, as if to signal "no way are you to publish what you witnessed." I smiled triumphantly, letting her know that the scenes I witnessed would be for me a useful bit of information I will definitely use as leverage, to get a live interview with RC. I was also doing my best to use non-verbal communication and disdainful body language to get the message across to her very clearly that I really and truly did not like her, her choice of shoes, her jewelry, her hair-style, or her fake designer finger-nails. On the sidewalk two steps outside the main door of the coffee shop RC's assistant handed him a fresh cup of hot coffee. For entertainment, I watched with anticipation to see if RC would spill the hot coffee drink, but no luck, how disappointing. RC took the twenty ounce Hot Latte' carefully across the street and gave the Latte' to a homeless man. RC knelt down and visited for the better part of ten minutes with that homeless man. When RC left, the homeless man waved goodbye to him and then focusing upon the coffee cup as if it was some warming campfire on a cold wintry day, he seemed to take great comfort in the hot coffee, warming his hands around the outside of the paper cup and slowly slurping the hot liquid and smiling, as if to show the world that deep down inside, his soul was warmed by the heat of the coffee.

I had never witnessed anything like that particular sequence of events in my entire life.

My mind was busy conjuring up what this guy could be: an ex C.I.A. special field operations officer, or a foreign exile given political asylum, or a former drug lord now turning states' evidence and in the witness protection program, or a top-secret financial market manipulator used by a foreign government to de-stabilize currency trading, or a movie director, or a mad scientist visiting Seattle to acquire Kryptonite for some dark military purpose, or a technology company Executive with an megalomaniacal ego, or a rich person from a foreign-country who was trolling for American women? What could he be in the real-world that there were a dozen bodyguards protecting him? And what is going on with his name: I mean, really ... what kind of a penultimate lame joke it is to claim you have a name like "RC?" Was it a jeeringly absurd word-play, something like turning inside-out the real meaning of the phrase "radio controlled?" Is he a robot? I got the creepily exciting sense that perhaps someone was filming a new TV Reality Show in the coffee shop, since the setting and events were disturbingly surreal to me. It was several hours later when I finally calmed down from my exuberant adrenaline rush, a moment that had the effect of a crushingly heavy sense of sadness and disappointment drowning me like a tidal wave after I have fallen off of my surf-board. The reality television show would never be realized with me as the star, since by early evening, no one offered to pay me and there were no cameras in the coffee shop.

For a brief moment I was distracted by the shiny shimmering earring jewelry worn by some of the pretty pouting prostitutes that walked by, too late to go for their famous attempts at trying to get close to RC. As a group, they seemed well-organized, all were smiling, preening, posturing in an obviously flirtatious effort to try to get attention from and access to, RC, yet no one in the management caste at the coffee shop bothered to inform them that they had missed entirely the person they were after. I quickly realized that for all of the dramatic display, their motivations were to get money from RC. I guessed that some of the hookers harbored distant hopes and wondered what their chances would be if they could somehow become his mistress. I calculated the probability also that at least three out of twenty-one of them would be hoping that they would become lucky enough to have their fairy-tale dream come true to get the privilege of using RC's money, spend him out of existence, then move onto the next rich guy. Maybe that was one of several reasons why RC had bodyguards, to keep away those people of ill intent who would harm his economic interests. I assumed that RC was another one of a common type of greedy capitalist. I was utterly and categorically incorrect. I would not find out how grotesquely wrong I was until years after that first meeting in the coffee shop.

With RC's departure and after the sights and sounds of his entourage faded into the distance, the crowd started again with their vocal boisterousness, returning to a cackling, laughing, disjointed series of competing conversations including some people saying "shut up dude" as their way of communicating that they were reacting in disbelief to a job interview story. All of it seemed background noise to what was going on in my mind. I focused my thoughts on the press secretary for RC. I hoped my impolite brashness would provoke a panic need for damage control by the press secretary and thereby ultimately result in an interview: for once in my life, that ploy worked well. She phoned me later the next morning to say that RC would grant me an interview, but only for one hour and only at the same coffee shop. RC required that his press secretary and one of his Lawyers would both be in attendance. They would get my binding acceptance to honor their detailed ground rules before the interview. If there would be the slightest hint of misbehavior on my part in the form of any deviation from RC's terms and conditions of granting the interview, then it would result in an immediate termination of the interview.

I did my best investigative journalist's homework that night before interviewing RC, by diligently searching public news information on the Internet about him. There was a lot of generic stuff about him on the web: but it was all tightly controlled, managed for a spin of understatement and restraint and protected from intrusive follow-up by a wall of Public Relations press people employed exclusively to provide services between the public and his several business interests. He had businesses that were successfully and actively doing all kinds of stuff, in over twenty-three different countries. No one in the several media articles I read could accurately estimate his total wealth because he kept all of his businesses as privately owned entities with no need for public disclosure of business information. In the electronic-ether there was a lot of speculation about him, but interestingly the guessing was not about things dramatic: I also could not find anything empirically verifiable, or illegal or scandalous. It was almost as if RC and his businesses were designed and functioned in a grand concerted effort to hide RC in plain sight of everyone. Despite terse biographical information, in the present day he didn't seem to be living in any one country, because it seemed he was mostly everywhere. Writing notes on paper and editing them in my mind before tapping them into my computer, and scribbling questions to myself while conducting research in advance of our interview, I scratched in red ink several jokes to amuse myself, along the lines of obnoxious one-liners full of sarcasm that only I should be acquainted with, including: "this guy should be called "O.O.C.P.S.O.S.H." which is an abbreviation for "Omnipresent-Omniscient-Capitalist-Patron-Saint-Of-Striving-Humans."

My collectively exhaustive research of public information about RC quickly led me to the most remarkable thing, which was the description of RC's business practices. He used technology and logistics in all of his businesses, training everyone in a specialty of their choosing. His technology related businesses involved software development for banking transactions, software programs that ran hi-speed stock trading (program trading), encryption systems for wireless communication, high-speed TCP networks between Satellites and terrestrial computer networks, encryption systems development and a variety of systems integration involving non-secret and non-sensitive contract services for the provision of basic utility services for governments around the world. After he started a business and made it profitable he then made everyone who was already an Employee a co-equal owner by selling his ownership shares to everyone involved.

Unexpectedly, the public record had plenty of information that showed a consistent pattern in that everything he did was not motivated by greed: he only retained a one-half of one percent interest in the gross revenues of the business after selling the majority of the business to the Employees. In media-speak, he used a weakly competitive form of capitalism. He insisted on structuring his new businesses along the lines of an interconnected social network of "mutually assured generosity" and made that structure active by transferring money and resources from the business by funneling revenues to those people who worked together to bring the new economic entity to life. He made sure that as soon as possible within the first few years of starting a new business, that the communities and countries allowing his businesses permission to operate, that those jurisdictions in return should be compensated with new educational and healthcare institutions located within a ten-minute walk of the business headquarters building closest to the new businesses. He opened to everyone the educational and health care systems he created, irrespective of their ability to pay for those services. They didn't have to be an Employee or partner of one of his business entities to get education and medical care: he gave scholarships and free medical insurance coverage. This guy behaved as if he was Santa Claus and that every day was Christmas Holiday for everyone.

To fuel the two crucial systems of education and healthcare and keep them working, he donated vast amounts of cash. The cash was not taken out of the businesses he founded, but out of his own pocket. Because of the majority of communities benefiting from his new approach agreed that outright subsidized schools and hospitals were a good start, but not the entire economic equation of a society providing the bare essentials for humans to survive, RC also developed an affordable long-term mortgage and new-housing construction assistance program to encourage housing development for as many people as possible. That seemed to be his blueprint for starting small businesses and launching them into the world: he used this model in several different countries.

The result was that after a few years of successful business operations and charity donations, several communities wanted to reward him and offer to RC many more opportunities to profit than he ever would ask for or accept. There were thousands of families helped greatly by RC's business developments in foreign countries. Among the publicly available news sources RC was portrayed by several other journalists as more of a humane utilitarian than a greedy capitalist who like almost all other capitalists routinely exploited foreign resources. Because RC did not exploit anything or anyone that made people react with astonishment when discovering that he was an American. He was genuinely written up as a humanitarian seeking the greatest good for the greatest amount of people possible, and doing that in different countries outside of America. The most accurate article I found was titled "At the gates of tomorrow:   full employment and prosperity for all." The article accelerated his un-wanted fame, and it also made him a lightning-rod easily targeted for criticism by those who felt threatened that he was setting a harmful precedent by practicing business in a way that was "too democratic" and that some said "threatens the very foundation of capitalism and the free-enterprise system."   Most of those criticisms were from ultra-wealthy people who would have been considered over one-hundred years ago as Robber-Barons.  Those were the type of persons who used references to Social Darwinism, Draconian levels of competition, and property rights far too often during interviews I have conducted several interviews with their ilk, in my past employment, as a journalist.  I remembered clearly the sensation from my past experiences with those demons, that after spending twenty minutes interviewing fierce capitalists, I had the emotional sense that I was in the presence of a sea full of sharks and that if I spilled one drop of blood, there would be a frenzy as to whom would be first to get property rights over my blood and use it for some biotechnological research that could in turn be developed into a profitable drug.

A few days later after I finished my homework, I realized that I had not slept for thirty-two hours ... so I went so far as to consult my Psychiatrist with hopes of getting a reality check. I was worried that I was projecting an imaginary RC onto paper as one of my psychological selves. Thankfully, I was relieved when my Psychiatrist did not laugh out loud at me when I explained my lingering doubts about pursuing this story and how from lack of sleep it seemed that I also had to battle myself over a wavering grasp on reality. She was a just barely good enough doctor to be willing to test my theory, and so she did agree (not out of a feeling of generosity) to go to the same coffee shop for my first interview with RC in a clinical effort to validate that yes it was a real person I was interviewing. All of this was conditioned upon doubling the hourly fee, with a non-negotiable payment up-front before she would leave the office and journey to the coffee shop. How embarrassing if no one would have materialized. Thank God RC did show up, flesh and blood, accompanied by that simpering wench of a press secretary. As you can tell from my earlier comments, I felt untrusting and was certain that RC's press secretary was somehow my enemy. Wow, after all of that time, effort and anguish, it appeared that the interview would finally take place!

At the beginning of our first interview, I asked RC's permission to first use a recorder and second to publish our recorded discussions. "Yes, you have my permission, but it is a question of timing. Please wait until I am dead and gone ... OK?" When I asked him several times why he wanted to have these conversations published only after he died, I can boil down his justification to these collected quotes: "I don't want anything disrupting my quiet enjoyment of what I had hoped would have been a quietly private life. I really only care about what my children think and feel and so consequently I truly care about how they may judge me and my life's contribution to humanity and what I have tried to teach them about how to be truly human and benevolent. My children need to live their own lives in a happy and meaningful way on their own terms. They should only have to make soul-searching judgments of their Father in terms of what their conscience tells them ... yet it will be less harsh for them and they will feel less guilt if it is done only after I'm gone. It will be easier for my children to resolve their feelings into something that they can live with after I am gone. So please wait to publish until after I'm gone ... long gone. I can tell you that the experience of my life feels like it was lived better than it will seem to be, when it is read from your upcoming story."

In his presence, disequilibrium and emotional discomfort are the things that I felt most, right through to my bone marrow. More precisely, it was the sharp stinging pain of subtle inferiority, in terms of emotionally feeling like my intellect had a certain capacity and weight as if it were tangible and as if I could also see that RC's intellect comparatively was much more intelligent than mine in exponentially more ways and in several superior ways. It was a burning feeling in my heart of doom or failure, or the gloom of impending failure to measure up, like when in school sports, you meet your opponents for the first time and they are five times more gifted, talented, skilled and certain to win at your expense and your pain. My role as note taking journalist building a historical record for future generations seemed inconsequential when I was in his presence: I felt like I was a messenger for a dying man, a town crier shouting profound insights on behalf of someone that hardly anyone else in the world could begin to understand, or more frankly would ever care about wanting to figure out. I don't think RC had a wish to be understood in a popular way of celebrity, fame and glory, but he did seem to want to convey important things to my readers, things that he worried would perish from the Earth at the time of his death.

Our first interview did not go well. "Mister Journalist, I don't want to hear you talk about yourself or listen to you talk only about questions answerable with my biographical information. There are far more important things to discuss, like the question: what have you done to help others less fortunate than yourself?" Without waiting for an answer to that question, RC began by motioning toward his public relations troll (I genuinely disliked her) and a Lawyer sitting on either side of him: "Mister Journalist, I see from your facial expression of confusion and revulsion over not being in control of this interview, that you are wondering if it is politically correct for me or anyone to be posing and posturing oneself as a Renegade Random Capitalist in today's modern society. You might possibly wonder if it is an unhealthy form of behavioral acting-out, exhibiting a psychopathological and cowardly form of skulking. Perhaps you assume I am some blue-blood rich-kid who doesn't want to get his hands dirty by working in the muddy Earth, or someone who fears breaking into a sweat while working. I will bet you a hundred dollars that you prepared for this interview expecting that you would be talking to a voluptuary, or a valetudinarian, or an introvert, or an egomaniac ... I wonder if you will be humble enough to look up the definitions of those words. At this moment, your facial expression conveys to me that you need to use the restroom and then frantically try and call a Psychologist for advice on how to use Neuro-Linguistic Programming methods to try and fool people into mindlessly doing what you want during interviews. Let me save you time: Operant Conditioning never works on me, in fact it just pisses me off." His public relations troll laughed at my red blushing face, while RC smiled, then he laughed and stood up quickly and excused himself to get a six shot espresso latte' while walking away from me he looked back and said while speaking over his shoulder that he promised to return in five minutes so that we could start over on a firm foundation of: "no messing around with half-truths. Instead of the usual interview games and your attempts at trying to pin down mercurial and theoretical topics like my economic payoff matrix and what really makes me tick, let's agree instead of that dead-end game to dispense entirely with prevarication. So let's cut to the chase and let's shoot straight in order to truly respect each other's time." Because RC said those things loud enough for other people in the coffee shop to hear, and I had some face-saving behavior to practice, of course I agreed to those terms.

RC returned in three minutes and asked me to show him "more examples of your writing methodology other than quoting to me what you read in the papers this morning, then by using your own words and original ideas, try this: in less than one-hundred words, disprove the hypothetical argument that capitalism is like the ocean which makes all boats rise with the rising tide of a new prosperous free-market and it does that better than any other economic system."

Often he enjoyed challenging my world views in mocking ways: "what's the matter Mister Journalist, don't want to get your hands dirty by digging in the dirt of reality's complicated gardens? Too much manure for your liking?" He was unique in that he was humane and kind to several honest and hard-working people, yet in the same hour he could challenge the people he perceived as being too weak and succumbing to the temptations of the seven deadly sins, most notably greed: he despised unbounded greed most of all. "In its extreme form, greed makes the few steal the most things from the greatest amount of people." He said for him greed was "Anti-Utilitarianism."

While stopped at the intersection waiting for the red traffic light to change, my flashback of that time over five years ago was caustically interrupted by cars behind me honking and shouting obscenities. Embarrassingly I smiled and waved apologetically, deciding to take a few minutes break from that flashback ... I looked around at the Seattle skyline as I waited at the next stop light. More gray clouds, a very typical skyline ... I had hoped that the clouds would part and that the golden sun would throw to Earth some golden beams of light, if only for RC's funeral. Driving too fast for the posted speed limit signs on the downtown streets, I was thirty-three minutes ahead of schedule. As I pulled my car into the parking lot of the Temple, the first thought in my mind was about the incongruity of RC's funeral being held at a Temple ... RC was not the most religious person, so maybe it was a ceremony planned by his new wife ... I mean, planned by his widow. I had a few minutes to wait in my car so instead of blaring the music on my car radio, I sat in silence. Another flashback took over my mind, again it was completely involuntary ... it almost felt like it was prompted by RC's ghost.

My second flashback took me to that same year over five years ago, about two weeks after our first interview (which I assumed would be our only interview). RC phoned me and invited me to attend a public relations event on a Saturday for one of his charities. It would be a demonstration of how one of his charitable foundations used aircraft for the "real-time delivery of humanitarian assistance worldwide." He said I could ride along in one of the biz jets while he flew a lead plane. The whole event was described to me as a quick trip in one of his jets from Seattle, flying over some of RC's favorite and most scenic mountains in Northern America. RC's jet would be accompanied by five escort chase jets as part of the demonstration. His private jet for the flight was an experimental YF-35 supersonic fighter jet converted to peaceful flying configurations with special modifications and a one-of-a-kind set of electronic equipment that RC engineered, built and installed with his own hands. The other two jets were corporate biz jets, flown by pilots specially trained by him. I was allowed to select which biz jet I could ride along in, for the trip. The two biz jets usually included friends or business associates. One of RC's assistants at the airport before takeoff mentioned to me, as if to ease my suspicions, that one of the jets would include a doctor, a government official from some un-named department of the U.S. Government and a few of RC's bodyguards.

It turned into quite a show. RC flying the lead jet started his fast take off by tuning up the music. His so called 'launch music' was "Pump-It" a song from the Black Eyed Peas. The passengers in the chase planes really did not know what to expect. RC must have already filed with the F.A.A. a pre-approved flight plan, because the flight path took all of us passengers away from Seattle East over the Cascade Mountains, the flat parts of Eastern Washington, up to the mountains of North Idaho and the big lakes there, then over the Selkirk mountains, onto and then over the Purcell mountains in Montana, then at Glacier National Park, where he abruptly climbed to steeper than a 45-degree up-angle and then he shot straight across the Canadian Border with orange flamed afterburners blaring. At the moment we crossed the border, over my headphones I could hear the pilot's radio conversations with RC, which RC abruptly drowned out with loud laughter as he switched his background music over to the musical sound of the song "Red Barchetta" by the band Rush. The biz jet I was in was full of passengers, young reporters from various newspapers. At my middle age, I tried to remember back to my twenties and what my journalistic ideals were at their age ... at that moment I felt very old and obsolete. Perhaps one reason the younger people were still hired and working in journalism is that younger people fresh out of college can be paid less than seasoned accomplished journalist veterans such as myself. Getting back into the moment, I sat close enough to the pilot to hear him laughing a moment before he got on the intercom: "folks, I suggest you buckle in tight: this is where the trip gets fun, and by the way, air-sickness bags are located in the seat-pocket directly in front of you." The pilot radioed some garbled jargon to the other chase plane so then they too climbed a modest 20-degree up-angle, they hit full throttle and gave chase to try and catch RC's jet. We passed over Banff Canada then RC dove steeply down into the mountain valleys, quickly circled back on the route to setup a vector behind and pointing toward the chase planes, then zipped quickly past the jet I was in. RC was going supersonic, showing us all what a shock-cone of vaporized air looks like, before we heard the concussive boom of the blast from RC breaking the sound barrier. All of that was done apparently with the purpose of demonstrating how quickly he could get to anywhere around the world. Things for the passengers leveled out somewhere high above the Okanogan region of South-Central British Columbia. Returning, all of the aircraft followed a well-defined flight path, gradually descending onto the Canadian Forces Air Base at Comox on Vancouver Island, British Columbia. By the time we landed, RC had already touched down there a full

20 minutes before us: he had a modest trio of large new tourist buses waiting to take all of his passengers to a rollicking no-host bar and press conference in Victoria. What a trip ... what a bizarre trip. RC received a great deal of donated money after that demonstration: he used the money to buy food supplies; which I later found out he took tons of that food and air-dropped it to a village of starving people somewhere in China by using his private air-force of cargo planes.

Having more than enough of involuntary flashbacks, it was time to go into the Temple for the funeral. Walking slowly across the parking lot, I realized I was one of the very few people who showed up alone. As I watched my exhaled breath rise like vapor into the cold January sky of Seattle I wondered if RC's last breath rose toward the sky in the same way. Thinking of RC I had a flashback to my article, 'A Soliloquy of First Light & Caffeine' which was the title of the article I wrote after first meeting RC. Later he would tell me he hated the story because of my sloppy writing. How charming. That comment by RC was on my mind as I stepped through the entrance of the large Temple, which was already full of people, to attend RC's funeral.

Stepping into the Temple doors for RC's funeral, I had an immediate sense that this was a high-security event. Metal detectors and guards were everywhere in the hallways and outside the main Temple. I also quickly noticed that too many people from too many different countries showed up ahead of my arrival: I had to sit in the overflow room which felt like quite an insult. Since I graduated from college with honors over twenty years ago, this was turning into the first time that I have had to be so far removed from an event I was covering for a story! I was embarrassed to be relegated to the lowly social position of only viewing the orchestrated ceremony on a widescreen TV. Not giving up, I had to show my journalist press and media credentials three times before the security staff allowed me to have a better seat in the Temple closer to the front podium where the funeral speeches would be given.

My first impressions from the speeches were that this whole charade seemed more like an overly stylized and glitzy press conference: it was unlike any funeral I had ever attended in my life ... it really was not a funeral. It seemed too perfectly scripted to be a realistic memorial of any human being.

Although several people were listed on the ceremony printed program to speak at the public funeral for RC, there was only enough time for his family members to speak, including only ex-wives and two of his many children. I recorded their speeches on my smart-phone and then spent quite a lot of time transcribing and editing for clarity.

RC's first wife was the first speaker after the religious leaders opened the ceremony somberly and spoke of RC reverentially. She was also the first of the family members to speak. She was tall, stunningly beautiful and appeared as if to have a likeness to a combination of the actresses Kareena Kapoor and Angelina Jolie. She wore a dark gray dress that looked like something a Conservative Parliamentarian would wear in London England to a funeral at Buckingham Palace, except without the fancy hats that are the style in Britain. Her speech was clear, but at a slower pace. That pacing was something distinctive that identified her speech origins to me as definitely from the Western part of North America: people there never hurry.

**The first Ex-Wife from Nelson B.C. Canada** - *"The American man still is the guiding light of my dreams...* I have known him the longest time of anyone here. I knew him for over 35 years. He was an orphan, raised by adoptive parents who were translators for the interred Asian prisoners of war somewhere in the central lakes region of British Columbia during World War II. The parents adopted RC from an orphanage and moved RC to the United States somewhere North of Seattle in the early 1960's when he was still a young child.

RC was very outdoorsy or "back to nature" oriented and physically active, climbing mountains and hiking and surveying precise altitudes of the highest mountain peaks in the area.

We met in the summer of 1981. He was walking at night along the outskirts of the town of Nelson British Columbia Canada. My first sight of him was in the orange glow of sunset light. He was carrying a red metal petrol can, heading for the nearest fuel service station. I asked my girlfriends to slow down the Chevy Nova and offer him a lift to downtown. We slowed down while my distrustful and suspicious friends were poised to hit the accelerator of the car to speed off to safety if the stranger was a threat. While my friend's Saint Bernard Dog leaned out the open side window and drooled down the freshly waxed Chevy door in between short

33

happy barking sounds, I said: "Hey mister, you need a lift to the service station?" I smiled and could feel my curiosity awakening several emotions that I had hoped were not easily noticeable to the stranger. He stopped, put down the petrol can, looked at me directly with his silvery soft eyes, smiled and said in an upbeat but baritone sounding voice sprinkled with a pleasantly American accent, "No thank you – I am enjoying the walk ... this place is paradise. Besides, who could resist looking at the sunset and the moments when the sky will be full of soft starlight?" I noticed immediately that the dog stopped barking when he spoke and I felt a warm rush of several physical and emotional things. He picked up his petrol can, smiled, waved and walked away toward civilization.

My friend driving the Chevy Nova hit the car accelerator. The dog slobber, the dog and my head collided as we left a cloud of road dust and went to cruise main street for attention and flirting, in that order. My friends were looking for some way to relieve their anxiety, so as all normal female teenagers probably do, they verbally attacked me for putting them in harm's way. "Why do you have to be polite and offer possibly psychotic strangers a lift to town? We could have been killed! And another thing missy, why would anyone in their right mind be enjoying, actually enjoying a walk down a mountain, I mean all of the bug bites, the sweat, the grime from road dust sticking to your nose hairs, sunburned skin? And did you notice the purple berry stains on his fingers? Who could survive on Huckleberries?" My friends were subtle communicators: I got the point - the American man was a bizarre sight, walking down the mountain, smiling yet still appearing to them to be a bum. The astonishing thing for me was that he did not ask for directions and he seemed to be amused at me: was it my appearance? What was it? I was curious, I felt strange, I wanted to forget about him but I couldn't get that first meeting out of my mind and heart. That same night in my dreams I kept hearing the distinctive sound of his voice.

I saw him the next day at my relatives' street vender food cart in town. He was ordering an unusual combination of foods: Huckleberry pie, buttered pan-seared Rainbow Trout rolled in a mixture of cornmeal and salt and sautéed Morel Mushrooms that were glazed with an apricot brandy sauce. I watched him from a distance, hoping that he did not see me or recognize me. He looked like he was cleaned up that morning, but still looked like a mountain man; suntanned, muscular, like he could swim the entire distance of Lake Kootenay from Nelson to Kaslo and still have enough energy after all of that to climb to the top of any mountain. On the sidewalk he stood with his back to me, so I dared to walk closer and closer to him. I don't know how he knew, but with his back still to me he stopped walking away, turned around to face me and smiled. He motioned to a street side table, sat down and I joined him. He ordered two glasses of Raspberry Lemonade and we visited for hours under the protective yet giggling gaze of my relatives. Someone watching this spectacle phoned my Father and Mother. Within an hour I had introduced him to my Parents and also to most of my Family. From my body language, my Mother could see I was not merely a nineteen year old girl anymore ... I even caught her staring at his muscles. I hope she was only thinking of the statistical probability of our union possibly resulting in grand-kids. My Father and uncle offered to give him a lift in their Ford truck to the mountain where his own truck was stranded. When my Father and uncle returned three hours later, they were both drunk. He had bought them several drinks as a sign of his appreciation for their help. Father announced something like "before he drove off to go home to Seattle that young man asked my permission to court you ... I said I would think about it. He gave me some Quartzite-Crystals that he found in a lightning-strike tree, burst open and burnt during the last storm from two days ago. Look at how beautiful these crystals are. He said it was a Buckskin-Tamarack tree. I haven't heard anyone use that term for a long time. That guy might be OK for you to see. Let me think about it some more."

With parental permission and bringing a relative to accompany me every trip, I visited Seattle many times the following year and after a long-distance courtship my parents agreed to his request for permission to marry me at our Mosque in Nelson B.C. Canada.

It was bittersweet for me during our first year of marriage since he was asked by the government to help with some secret logistical projects in the Persian Gulf and throughout Central Asia. When he returned from seven months being overseas, he was entirely more serious, yet still dedicated and faithful to me. I strongly resented the business people and government people that he had buzzing around him like insidious mosquitos: we were interrupted with requests for decisions and phone calls and teleconferences constantly. I knew it was a trade-off between losing time in exchange for the work and the pay and how well he provided for the children and me, but I still thought work should be separated much more from family time.

We had a few beautiful children. Life was mostly happy for my children and me. He was at times pre-occupied with a business that he was secretive about, yet his time spent "doing business" provided a lifestyle of wealth and privilege for us, that my family, friends and I had never dreamed of. He took care to diligently and consistently provide for me, my kids and my relatives in Nelson B.C. after our divorce. He paid off all mortgages of all my relatives in cash. The banks in town loved him. We divorced when our youngest child turned eighteen. The divorce tore him up emotionally, but he said that he could see I was no longer happy and that we had naturally evolved into different people and that our paths in life were meant to go different directions. He kept all of the divorce legal stuff respectful, amiable and agreed to generous divorce terms.

After our divorce, I moved back to Nelson B.C. and worked hard helping my relatives get their special recipes into a cook-book. Most of our children moved with me and I have enjoyed having our grandchildren close to me. He visited every time that he was invited and was still a supportive Father and a helpful ex-husband. He thoroughly enjoyed being a wonderful Grandparent.

I still miss him: the happiness and the conversations I mean. I miss those things from him, the attention and care and love. At night I can still hear him in a recurring dream of mine, singing a silly song to cheer me up, as he often did during our marriage: "I first met you as a foreigner, a needy American out of gasoline, out of lighter fluid, walking past your home in the darkness, miles away from my own country, feeling the heaviness of lonely starlight silence, I measured everything alighted from the Heavens as heavy and far but then I saw a pretty girl in a Chevy Nova car, that girl smelled of courtly fragrance ... wait! Stop the music! Tell me what word would rhyme with the phrase, lilac flowers and peach pancakes?" He used to describe our first meeting in absurd prosody: "She wore perfume that made her presence known first by the aroma of Lilacs and Peach Pancakes, second by her soft laughter and third by her symmetrical and beautifully proportioned physical appearance." Wow, it is amazing what lives on in your memories."

After Ex-Wife #1 spoke, there was a great deal of applause. Although there was an obvious effort on her part to be stoical and force a smile for the benefit of the crowd, she was in tears as she made her way back to her chair near the front of the Temple.

Thinking about how the first ex-wife's comments would possibly make the other ex-wives feel, I was bemused and wondered if the speeches would become competitive, showing how each wife might portray her impact on RC's life.

The next family member to speak was one of RC's daughters. She looked similar to an amalgam of the actresses Mindy Kaling and Parminder Nagra, along with several of her mother's stunningly beautiful features and she was tall like her mother too, yet what was haunting to me about her appearance was that she had RC's silvery colored eyes. Like her mother, she too wore a similarly conservative outfit, yet it was slightly more modern and definitely something that I have seen available for sale at the Nordstrom's store in Seattle. Her speech patterns were solidly Seattle, complete with the vowel enunciation that is as mellow as the gray clouds that take their time leaving the waterfront at a pace of their own choosing.

**One of RC's Daughters** - *"He was a positive, spiritual and intensely supportive Parent...* I am stunned by his tragic death to the point that I can't tell what time it is anymore: I mean in a natural sense, my sad feelings and grief keep me up awake at night. I cannot acknowledge that I feel tired enough to naturally fall asleep. My Dad was also a living part of my conscience, someone I confided in constantly about a variety of life's challenges. I have always felt he focused his care and concern and love on me like I was the most important person in his life.

Our Father would take pride in providing for his family by cooking with care: his love was evident in simple things like making the morning breakfast pancakes, made from scratch, mixed by hand; he would pick fresh Huckleberries and put them in the pancakes at the right moment. I can still remember fondly the hissing sound of pancake batter hitting the hot frying pan griddle and especially I remember the aroma of those pancakes filling the air accompanied by eggs and bacon and cinnamon rolls with cream-cheese frosting. With a breakfast like that, we all knew our Father was happy about being alive another day to take his family outdoors, to show us picturesque mountain valleys, waterfalls, lakes and old-growth trees. Especially in the summer months, my Father smiled when the song of birds filled the air. When we finally made it to the mountains, he would breathe in deeply the pure air and smile: the aroma of Spruce trees made our lungs feel like they were in Heaven. Our Father showed us the importance of spending time outside, enjoying the tranquility of being off the grid and cherishing the joy of swimming in the lake.

When I was a little girl he and Mom would take a lot of time to play any game or read any story or draw any picture that struck my interest. He could talk to me in a straightforward way about anything I was curious about. He had some hilarious ways of teaching me about the world through more than intellectually motivated and theoretical conversations. He sympathized and understood well, when talking to me about the underlying causes provoking my turbulent emotions and formulating several possible solutions to act in my own best interests. He was the only human male I could turn to for objective advice about "what in the world are young-men thinking?" More specifically, when my teenage boy problems were not solved by talking things out with mom: she would say "let's sit down and talk about it with your Father – he always has a unique and helpful solution no matter what the problem is or will be – he can solve problems in the present but also anticipate and prepare in advance for what is coming around the corner at the next turn in the road of life." In my family, Mom was most often right about all of the questions I asked of her, but Dad was already thinking ahead in multi-step and statistical ways about how the odds would fall or fly in the real-world for me and he helped open my mind and heart to preparing several simultaneous solutions to most of the normal obstacles in a young person's life and to overcome them in a way that did not diminish myself and in a way that certainly did not make anything worse for others. One of the unusual ways Dad would help me think of obvious things in terms of solutions that were non-obvious, was to use a naturalistic and somewhat primitive allegorical image: "intimacy is a positive and sacred thing, it's about quality not quantity ... intimacy is photosynthesis of flowering plants embracing golden sunlight on a perfect summer day, intimacy is silent gray clouds embracing high granite mountain tops, with both of them turning orange in the sunset light – think about it, a silent and secret embrace that has been going on for millions of years: high altitude old rocks embraced by water vapor that has been recycled in the air and clouds for almost as long as the mountains have been around." It took me awhile to try and assimilate the meaning of what he was saying into something that would help me with my problems. Now that he is gone I also have several regrets of losing moments discussing the things that we can never talk about now: like the topics of his own mortality, his Religion that was lost and never fully grieved away healthily, his time spent in the military that he always said he "wanted all of that time back" meaning that he wanted a refund of time in order to re-live it in a more meaningful way. Whenever I did bring up those topics, he replied with a look of pain on his face "those subjects are buried deep in the murkiest depths of my soul ... and because life is short for all of us, let's not waste any time talking about those sad subjects.""

She had more to say but was overtaken by emotion and so she cut her speech short and ended early. Her mother had to stand up and help her back to her seat. The audience was applauding in an effort to try and console her.

The next person to speak was one of RC's sons, his oldest child. He looked like a more ruggedized version of RC but much taller and muscular and more imposing than RC, if that was possible. He too had silvery colored eyes. At first sight, the guy looked like he could break through brick walls without too much effort, yet he didn't appear to be a Neanderthal. He had a similar speech pattern to his Father's, including especially the distinctive way of saying the vowels in his words that was identical to RC. He looked like a combination of Fareed Zakaria from CNN and the actor Sven Ole Thorsen. He wore a custom-tailored suit that was black, with a dark red tie knotted into a distinctively precise Double-Windsor tied knot, framed with a British Cut lapel vest. He was attending Oxford but was home for the Christmas Holiday and in his speech I detected a hint of a British Accent creeping through some of his spoken words, which I guessed was a common thing picked up by osmosis by every student who spent time at Oxford.

**One of RC's sons** - *"My Dad was an over-wrought humanist born at the wrong point in history, pursuing the wrong vocation in life...* My Father was my best source of finding meaning in life when my well of hope ran totally dusty, dry and barren as a desert. I cannot find the words that in any way convey the profound loss I am feeling. I should say a few words about what he meant to me.

He put forth so much effort when speaking to be clear and use naturally direct speech with me and those whom he loved. He wanted to get you to understand things quickly so that you would not be stuck in a state of confusion or worry or any kind of negative state of mind.

I find in my sad duties of being executor of his Estate that those qualities and motivations carried over to his written documents. His legal papers and financial documents are easily understood, but I had to hire Lawyers, Accountants and Trustees to help me sort through the complex implications of clearly written legal directives. He seems to have been greatly preoccupied and worried during his life with the duty and task of making more than enough money to take care of those he loved after he was gone. As his son, I am humbled to discover the facts of how far he had reached the accomplishment of those goals and to see the fruit borne from decades of his hardworking yet tryingly anguished labor so that those he loved would be better off than he was.

Of the several wonderful and profoundly meaningful memories and feelings I have of him, it is apparent that he loved me, respected me, was proud of who I am and he was genuinely interested in me and always asked what my thoughts and feelings were at all stages of my growth. To me he was the most patient and careful person that I have ever encountered in life. He enjoyed teaching me about life through a variety of methods, mostly through an upbeat and irreverent but thorough discussion of ideas, always honoring my emerging independence and respecting my own views that diverged from his. Until this moment, I had not been able to articulate how much he helped me in the formation and development of my own conscience and ethics and moral beliefs. He challenged me to balance my diverging views by always seeking truth and beauty simultaneously with a firm grounding in love: not only love for what I want, but love that would help others too. "Love of family means feeding those you love so they never go hungry no matter if you yourself as a responsible and productive adult have to starve in order to do that every day – always feed the children first."

He made sure I was aware of how to avoid a common failure among people who lead an intellectual life that "you still need to be able to grow a red rose plant and give the roses you have grown with care to a woman you feel for and from that gift to possibly make her swoon, instead of talking about sterile intellectual concepts that are too theoretical to be in any way helpful and emotionally meaningful to flesh and blood humans." The accomplishment of instilling the kernels of a budding conscience in a young person: that is subtle but a permanent gift. He accomplished that by going far beyond encouraging this son to read everything and rely on questions to organize data and then make thorough analyses of the structure and function and outcome of what you understood and how it helped you act benevolently in the world.

Without expressing it directly to me, I discovered from reading his personal journals kept in meticulous detail throughout his adult life, that he was able to pursue a coherent distillation of benevolent philosophies without appealing to any principles that were religious or medieval. He figured out how to be a good humanist without rejecting technology. Although there was a war within his soul, he was OK with continuing his personal daily battle of trying to solve the contradictory forces and internal turmoil he experienced from the warring elements of his mind, body, character, psyche, spirit and conscience. I would often and constantly point out with triumph how glaringly and intensely opposite that all of his contradictory selves were. He would laugh in a kindly and gentle manner at my recognition of irony. The foundation of his soul seemed to be a pursuit of truth in that he was unequivocal, truthful, direct and honest in all things. What I didn't understand was how someone so truthful could be so shattered and contradictory from the inside of his self when viewed from people looking at him from the outside world.

The search for meaning by a complex soul is what he was all about: that is something I could not comprehend until now, yet it is and was, I think, the answer I would give to define the resolution of my confusion over how to understand my Father. Taking ideas from the Heavens and bringing them to life here on Earth, his soul simultaneously had vast amounts of space, time and room to enjoy and absorb Art, Music, Poetry and their opposites, Math, Science, Reason, Logic and common sense, practicality, frugality and on and on...all of that he pursued intensely with colossal amounts of motivation from sources unknown. I would hear him recite his favorite poems then he would turn to me and encourage me to do additional reading after my homework assignments were complete. He often exhorted me toward the knowledge one could gain from reading Polya the Mathematics teacher and Tufte on how to communicate information clearly. Typically, in one weeks' time he would go so far as to suggest that I read *The Fractal Geometry of Nature* by Mandlebrot, followed up by the book *Insight* by Bernard Lonergan, however if in the middle of my homework studies, any of the TV series 'The Day the Universe Changed' and 'Connections' by James Burke, or The Western Tradition by Eugen Weber was on TV, he would ask me to drop everything and watch the half-hour documentary with him. After suggestions like that, I was confused and emotionally all I wanted to do was play with finger-painting on a blank canvas, instead of trying to grasp the many and profound ideas that were obvious to him and non-obvious to me.

He would ask my mother and me to go with him for a walk before sunset throughout all seasons of the year. Walking together during Autumn, he would say things like "listen to the rain falling on the leaves that are themselves already fallen and frozen to the cold ground: it is like warm tears from Heaven giving a last breath of life to the leaves and to literally give them the sound of applause for their last effort to make the world a beautiful colorful place by giving their final light of beauty before melting away. The colorful leaves of autumn really know how to give a performance."

My Dad spent a great deal of time with me when I was young, having his work brought to him and he always placed my needs for and demands upon his time, never as an interruption, but always as a chance to stop work and happily give me his undivided attention. My Father would have people who worked for him, follow us around on our travels, bringing him his work, as he flew us and drove us around the United States, Canada and Europe for long vacations that involved several pilgrimages to libraries, astronomical observatories, museums and historical or scientific sites of all kinds, both renowned and obscure. My Dad had nothing but disdain for following any mindless conformity of a popular aesthetic regarding anything, so he was independent and comfortable trudging us to far flung remote areas, especially if it meant combining an exciting adventure with an educational experience, with a certain goal of helping us formulate our own individualistically unique view of the world.

As my teenage years provoked feelings of embarrassment and passive resistance, he encouraged me to explore on my own, in my own independent way, encouraging ethical use of the Internet and World Wide Web to broaden my mind. He expended his utmost and unfailing best efforts and resources to give me full and fair access to the finest knowledge available on the Earth and in the Heavens. My Dad loved libraries and learning about everything, I mean every possible thing that existed on the Earth and in the Heavens.

When it came to the tedious duty of grinding out my homework assignments my Father never ever did the work for me as most other parents did for my classmates. I thought at the time it was cruel torture but he really showed me that I had to rely on myself, to do my own thinking: "having someone else do your work will destroy your soul and sense of worth my beloved Son. You need to develop your own insights, find your own knowledge and develop your own unique views on everything, so that you can act according to what you know and believe is true, good, right and do what increases the amount of love and benevolence in the world while still being fair to yourself. If you only copy what others have written, you are only mindlessly regurgitating someone else's originality by stealing their creations: that would make you a thief of the worst kind."

I remember feeling full of pride, during the few times I had classmates over to the house, my Father would walk by as we were sitting at the kitchen table, doing our home-work assignments and my classmates figured out that they could make a game out of trying to ask my Dad a technical question and challenge him to say the correct answer on the spot, without any chance to look it up. My Dad had a perfect record of answering 100% of the time correctly no matter the various subject matters that the question was from. My classmates would wait silently as my smiling Dad walked out of the kitchen after correctly answering their questions while balancing a cup of coffee in his left-hand. It was an understatement to describe the reaction of my school-friends as stunned silence. My classmates would say in a whispered voice: "... dude, your Dad's an alien."

In moments when my friends commented that they thought my Dad was an alien, I realized that one of Dad's unintended achievements is that over time I found the truth in the platitude that as a child grows older their parents in retrospect seem less idiotic and instead are truly wise: in the sense that they took a long term view of educating a child in a present moment to help the child their entire life.

For all of the philosophy and search for truth we were encouraged to pursue in our intellectual lives, it was also extremely important to my Father that I follow his example of being realistically grounded in the real-world; paying attention to the practicalities of life and common-sense, which according to my Father, were essential to becoming a responsible adult.

Here is an example of what he encouraged me to be. My Father took me along on several of his day-hikes in the wilderness. We would get up early in the morning, he would cook a high-fat breakfast of bacon, egg omelets, pancakes, juice, coffee, he would pack a lunch made from home-made bread and four different types of sandwiches, then we would drive for about three hours in a random direction, heft on our shoulders a heavy backpack full of all kinds of survival gear and photographic and scientific equipment. We would hike along lush green forests to the top of several mountain peaks in the area. Once during late summer near Nelson B.C. I found some Native American arrowheads stuck in the sand of a remote mountain lake. Sifting down in the sand I also found an Obsidian-arrowhead. I dug around and we found about a dozen more arrowheads of various shapes, most of them cut from flint. My Father said the honorable thing to do with my discovery was to mark the location with our hand-held GPS device to get accurate location coordinates of Latitude and Longitude, take the arrow-heads back home, then contact the local Native American Tribal Government and hand over their artifacts. He helped me make a detailed map showing the location of the find and he drove me the following weekday into town to hand over the artifacts. At the time, I was a teenager and I was beginning to understand him as someone I should listen to and learn from. He thought it more important to respect the cultural traditions of the descendants of the Native Americans who made those arrow-heads: it was much more important to return those items, than trying to be a treasure hunter with a perverse sense of opportunism by making money off of a cultural find by selling those things.

As a sign of his love of knowledge and technology, he invited me to watch on a video-link the live coverage of the launch of his twelve Satellites carried on rockets. As the rockets launched, he was reciting in Greek a few lines from a poem about the music of the spheres. I would guess that his Satellites' launch was quite an accomplishment for him on a professional and career level, but he was more interested in what I thought about the presence of technology in modern society and how I would like to use it in my near-term future. "Son, you would be amazed at the amount of good things you can do in the world for lots of people everywhere on Earth, by using Satellite technology."

I never did figure out how he made the jump from private business man to owning and running a far-flung space Satellite Corporation and several banks and lots of other businesses; however my Father was an amazing man, whom I learned to never underestimate.

During my young adult years, my Father showed me that it was good to be developing all of your interests as long as you caused no harm to others or to property rights or break any laws. He showed me by example that it was OK to be several things in your life, to go ahead and be an outdoor-oriented Naturalist, a Conservationist, a Biologist, an Astronomer, an Artist, a Scientist, a successful business person: "but first and foremost, you should hold as your top priority always, those you love, especially your children and looking out for their best interests."

Those fond memories help me and comfort me greatly, although I am still stunned about his accidental death. I am un-consolably mystified as to why an accident would happen to my Father ... especially after all of the good things he has done in life for others.

When I was called to the crash site, I went with the Coroner and after their formalities, I took what was left of him and we cremated the remains ... his ashes I took to the only place on Earth I remember seeing him relax enough and show a contented behavior of "being at home," it was an alpine lake that is the only lake cut-in-two by the British Columbia and Idaho borders. I remembered that seemed to be one of his favorite places. His body and spirit are together and home now in the alpine water, evaporating into the wind, flying around the Seven Heavens."

The son received a standing ovation from the audience...perhaps the crowd was all afraid that if they didn't show their appreciation, that it would upset the son and he might tear down the whole Temple, which of course was not true. He left the podium with tears in his eyes, but he too forced a smile as if to signal to the audience "thank you for attending." He seemed to be a perfect English Gentleman, a giant, but also an intellectual who was highly civilized.

The next speaker was RC's second ex-wife. She looked like a combination of the actress Meryl Streep and the singer Jewel. She wore a dark brown semi-formal business suit that would be appropriate for a fund-raising event at a stodgy museum. Her speech was solid Chicagoan.

**The second Ex-Wife from Chicago** - *"My Bodhisattva now silently swims in the mists of time...* My beloved husband was a Bodhisattva to me. No one I have ever met was anything like him at all. We were married for a brief one and a half years. Those were incredibly happy times full of travel, painting, photography and an ungodly amount of time in "the great outdoors." The nightmarish parts of that time came from his business activities that could never seem to be put out of our life together.

Whenever I hear the sound of the ocean I remember our times spent together laughing and being in love like newlyweds. We traveled along several Pacific Coastal communities from Glacier Bay Alaska to Baja California.

Often, after a full day spent outdoors, he loved going inside to try the food of a different restaurant each night: especially the ones with a fireplace and a roaring fire of natural wild wood from real trees. That 'enjoying the outdoors' part of him was totally foreign to me, I was a city girl my whole life: it seemed primitive to me, but it worked for him well. Anyway, he seemed to live for enjoying desserts – he was giddy like a little kid already high on a sugar-rush when the dessert tray was brought over to our dinner table. "I will try this and that and also that one." The man could put away berry pies like he was carbo-loading before his own execution. What he didn't tell me was that the brain cancer he was battling was interfering with his sense of taste and smell and so at the time he obviously was trying to overcompensate for the loss of those senses, especially a keen sense of taste, by increasing the intensity of flavor he was trying to experience, but couldn't, through boosting both the quantity and quality of desserts.

We split because of his intrusive work and several work related things he kept secret from me. Whatever he really did but could not or would not tell me was that although he was physically within walking distance of me most of the time, work was something that stole his focus away: it bothered me greatly that he seemed that he was mentally away from me far too often. I thought it was another woman, but it was his work. I would follow him around and he always was in his office, his communication center, making international video conference calls and arranging all kinds of secretive transactions. During our travels outdoors he had business associates with backpacks carrying communication equipment and Satellite phones. They constantly interrupted our happy moments. It was infuriating to me.

I loved him, I miss him, but I am still angry at him. I should have been more important to him than his work. When I heard about his death, it has placed me into a dizzying state of grief. I honestly have not gone past my grief, at least not fully."

The crowd applauded politely, yet they didn't seem too impressed with her and they were not all that sympathetic, in reaction to her self-centeredness.

The next speaker was ex-wife #3 from Athens Greece. She looked like she had features of the actresses Brigitte Kahn who played the character Christina Santos in the British Spy series "The Sandbaggers," and the actress and producer Nia Vardalos. She wore a black business suit with a white blouse and she spoke English OK, but her speech still had a heavy Greek Accent. I was trying to decide where I heard a voice similar to her voice before, but then I decided that her voice sounded exactly like the same as the pitch and tenor of the natural voice of the actress Nia Vardalos.

**The third Ex-Wife from Greece** - *"Our daughter asks me when RC will be back again to visit...* RC was my beloved husband. I met him in a restaurant he had recently purchased in downtown Athens. I was there with four of my lady relatives. They visited me on a lunch break from my job at the Ministry of National Defense. He spotted me and smiled then walked over to my table. He politely introduced himself and it was clear he was intent on going out with me on a date. He was charming and persistent and so interesting.

I went out with him and accompanied him on his business dinners, his art buying trips and his several flights back to his homeland in America.

We were happy during the time he was visiting my country to set up some of his new technology businesses.

I fell for him. We were married for only two years. We had a beautiful Daughter together: she is here with me today.

The only thing RC feared was Mincemeat-Pie.

He provided well for our Daughter and me. In Athens and here in America, wherever we go, we have escorts for security.

He made it to visit us one weekend each month: he was a good Father and husband.

We divorced because he refused to convert to the Greek Orthodox Religion.

He left me more than enough money to make me the richest woman in Greece."

She also stopped her speech short and could not finish because she was overcome with tears. The audience applauded politely. Her young daughter sat next to her near the front of the Temple. I noticed the daughter had silvery colored eyes.

The next speaker was ex-wife #4 from Russia, her speech was the most difficult to hear and to follow, because her spoken English was clear but it was interrupted by her attempts to pause and to not let emotions overtake her while she was speaking. She was of medium height and wore very plain but professional looking clothes. I cannot remember what color her outfit was, because it was so understated ... gray colored, I think.

**The fourth Ex-Wife from Russia** - *"My family often asks if I wish for my husband back here with me...* I was a translator for business matters in Abakan. So I met RC during his visit to Abakan. He landed at the airport in his private jet. He had another five planes land with him. Russian bodyguards and local police and military with machine guns protected him and all of his own bodyguards. He came to my home city of Tashir to buy land. He bought enough land to start his own airport and Satellite-dish-antennae and Cell-phone towers. He hired me to be his official translator for the local dialects when he met with leaders of different local villages.

We spent so much time together that we got to like each other. I was totally in love with him. After a few months he asked me to marry him. We were married for one year. My relatives are a big group of people. They worried the American would quickly forget me. That didn't happen. My Father worried about RC if he was American Spy. I laughed. No it is worse, I said: "he is a businessman!" My family was proud when he wanted to marry me. He had a lot of history about him: about his past and what he has done. He did not tell me everything about him. He was mysterious to me.

After he built his airport and his businesses across several sites on the ground from Tashir to Abakan, he had to go back to America. He asked me to come with him. I could not leave my family relatives here: they need me. I wanted him to stay with me, but the world demanded him to be away. The long distance relationship was too difficult. I was sad, we divorced. He took good care of me financially. He left a lot of money for me and my family to prosper. I miss him. When his death was given as news to me, I felt very crushed ..."

She was unable to speak and could not finish her speech either. The crowd sensed she was in a lot of pain, so they gave her a standing ovation. She sat in her chair with her head cradled in both of her hands for the rest of the funeral service.

The next speaker was ex-wife #5, an American from Portland Oregon U.S.A. She appeared to be a combination of the actress Emanuelle Chriqui and the singer Nelly Furtado. She was about six feet tall and wore a button down dark blue business suit with a narrow dark maroon tie: overall a modern and trendy new style that was popular in New York. Her speech was plain and clear, making it easy to understand.

**The fifth Ex-Wife from Portland** - *"He laughed when I thought of taking up numerology in order to manufacture more meaning in my life...* I am a musician by vocation. RC was a gifted musician in a 'primal and instinctive or intuitive' sort of way. He had real raw rhythm although he was not formally trained in the mechanics of precise use of musical instruments. He had a sincere sound to his music, which is another way of saying that he composed his own music according to his own style preferences. He didn't mindlessly practice repetition of the work-product of someone else's creative arts.

I had hoped I would be his muse, in the sense of a Greek Goddess way of the mythological allusion, but his true inspiration was the several pressures inside of him, his thoughts seemed to build up pressure waves that he had to constructively act upon to build, rebuild and by iterations rebuild again and re-assemble himself into some kind of superlative man. That sheer effort was willful and it seemed to be something akin to watching a huge piece of road building machinery powerfully plodding through tons of Earth and dirt.

Nothing involving finesse or highbrow aesthetics had any part in his music, although he did try to be open to his creative impulses of expressing feelings through music. I always had to forgive him his lack of dexterity when trying to play the guitar: he moved too quickly through too many complex chords – it was like hearing a screeching train-wreck because the notes and rhythms collided into something that was noise, not music. The cliché that you can tell a great deal about a man by his music, did not apply fairly or accurately to RC. It would miss the complexity of his eclecticism and creative juxtapositions of musical styles.

Early on in our marriage, I noticed symptoms of, and I often worried that, he had a brain tumor or that he had begun to develop hearing problems, or perhaps he would become an example of some bizarre neurological diseased man in some medical text-book. One time I overheard him take a seldom seen work break, by cranking up some music, while he was still sitting at his big oak desk. The funny thing was that he cranked up the volume and simultaneously tried to listen to seven different songs. I was so offended by the raucous sound that I went upstairs to his office and asked him what was going on: "are you deliberately trying to ruin your hearing and your mind at the same time?" It was apparent that his usually ready wit and sense of humor was being taken away by his cancer and his speech was sliding towards technical jargon, not always easy to comprehend. When I asked him what was going on, he stopped all of the music, saying stoically, *"sorry to disturb you, but I was trying to save time by accomplishing several things at once instead of doing those things sequentially ... remember the other day when I was telling you about polynomial time? Well this is the same thing: it was a buy one get seven free deal. My dear the combined songs reminded me of the Greek Mythological story of Icarus, I mean his heart was in the right place and he showed courage, but think how things would have been different if he had used a polycarbonate resin instead of wax to bind his artificial wings together. He could have flown around his country and began airborne deliveries of Baklava."* We both laughed at the absurdity of the image and the intent of his joke, something so far "out there" that it was intended to provoke a laugh as a way to cover up the emotions that often lead him to cry in private moments so as not to scare anyone. His cancer was taking away some of the best parts of him. After encountering momentary self-awareness of his rapidly accelerating mortality, he would watch on his computer, videos of the British TV series "The Prisoner" starring Patrick McGoohan. Then he would watch anything involving the British Comedy Troupe "Monty Python's Flying Circus" and from the sound of his laughter, I could tell that those old shows somehow helped him, in ways I did not understand, at all, ever.

That story is one of several I have about how mystically enigmatic he seemed to be to me. I never met a man like him, before or since.

He was a private man, exceptionally intelligent, insightful about human nature and personality theories and he was also consistently empathetic towards others emotions and feelings, although I wonder if deep down he truly ever understood himself.  His focus was outward, outdoors, beyond himself.  Looking at him, others seemed to compare themselves to his abilities and almost always I noticed that they ended up seeing how far they fell short and how different they were in several respects.  I guess that was one of his involuntary gifts to the world: provoking a self-assessment of meaning in one's life.

It is no difficult thing for me to figure out that my best music was composed while I was married to him.  We were together for a year and a half: at first I was extremely happy and thought I could help tame this magnificent specimen of a man who tormented himself by agonizing over so many things, but I was wrong.  The best music written during our time together was also my best selling music too.

On my remix release available next year, I will be dedicating my best selling song to him as my inspiration for the song titled *"The Sacred Spreadsheet of Numbers."* Selecting that title is my way of paying homage to RC's ironical word-play and to help me remember the Metaphysical reasons why RC attempted to replace the emptiness of his lost Religion with Math and Science.  I think that from whichever Heaven he has gone into after his death, he is looking down on me and laughing endlessly at me and at the intended meaning behind that song.

His laughter as I hear it in my nightmares sounds the same as the time when he laughed at me when I shared my efforts to study numerology as a way to manufacture more meaning in my life.

In my recurring nightmare, RC is with me, it is winter: he and I are inside of a warm mountain cabin with a roaring fire in the fireplace however he is standing near the windowsill, looking out on a frozen landscape.  I ask him what is wrong with this picture and without making an effort to face me and make eye contact, in the dream he says to me in an emotionally heavy and gasping whispered voice *"my dear, I am brooding in the heavy depths of frozen alpine lakes, pondering all things distant, heavy and far as a recurring echo in my soul: I cannot figure out where all of the time in my life has disappeared to or how to get it back.  The full breath of life evaporates away from me until I am an invisible whisper of fog, rising to join the clouds."* In the dream, I know how to make him snap out of it, so I go into the kitchen and start baking some of his favorite desserts, but as soon as I turn my back and lose sight of him, he disappears. The dream ends and I wake up crying when the final dream images of me having to get dressed in heavy winter clothes and to walk several miles in the deep snow to make it back to our warm home in the city, only to find that all is silent, no wind, no whispers, nothing of him remains at home or anywhere.

I asked for a divorce because I knew I had failed him as a soul-mate: he was too complex for me, too far to reach despite my intentions to meet him half way to anyplace he was at mentally. I only experienced nothingness and we went nowhere. He was a shadow to me in life and now he is long gone and not a whisper to me anymore. He is a recurring image in all my nightmares."

I think the crowd was tired, because they really didn't like her speech at all ... she got a few half-hearted clapping sounds of applause. But most people silently appeared shocked, gazing at her wide-eyed, as if she had committed some act of sacrilege that the audience all shared in feeling, but that the speaker had no awareness of at all.

The next ex-wife to speak was ex-wife #6. She was of mid-range height but was curvy, that was obvious and noticeable through her black dress that looked like something from the 1960's styles ... it was very retro. She looked like a combination of the actresses Eva Mendes and Salma Hayek. She wore too much makeup though and wore too much gold jewelry: especially overdoing gigantic sized loop shaped gold ear-rings. Her fake fingernails were glittery and it was mesmerizingly difficult and challenging to not let your eyes get fixated upon trying to count how many sparkles there were on each fingernail that glittered from a far distance. She had decided to wear these incredible stiletto high heels, maybe someone forgot to tell her this would be a funeral, in a Temple, where most people take off their shoes before entering as a sign of respect. She delivered her speech in Spanish and an English translator then read her speech aloud in English.

**The sixth Ex-Wife from Brazil** - *"My husband RC was a saint. God sent him to me...* I cannot believe that he is gone already, but I am sure he is in Heaven: he was such a good man. He helped so many people in my city of Natal, Brazil.  I met him when I was working at the airport near Parnamirim.

RC started a computer communications company in Liberdade.  He would have business meetings at my restaurant located at the far Eastern end within the airport terminal.  I was the Manager of the restaurant and he was always such a gentleman to me and others.  I have never felt more respected and listened to by any man.  Most Americans are preoccupied with only a physical relationship, but RC was genuinely interested in my spiritual views and my way of seeing life.  He made eye contact with me.  He was interested in my mind and emotions.  He wanted to meet my family.  He wanted to visit with people that were having a hard time in life and genuinely understand their problems, to try and help solve.  He asked me to go with him to see the city.  The more time I spent with him, I knew he was a special man.  He wanted to have a big family, a traditional wife.  I worried that I was not enough of a woman for him, but I said yes when he wanted to take me to dinner.  I said yes when he wanted to take me to Paris for a vacation.  I said yes when he wanted to get married in London.  He flew me all over Europe and America and we also then spent a lot of time with my family in Natal.

He funded small businesses around my city: he helped so many people.

I knew I was slowing him down.  It was a devastating thing to ask for, but I had to divorce him.  If he stayed with me it would have meant other people in the world would not have been helped as much by RC's money and generosity.  We divorced after one year.  I am still regretting that decision.  I still look for him every day at the restaurant.  He left me so much money, but I keep working to keep my humility.  I miss him.  I am so sad that he is dead."

The crowd applauded, but they seemed to be holding back less than their 100% approval.  Perhaps it was a way to signal some apprehension as if to vote on her style choices in dress and appearance, or maybe they were exhausted from hearing from ex-wives and wondered how many more hours this would go on.  I am unsure of what it was, yet it was a subdued applause and I could tell that ex-wife #6 was offended.  She sat down, but I could see from her facial expression, that she was silently fuming with rage at such disrespect.

The last speaker was RC's widow, obviously the current wife married to RC at the time of his death. She was the most interesting speaker among all of the wives. She wore a conservative black colored Shalwar Kameez along with a fragile appearing grayish colored Duppatta Head Scarf. She had designer glasses on, yet through all of that, she appeared exquisitely beautiful and spoke both intelligently and from the heart. She wore a simple gold wedding band and used that hand to gesture toward the audience while she spoke. Her hand movements were graceful, yet the body language conveyed to the audience very directly her sincere thoughts and feelings: none of it seemed like a contrived or overtly dramatic act.

**The seventh and Current Wife (Widow) from Bangladesh -** *"RC funded more cancer research for me than anyone...* I am RC's wife. We were married at the time of his untimely death. I am a Research Neuroscientist specializing in Brain Cancer. My special research clinic is today located near Khalikur Bangladesh.

When I met RC it was in America. I was then in my final year of a PhD Research Program in Boston Massachusetts. RC appeared without any notice at my apartment door, one evening in the summer. I was surprised that a well-dressed and well-mannered American, who apparently had too much money, one who had bodyguards with him, was interested in my research project. He introduced himself and asked if I would be interested in discussing funding for my research. I thought it was a prank. He detected I was suspicious. He gave me his business card and a private phone number and then he apologized for disturbing me in an unannounced manner. I was impressed that he was empathetic enough to detect my defensiveness as a survival instinct. It was a curiously strange visit.

The next day I mentioned to my research staff about the mysterious visitor and a potential for funding. One of my research project colleagues opened her laptop computer as I was speaking and searched the internet for available public data about RC. We found plenty of information about RC and at that point, I was then convinced from the evidence that it was RC who visited me and that he was not joking around. The internet search showed that he had business interests all over the globe and tremendous amounts of money. I thought I would, out of curiosity, see what his funding proposal might be.

I phoned him begrudgingly. What did he really want with me? For our first business meeting he asked me to join him for lunch in New York. I told him that I did not have time to drive that far for lunch. He replied that he would send transportation and that he would not take more than three hours of my time. I tentatively agreed to meet for lunch, since it would be occurring at a public restaurant. The day of our business lunch he showed up in person at my apartment in Boston. The transportation he provided was a limousine to the airport and a private business jet ride to New York and then a helicopter ride downtown. He somehow reserved for us a table at Le Cirque. They were able to accommodate my vegetarian preferences. I ordered the most expensive lunch on the menu to test him: yet it did not bother him at all. During the discussion, RC listened most of the time: he posed questions and wanted to hear about my research purpose, my findings and what funding would be needed. I could tell by his questions that he had done his homework and he understood several arcane and technical aspects of my research. He was the only person I met who questioned the efficacy of my 're-switching DNA phasing method' to target specific cancer cells in the brain. Most other people in America I speak with get lost quickly when hearing the scientific terms. However he posed clear and cogent questions to me that showed he truly understood the words he was using. He also understood the outcome of the experiments I had documented as part of my research. I was impressed. He seemed serious. This was not a prank.

He then told me that he himself had brain cancer and that he knew the only way he could make the disease turn out to be an event that would be a positive thing for other people in the world who might get cancer in the future, was if he helped fund my research.

I was worried that he had some optimistic do-good-wish acted upon from a place of vanity and hypocrisy, or that he would want to make a documentary film out of the whole thing ... however he also was realistic in the sense that he was aware how many years it would take our industry to find a way to treat the type of brain cancer he had. He did not expect to personally be cured or in any way reap the benefits of his potential investment in my research.

One request he had, was that part of the money be used to sequence his entire DNA so that it might be possible to identify predictable markers of his unique type of brain cancer: he hoped that a cure could be found sometime in the future.

Our lunch proceeded much better than I expected.    I did understand his urgency, since he himself was handed a death sentence by the brain cancer diagnosis.    Our lunch sitting at a restaurant table only lasted thirty-eight minutes.  I was more impressed with him after he said he would have a written funding proposal to me within a week.  He did fly me back to my apartment and true to his word I arrived within three hours of my departure.

Again acting faithfully and honorably as a man of his word, he delivered in person a fully funded research trust with fourteen million British Pounds Sterling, to be used for my basic and applied research.

I was stunned, I was angry, I was grateful: yet from the mix of emotions, my only available response was the last thing I wanted to do and so all I could do was cry.  He felt embarrassed but was comforting and supportive.  I collapsed into his arms.  He helped me calm down and encouraged me to think about all of the good I would do with the money. There were no strings attached, nothing that I would owe him.

Over the next few months our communication started as professional and business-like, however with his frequent visits to my research lab, we developed a friendship after our first year.

Then during our second year of communicating, we enjoyed each other's company so much we decided to start a love affair.

I married him within six months after that.  We traveled often to Bangladesh to visit my extended family.

Several of my family members were able to immigrate to America because of his sponsorship and financial assistance.

RC was always good about going around and seeking out orphanages to give financial aid and assistance to all of them who would accept money from him.

I admired his sincere Philanthropy, his down-to-earth manner of wanting to help others without expecting anything in return.

We have been married only two years, we have divided our time between Seattle and my home in Bangladesh near my Research clinic in Khalikur.

A few days ago in December, I made my way here to America, traveling to Seattle to be with RC over the New Year Holiday. Our plans were to settle in Singapore and start our new family ... he was going to leave the business world forever.

I want to sincerely thank each of you for attending the funeral ceremony today: RC would have greatly appreciated your kind and loving attendance and I am sure he would have proudly introduced each of you to me. Please join us for a catered luncheon after the ceremony. Please accept my gratitude for your presence here: it is a great comfort to me." She began to let a few tears fall as she left the podium.

The audience loved her speech. She received a standing ovation, it was if the crowd was cheering her on to conquer the world with their collective blessing and find the cure for brain cancer.

As the ceremony ended (after two insufferably interminable hours) the crowd was enthusiastically concentrating on the current wife. Several people walked slowly past the closed coffin. That was a curious ritual to my way of thinking, since I could not understand why there was a coffin there in the first place: the Son of RC said in his speech that they had cremated the remains gathered at the crash-site. Some people showed enough courage to go and respectfully shake the hands of the ex-wives and the current wife from Bangladesh, offering their condolences and briefly saying how RC had impacted their lives.

The post-funeral luncheon was catered and featured plenty of non-alcoholic healthy beverages and ethnic foods from over twenty-three different countries, all of it incredibly delicious. I returned to the food tables for three full plates of food, in between trying to get people to let me schedule a future interview with them.

I was approached by a few people from RC's past: they had heard somewhere that I was doing a book on RC and wanted to make a contribution of information. One thing I expected to hear rumors of was the possible scenario of each ex-wife having a copy of a different will: no luck, RC had extensively planned out each pre-nuptial agreement, divorce decree, trusts, and had only one final "Last Will and Testament." Everything was so detailed and the wives were so well compensated, that the competition among the wives was directed toward a class action lawsuit against the people who killed RC.

Driving home, I reflected on what I heard at the funeral.

Almost all of the speeches were seemingly and most likely fictitious stories of RC's benevolence spun eccentrically out of control by family members grief-stricken over the loss of RC. Considering the content of the speeches, I was simultaneously curious and confused; there were enormous contradictions in the facts mentioned by each speaker, and it was too much distortion, even if the speakers could be excused for speaking from the heart during an emotionally troubling ceremony...my problem was that they described too many different people, and it was not believable that all things added together could be interpreted as disparate elements of RC as the true one-real-person.

Internal discomfort and disgust are things I have learned to rely upon as feelings that instinctively alert me that there was a deep problem hiding beneath a story I'm pursuing. It is also my immediately intuitive reaction to spurious public information I have analyzed in the midst of researching a story. With each obsequious and overly reverential speech I heard, my gut felt increasingly queasy and it was a feeling deep inside me, within my soul, that simultaneously was accompanied by a feeling of disgust. The kind of palpable revulsion provoking my urge to vomit, a feeling similar to the involuntary physical reaction to revulsion I experienced when I have stepped in a pile of Manure at a Rodeo. That is the best description I have of my assessment of the funeral speeches: they were a pile of lies, or so I mistakenly concluded at that point in the journalistic investigation.

After the funeral and half-way through my drive time home, I promised myself several things: first, I was going to talk to my Jungian Psychiatrist about how to best deal with the possibility that despite the revulsion I felt as a reaction to the speeches of the family members of RC, why was I bothered most by a heavy burden of doubt about whether or not I had the whole story about RC before his death? Second and most important, I felt that I was still misunderstanding essential things about RC, which may have been my way of dealing with remorse and regret over not capturing more information from him before his untimely death. Could I have missed so many things about RC, the things that those people spoke of at his funeral? Was there a shred of truth to the virtues they extolled? Was I losing my ability to ferret out the truth?

My skepticism was in high gear at the funeral. If I was willing to cut some slack to the grieving rich people in the audience, (which I wasn't), I still detected a single unifying theme of darkness and untruth behind the orchestrated efforts to sugar-coat the information about RC's supposed benevolent life. During the funeral speeches, the confusion I experienced was the exact opposite state-of-mind I experienced while interviewing RC when he was alive. RC showed me consistently truthful information, answers and motivations during all of our interviews: there was never any effort to deceive me.

After RC's funeral I interviewed some of his family and friends over the course of several months. My top priority was to try and get interviews with the pilots who were in the chase planes escorting RC at the moment he was killed, but no one at the funeral claimed to know how to get in contact with any of them: how incredibly disappointing that was for me! However, I gained the satisfaction from feeling that I was closer to the truth, when I finally tracked down additional persons of interest from referrals made by the few people who supposedly knew RC well over the course of his unorthodox life. I made great progress by saying things like "do you know who could answer the questions I have about RC's early days, or about how he went from being a poor young man in America into an international business man of extreme wealth?" I persuaded most of them to grant me interviews, and freely speak about their memories of RC. From my interviews with those people who voluntarily agreed to share information with me there emerged some unexpected background information that I found interesting and informative. What follows are the interview highlights from several discussions.

The first person I interviewed from RC's past was a college professor. I didn't have time with my scheduling conflicts to fly to Boston Massachusetts so we visited over Skype and my new video webcam. She was delighted to visit with me about "the old RC before he became world-famous." She was near retirement, yet her memory of RC made it seem like her mental engines all seemed to be functioning well. Through the video webcam I noticed that she had visibly contrasting shocks of gray and black hair neatly gathered into long braids, one braid falling on each side of her ears like waterfalls over craggy granite gray cliffs and she wore gaudy ear rings that were popular in the 1980's.

**A College Professor** - *"Sometimes passive, always intellectual, RC was exorbitantly complex, simultaneously full of good intentions: he showed admirable, heartfelt, sincere motivations to help as many people as possible...* I am a college professor in the fields of Mathematics and Economics. Way back in the day, as a new female PhD during the late 1980's, I can truthfully say that RC was my number one source of dread and foreboding among all of the bright minded students that showed up in any of my classes. I mean to say precisely that he was my all-time greatest frustration because of the chasm between his intellectual potential and that part of total potential that he meagerly brought to life in the real-world. He didn't fully become himself during his college days.

Imagine how I felt, seeing someone like RC with the sharpest intellect in the whole school, having the most sensitive awareness of what it is to be humane and then combine that with perpetual passiveness, being non-committal, detached, mellow, so as to process and analyze all points and counter-points with equal care and scrutiny. My view was that his mind reached toward the goal of going everywhere all at once from all directions on and through all things. I asked him point-blank if he was doing drugs before my classes. He had a wounded look on his face for a millisecond and then lapsed into another serene state of malaise, before replying, "I love my brain cells too much to destroy them that way. No I do not do drugs, ever." My exasperation with RC was vocalized one time too many to my fellow Professors. "Wow, don't mess with that guy: he can out-do anyone at this school in anything, so I think we should encourage him to develop his innate talents and abilities towards something good, so let's not provoke him into anger or do the slightest thing to discourage him."

His written papers are the documents I have preserved and still use to this day to show new students what a well-conceived and clearly written paper with concise logical argumentation should look like, in its structure, function and content, if they want to get an A+ from me. All of his papers in my class were incredible. I was surprised, since they were the product of an extremely intelligent and practically organized mind. His all-time best paper astounded the professors of the day, since it gave us all a glimmer of the complexities of his heart, mind, soul and the essence of what it is to still try and act in accord with a benevolent conscience in the modern world. His best paper candidly and convincingly raised the topic of the troubled condition of humankind's existence within a society and economy involving competition-based rewards. The subtext of his perspective and thesis boiled down to a utilitarian critique that evaluated the cost-benefits of the then in power decision-makers in society, concluding that for their exclusive self-interest, they systematically engaged in lying cheating and stealing: he concluded from the several lives that were destroyed by the consequences of their economic decisions, that the leaders were "cold-hearted thieves." At the time, the phrase he used was "self-interested politicians committing the cardinal sin of skulking towards profit in all things based on the perverse incentives and economic rewards for the privileged few at the expense of the many." Although sometimes bombastic and irreverent in his writing style at the time, he made logical arguments in a unique way by deftly plowing the data among the intellectual fields of Economics, Mathematical-Economic Game Theory, Psychology, Ethno-Centric-Biology, Religion, Philosophy and (of all things unexpectedly added to that list) he also appealed to the Laws of Physics. From that varied survey of fields, he beautifully wrote in direct, natural, simple language, so that we could as quickly as possible grasp the propositions and new ideas he brought forth. Concerned with the welfare of his fellow human beings and overwrought at how miserable life is for a large number of good people, his most convincing points revolved around the painful fact that "capitalist society and every one of its members should be further ahead in every conceivable parameter of existence because of technology, free markets for goods and services, but most especially the free expression of ideas, opinions and information, which is infinitely priceless."

By the time he reached his final year in college I was convinced, along with my colleagues, that he was a true Polymath: someone expert in several specialties. I had expected him to develop into a college professor with an exemplary set of academic accomplishments, or to become a wise and just leader in a democratic country. In classical terms, he would have been considered a warrior-poet or a philosopher-king.

All of my hopes were in vain, since RC was not the slightest bit interested in any job that would require him to stay indoors too long without seeing the sky and the mountains. And he made it clear that he worked alone. "Besides" he would often say softly, "what does any of that materialistic stuff matter anyway?" The daily hours spent in college classes and inside doing research and homework, meant that he was being confined to an indoor space smaller than the size of the Pacific Northwest United States and Western Canada and so the study room was its own prison and seemed too oppressive for him. He grew more outwardly optimistic and 'joyously-smiley-faced' when he could get out of college at semester's end and fly back home to his beloved Pacific Northwest, to breathe the fresh mountain air and see the sky again.

As far as questions about the origins of his nickname "the Renegade Random Capitalist" it all began as a bad joke. I could see that since he outwardly was an egalitarian and truly believed in representative democracy in order to improve the human condition in a benevolent way, that his college buddies sarcastically coined the nickname to be ironical and rude – it was their way of mocking someone who was stellar intellectually, yet their true problem was envy, since RC did not have to put forth as much effort as they had to expend to get the course work done, and no one could expend any amount of effort or time to keep up with RC's academic achievements: they all realized he was a one-of-a-kind intellect. The nickname was much simpler and 'user-friendly' to pronounce than his real name, so it stuck, if for no other reason, because it was a selectively simple and a highly efficient mocking way of communicating "make way fellow mediocre humans, here comes the genius, but we think he should suffer the weight of our cruel disapproval, though he is 50 times more productive, inspired and creative than we other students are or ever could be." Those comments were made behind his back, because RC was physically imposing and looked like he could take on anyone in a fight and win within seconds. The comments did not bother him because RC never sought approval from others. To show that he had no ill will toward those who were not 'fans' of RC, he mentioned to me that he knew of some students who were running out of money to pay for their college fees and he asked if I could anonymously pass on cash from him to help keep them in school. "Please don't let anyone know I am behaving like Santa Claus: the people that need the money would have their pride hurt if they knew the money was from me. Let's keep everything anonymous so they will stay in school and maintain their self-perceived dignity."

We kept communicating over the years as 'email pen pals.' His family was the most important thing to him: nothing else occupied his heart, mind and soul more so than his children and their best interests.

People have asked me about the true nature of our relationship. RC was like a son I never had, I took a maternal interest in him. As early on as his first year in college I was maternal toward him and perhaps his primal doubts of who his birth mother might be, kept him at least communicating with me. I was never able to conceive children, RC was not my long lost child and I thought he was brilliant: I admired him and I wanted him to do well."

She seemed wistful and nostalgic in most of her comments, but it was clear she was a big fan of RC and she was visibly saddened by his accidental death.

The next person I interviewed after the funeral was a co-worker of RC's from his early days of being involved in some clandestine activities for the U.S. Government. I had never visited Alaska, so I eagerly flew to Anchorage International Airport and drove to one of the downtown Anchorage office buildings, to meet someone who claimed to be able to give me some insight into RC's spooky and murky past. He asked that I not use his name, since he was still involved with private and secretive contracting work for the government, and "they would not be too pleased to find-out that I had talked about my friend to a member of the press." He was almost seven feet tall and very tough looking for a man nearly fifty years old. He too had bodyguards, yet not as many as RC had. We met in a vacant office at the top of one of the tallest office buildings in Anchorage. I couldn't help notice that he selected the vacant office with a direct stairway exit to the roof of the building, where his helicopter was waiting for him.

**An Ex-Military friend from Alaska** - *"We fell from the sky to measure the limits of our mortality by hopefully not bouncing off the ground...* I first met RC in the late 1990's when I worked with him both during the Persian Gulf War and then later at a special military site in Alaska. I was transferred there as part of the process of getting honorably discharged from the military. RC was sent there for only one reason. Although he was a civilian logistics contractor with top secret clearance, something had happened on one of his secret missions and the only problem I detected was that RC inconveniently showed up alive after the military mistakenly listed him as Killed in Action. His contract managers in the field were C.I.A., but he also worked with military Commanders in the field who seemed to think RC was freakin' crazy, although we all knew that he really wasn't crazy: he was the sanest person there but his extremely intelligent mind was viewed as a threat. The paperwork mistake over his supposed death had really pissed him off. "Those bastards don't know anything except self-preservation and blood-lust for political power" he often said to me, when I asked him why he looked angry. The military commanders had recommended that RC be sorted through a psychological evaluation before being let back into America "because he is angry at the leadership of the military contracting directorate over misclassifying him as deceased and he may have some post-traumatic-stress-disorder bordering on rage, which may be problematic when measured against current standards of civilized society and may undoubtedly and egregiously lead to lawsuits against the U.S. Government which could interfere with the interests of the military."

The Alaska site we were at was a mental health stopover for psychological stability testing before the powers-that-be would begin to consider letting us Vets loose again into polite society in the lower 48 states. Whether you were sane or not, you still had to go through the testing and monitoring process for three months, because the type of stuff that a few of us did in the war was considered high stress by the academic Psychiatrists back in Washington D.C. U.S.A. Compared to the other dozen or so of us, RC was the most sane, however he was simultaneously the most difficult to figure out. I think that is why his Commanders in the field sent him to the psych evaluation camp in Alaska, to get a complex person who was smarter than they, out of their way. The military only rewarded mindless conformity as the highest virtue of those days: however RC being the most independent minded person I have ever met, was in no way willing to fit into that mold at all.

Most of the other guys were withdrawn and aloof as a way to try and not show how twitched-out and teary-eyed they were. Everyone processing through the screening protocols there had trouble sleeping. It was during your dreams that the worst images of the war came back to try and grab your soul and humanity and turn it inside out.

I knew RC was the best-of-the-best among each individual in the group when on the first day at the Alaska site, a Psychiatrist invited everyone to sit in a circle around a campfire and to begin talking about what was bothering each of us. The Psychiatrist looked too young to be a doctor, so we all thought he was a plant from the C.I.A. primarily because his questions were inane, such as the question: "do you know why you are here?" Everyone answered 'yes sir' except RC. He started laughing uncontrollably at the situation; it was a mocking laugh that showed he was never going to behave like a sycophant and his laugh provoked in us all to respond in kind, giggling along too. With a painful attempt to hide a contorted facial expression of embarrassment, the Psychiatrist asked RC to please explain.

RC stood, cleared his throat and then over what must have been a ten minute oration, RC recounted the top five leading Psychiatric diagnoses and treatments of 'combat stress' and broke it down to these words: "listen carefully Mr. Physician: I am only going to say this once. You are obviously trying to see if we can self-regulate our primitive actions driven by the limbic system in our adrenaline soaked brains and put the evil-genie-of-war back into its bottle before you will allow us to go back and play in the sand box with all of the other well behaved children, unless of course you want to pursue the short-cut method of drugs and electroshock therapy. In a phrase, the test is: 'can these men get their head on straight and prove they are not a danger to themselves or to other members of capitalist society, or do we need to lobotomize these brutes and thereby dismantle the machine of war, so that the general population is safe?' The flaw I see in your assumed method of confirming and treating a hasty diagnosis is that surely your approach does not include an updated look at our unique medical history and physical assessments since we have been removed from combat. Thus far all I see from you is that you don't realize that we have already been beyond stressed-out; so you are over doing it in the wrong direction if you are going to stress test us again ... that will only induce high performance combat readiness, showing how well we do in battle, it will not show how we would behave in a sedate social setting. Ultimately your little experimental camp here would therefore be putting on hold the real environmental stimulus, or lack of the proper relevant stimulus, that could remotely or possibly trigger anti-social ideation and behavior, of which you and your bosses are so mortally terrified of seeing from us, the Savage-warriors. I calculate that the odds of achieving any clinical efficacy in your approach to us either collectively or individually is seventy three thousand nine hundred and two, to one. Personally, I think you already have failed. I am not going to do a damn thing you say to do." The Psychiatrist was speechless: he tried to wrap up the session quickly. We never saw that particular Psychiatrist again.

I never noticed RC to be mentally imbalanced. Was he sad? Yes. Was he melancholy and brooding – well hell yes, always during the time we were there ... you would be that way too, if you had accomplished close to one of his twenty plus missions during the Gulf War and lived through some of the devastation. What I want to emphasize here, for the record, is that the unusually virtuous things about RC during that phase of his life are what I will use to illustrate examples of how humane and kind he was deep down.

After the first week, after RC destroyed the young Psychiatrist's confidence in the proposed treatment and therapy, the military 'superiors' scrambled hard to find a Psychiatrist who knew what the hell they were doing with a military group of soldiers who needed post-combat psychological testing and assessment for social transitioning or *"re-enculturation-al-ism"* as we mockingly referred to it.

Five new Psychiatrists were brought in to replace the ineffective doctor that they tried to foist on us during week number one. The 'Five new Shrinks' asked if we could all meet at the mess hall for a half-hour meeting. There was a lingering smell of burnt beef in the mess-hall, which made a few of us have flashbacks to a bombing site that involved a dairy farm during the Persian Gulf. No one wanted to open up and talk.

RC, however, had the courage to get the ball rolling and it made a big difference in my life and had a good impact on all of the other guys too. Looking squarely at the Physicians, RC said, "gentlemen let's consider the option of cutting to the chase, to save everyone time and save our government money. I will go first and let you know what symptoms I am experiencing from my combat activities OK?"

RC gave another honest but an altogether more detailed speech that sparked several other men to see it was OK to open up and talk about their feelings, describe their unique nightmares in detail and describe our personal interpretation of our dreams: if for no other reason, to support the conclusion that being emotionally communicative meant trading away the risk of being seen as vulnerable in exchange for expediting their own freedom of "getting the hell out of the rat's maze of this isolated psycho-fix'em-up camp" as RC jokingly said.

Here is what I can remember of RC's original speech that he volunteered to make in front of all of us and all five of the new shrinks: I think it shows you what kind of man he was. "Honestly, I am having quite an impossible time controlling the timing and expression of my emotions: not in terms of harm, but in terms of the emotions getting expressed almost immediately ... what I mean is that I am on edge emotionally because I cannot sleep soundly. Whatever noise I hear in the external environment is instinctively processed in my central nervous system as a threat and so automatically the fight-or-flight response means I immediately wake up fueled by adrenaline and rage so that physically I am always swinging, kicking and grasping for anything that can be used as a weapon to counter-attack the source of the noise. My other senses are out of balance in terms of my emotional response to unexpected noises ... here is a concrete example of what I mean. Here we are in Alaska and I cannot hear the crickets singing their hearts out in those precious moments before sunset and there are no skunks around here and the birds sound pretty when they sing but there are not enough of them to offset the sounds and sights and smells and sensations that are constantly streaming in from my senses to my brain when I try to sleep, which is too impossible, especially when it is twenty hours of daylight here! It is an overwhelming amount of sensory information overload. It's like when I don't sleep I cannot be myself and I cannot be myself if all I am focused on is this athletic combat use of my heightened senses every second of a perceived situation of being under attack and if it is a life or death situation. I expend all my energy to force myself to be in a heightened state of perfectly defensive vigilance, and I have to rely on adrenaline to keep my muscles finely tuned for a counter-attack at any moment. My freewill is OK with surviving: but is that all there is left to my existence, to survive another moment only to barely survive in another future moment? The logical part of my brain is also there in every moment, questioning whether my body is going to be consumed in adrenaline and nightmares and images in my dreams. Is my purpose of existence now to keep clawing and fighting and primitively regressing into something subhuman? It is <u>not</u> that I cannot turn off or restrain the caveman's immediate and lightning quick response to kill-or-be-killed: it is a crucial point to remember that it will take a while to get to the point of feeling safe enough to sleep and once I sleep then I can get rested and get repaired. For me, my repair time has to be spent in the great outdoors, where I can see everything near and far. Right now, it is important to realize that all is darkness in my mind, when I am trying to sleep and dream, and sleep is only a few minutes, if at all. What would be a good therapy? Adrenaline charged experiences that lead to an enjoyment of life, if only as a transition mechanism toward re-directing the ultimate results of adrenaline charged combat action. Doctors, let us go sky diving out of the helicopters, let us hear the chopper sounds, let us while we are falling choose life and choose to open the parachute. We should have the sole choice of falling from the sky to measure the limits of our mortality by hopefully not bouncing off the ground. We should have the sole choice of growing and caring for plants in a garden to grow food we can eat. We should be able to have plenty of space between us and another human being during this transition time, so we can build our own cabin and have a little bit of our own territory to exclusively use, enjoy, and relax upon, until we can regain the sense that all life is sacred again."

The new Psychiatrists quickly zeroed in on what RC was trying to communicate and they responded fairly and in helpful ways to get all of us to deal truthfully with trying to become civilized once again.

The doctors were the crazy ones because unbelievably they let us go skydiving from the helicopters. Flying through the beautiful blue sky high over the alluvial fields near Palmer Alaska, located a pleasant driving distance North of Anchorage, we asked the pilots to climb the helicopters to 23,000 feet, (to avoid passing out we had to use oxygen masks like the fighter pilots use), so that we could see the Blue-Ice from the Matanuska Glacier. A moment before we jumped out of the choppers, RC pulled his oxygen mask so he could talk loud enough for me to hear him, yelling to me "this is the way I always wanted to go out of this world, flying like a bird to see the beauty of mother nature and then falling into the arms of mother Earth, sped by gravity's greedy embrace ... gravity has never been my friend: it steals time and distance from my soul. All I have to lose now is gravity and then everything will be fine." He smiled, put back on his oxygen mask and then with hand-signals he showed all of us that he volunteered to be the first one to jump out of the chopper. With a double thumbs-up signal, and a rogue's smile, he launched himself into a swan dive out the open chopper door and then assumed a flying Eagle position of diving headfirst straight down toward the Earth. At what must have been only 1,500 feet above ground, he popped open his parachute, much to the nail-biting relief of the new Psychiatrists monitoring the whole 'therapeutic jump' from the ground below us.

When those of us that were still high above in the helicopters could see that RC made it OK, only then did the rest of the men have enough courage to step up and take their turns jumping: all of us chose to open their parachutes, so all of us chose to live. At the time I couldn't fully understand what RC was saying to me, or showing us, by his actions ... in hindsight, it all now seems profound and humanely transcendent. I can tell you this about RC: the wind was his friend, more so than any other force in nature; he flew and fell like an Eagle that day.

A few days after that therapeutic parachute jump RC seemed to be bored 'I have had enough of this place' he said, smiling wryly and mischievously. I knew he was up to something, yet he did not share any details with me. I laughed hilariously three days later, (even today I laugh admiringly at this story about RC) when several people from a Congressional Investigative Audit Team showed up at our Alaska transition site, complete with their own armed guards, new Physicians, Lawyers from the J.A.G. Corps and some computer technicians from the National Security Agency. They took all of us immediately by a chartered jet to Andrews A.F.B. in Washington D.C. for the purpose and process of getting our testimony about the Alaska transition experience. After two weeks of daily legal depositions and testimony, then they let us go free with Honorable Discharges. Apparently, as I later found out from speaking with the other guys there with us at the Alaska site, RC was the one who sprung us all out of our situation in Alaska. RC was quite talented with computer stuff. He had stealthily commandeered a truck and drove it off base in order to 'borrow' some computer equipment which he brought back on base. While the military leadership was sleeping, he somehow used the borrowed computer equipment to get into their entire computer system, copied all of the files for expense reports and medical records (except his records and my records) and then he transmitted all of it electronically to the U.S. Government General Accounting Office and to all of the secretaries of all of the Senate and House of Representatives in Congress. Believing strongly in freedom of the press RC thought he should also share the computer files with the New York Times newspaper. Irregularities in expenses and unauthorized disclosure of protected medical information discoverable in the electronic files were highlighted by RC and easy to detect, which obviously got the Alaska site shut down in record fast time and resulted in several judicial punishments for the military leaders of that site. Three nerdy guys from the National Security Agency eagerly wanted to interview RC and learn how he breached the Government Cyber-Security and, I suspected, that they wanted to recruit him for some special work. RC said that he would show them how he did it, but first they had to help him return all of the computer equipment that he 'borrowed' to its rightful owners in Alaska.

One thing was clear to me and clear to all of us who were there: for each person's own good, nobody wanted to, or more importantly should never try to, mess with RC or cross him in the slightest way. RC didn't want to be liked or treated differently or worshipped: he just wanted to be left alone to do things his own way. I also saw a clear method to RC's madness ... he was deliberately giving the National Security Agency his calling card by proving he could hack through the government secure computers. It was, in RC's way, communicating a fair-warning message: "you had better think-twice before spying on me...my pay-backs will be hellish for you."

I also remember the times before we were at the Alaska site, out as a large group on combat missions in the Persian Gulf Region ... RC was the one person almost all of us went to in order to get help solving a problem that no one else could figure out (he solved every problem brought to him within a few minutes), my discussions with people who knew RC over the years and in comparing notes of our experiences, it is truthful to say that during his contractor days for the military, most of RC's military contract managers back in those days, could not stand him at all. The common thread of the insufferable-ness was that RC had to do things his way, he worked alone and his way turned out to deliver better results through superior solutions ... he always seemed to have unique contributions to several human efforts at improving everything, all the while encouraging individual creativity. RC often commented that dealing with the military 'superiors' or civilian people in positions of authority, was for him, like "trying to deal logically with impossibly angry monkeys, stuck on their self-centered egos at all costs – they really refused to take a broader view of something beyond their own consciousness, of what alternatives and unorthodox options would benefit the most people with no harm."

Whenever I was called to go into battle of any kind, I requested that RC be hired to lead the charge: I was absolutely convinced that since he was too much of a humanist at heart; RC would never leave anyone behind, he would never diminish anyone and he never would quit or give up on the mission. The parts of RC that would never quit seem to somehow live on. I remember him well."

I was amused at the story, in terms of the admiration he felt for RC's accomplishments and anti-authoritarianism, yet the cloak-and-dagger theme was disturbing. His story raised several troubling questions for me about RC's real work during the Gulf War. My main questions were, why did he fight to correct the records that he was killed in action? Would not a secret spy want to be declared legally dead, in order to benefit from the legal protection that in America, you cannot prosecute a dead-man for a crime? That was the origin of the spy world name for someone who was declared legally dead on paper yet was still alive in the real-world and doing top secret missions: a spook, or spooking around. Why did RC fight against that? Perhaps the military and the government were trying to make him an involuntary spook.

Flying back home to Seattle, the three and a half hour flight from Anchorage to Seattle at sunrise left me feeling too tired and exhausted, yet my troubled mind was racing with so many questions: once again, I had to write down each question so I could quit worrying about forgetting something and try to force myself asleep. As I finished my list of seventy-four questions, I hoped that my next interview in Portland with one of the financial people RC associated with, for U.S.A. based business transactions, would shed some light on the parts of RC's life that made him most famous: his financial investments and private equity mergers and acquisitions. I needed a great deal of coffee to keep me awake for my three hour drive to Portland. I arrived in Portland around lunch-time, and met my next interview subject at an old-fashioned restaurant near the airport. He too asked me to not use his name, as he had several confidentiality agreements with RC that he wanted to honor. I thought that was an absurd thing to say, since RC was already dead and gone, yet I was too tired to put up much of an argument because I wanted to get this interview over and take some sleeping pills and try once again to sleep. After ordering a New York Steak and Eggs, I turned on my digital recorder and encouraged him to talk away while I ate ... funny thing, I could hear my gulping of food sounds in the background when I later listened to the recording of our interview. This guy was wearing a typical black business suit. He looked like a generic stock trading clerk to me.

**A Business Agent from Portland** - *"RC invested with great success in many different countries, markets and economies...* In a phrase, I would describe what I admired most about RC was that he was an incredibly creative investor. He seemed to be an economy unto himself, investing in businesses within several different countries. Compared to all of my other financial clients, he was the only one who didn't lose all his asset value during any of the several market crashes he weathered throughout his brief life.

None of the standard economic and financial analytical methods and tools used by the rest of us mortals seemed to be of any relevance to RC in his investing activities. "If everyone uses the same payoff matrix and mathematical game theory, then the market is in a stalemate, or in direct terms, when Lemmings can't decide which cliff to jump off of, then no one jumps at all. What a terrible result of group-think!" That image of Lemmings did not seem very direct, to me.

RC acted in the business world as if he was answerable to no one for his decisions and transactions: no one had a vote or a veto over him; yet although he did things as he pleased, what gave him a sense of meaning was when he helped others become financially independent by educating them in how to work their own way up to the self-imposed limits of benevolent capitalism and humane treatment of others. That was another thing that bothered me about RC: he was too restrained in his acquisitions and investments ... he could have been richer than God, but profits were not his ultimate goal.

When I first met him, his magnanimous generosity with his money was repugnant to me: if he would have given me half of the money he gave away, I could have created an empire of my own. I tried to understand the motivations and decision-science methods behind his successful transactions, but I often reached the point of getting a headache instead of figuring out how he invented new data analysis tricks-of-the-trade, that consistently out-performed any other methods. He carried several secret mathematical methods in his head, sometimes using a computer but mostly calculating things silently in his mind at lightning fast speed, which was scary-cool (as my teenage daughter says), during the times we were in meetings and he needed to make decisions. He would ask for the data, glance at it quickly, ask a few questions, and as we were speaking the answers to him, he would be listening but also simultaneously calculating the best path to take for any particular decision. He had a rationalized approach to using math and statistics and wanted current and accurate data, but the one thing he seemed to add to his mysterious methods of making decisions, was a lot more data that he said was "factoring in to the analysis, also the essential human equation, trying to do the most good for all people while simultaneously harming no-one."

The transactions of RC that I studied were multi-million dollar financial investments in non-violent business activities. The underlying companies had to be non-exploitative of workers, fair and reasonable and law-abiding in all countries they did business in. Whenever I tried to delve into details, I discovered that he had several accounts for investing and the payments and streams of cash flows seemed un-traceable, starting from an original site in the U.S. then moving outward to international banks, all of it done electronically. RC said that he had developed some customized computer software program and had his own proprietary network, using at least seven high-speed electronic cut-outs over the internet and into banks in several jurisdictions that were tax havens that encouraged and protected his confidential banking transactions. He also used off-setting risk neutral transactions where funds would be borrowed against cash-basis asset values. He swapped hybrid mixtures of asset funded convertible securities. He hedged all of those things with investment contracts that were insured by money in futures and options. He ran foreign currency investments and exchange arbitrage security investments so efficiently that any currency volatility problems in the markets would still be opportunities for him to make money for his businesses. All of the accounts and interlocking transactions and investment securities ultimately ended up being held exclusively for RC's benefit in a series of numbered anonymous Trust and banking accounts in Vanuatu and Singapore. Only RC knew all of the accounts and was the only one with access rights and password codes to control the authorizations for complex encryption/decryption protocols for each high-speed series of transactions. Combining everything together, the tax-free status of his profits from all the transactions offset the transaction costs and also since he was an investor in the institutions he used, he could truthfully say that he made money off of doing business in any type of market, whether the prices were trending up or down.

For me, the most bewildering methodology behind some of his more obscure transactions, involved his purchases on the spot markets around the world of actual commodities: so what I mean is that he bought and shipped and delivered tons of rice, thousands of gallons of Milk and Computers and Copper-wire and live farm animals, given to people who were at risk for starvation and war-torn hardships.

I was never able to find another private individual who could routinely write a check for $100 million U.S. Dollars without first having to sell major assets, but RC could do it several times a year. I did find out that all of his commodity purchases were shipped to charitable organizations, those entities that could help people suffering in abject poverty – he spread his gifts among several countries. The unofficial joke was that RC could outdo the United Nations for humanitarian relief. What I saw made me believe it was true: it was no joke.

I never had access to, or saw even one-percent of the entire universe of RC's transactional information: fragments of his information that I saw were protected by compartmentalization. I never had access to any of his tax returns. I wanted to learn more from him, but he seemed to be a secretive wizard: my impression of him was that of those transactions I could understand, it was just the tip of the iceberg with this guy – it was kind of scary; I mean how well he did, how he could manage it all on his own.

He used technology for good in the world, which seemed rare to me. Profit was not important to him to keep and enjoy on his own. Using his profits to help poor people become self-sufficient and to help real people in need was of the greatest importance to him.

Before he died, he was mentioning to several of us in my investment firm, that we should look seriously about investing at least 20% of our portfolios into Singapore based technological and bio-technology based companies. "Singapore is poised to become quite a prosperous country in a few years" he would claim, "yet also have bank accounts in Australia and Canada: people in those two countries consistently enjoy banking systems that are very solid and reliable. Besides, the higher tax-rates mean that the government will have a greater moral obligation to fund and operate social support services that will take care of the most vulnerable people in their society."

Let me close with what I think is the best example of RC's philosophical perspective when pursuing his own type of nice-guy-capitalism. One time in New York we had a big business dinner and RC made decisions that would bring him over thirty billions of dollars. He seemed sad at the end of the dinner. A group of we Lawyers and financial people were with RC, after the meeting, and to finish some firm decisions before submitting our legal papers for the merger, we needed to have RC tell us which way to go. RC walked everyone outside, hailed a Handy-Cab horse drawn carriage back to the hotel and as we all crowded into the carriage, RC looked at us, then looked at the horses and said: "most business people, managers, executives, supposed leaders, view their

Employees in the same way that most people view the horses pulling this carriage – the Employees in their view are merely work-horses, there is no effort on the part of the executives to make a human empathetic connection so that they could try to understand what their Employees need and then decide how best to help them. Every one of those people at dinner has that problem. They view the Employees as workhorses and have no qualms about whipping them into shape. They will never figure out that most of their Employees are struggling mightily to survive financially and they strongly resent being treated that way. Who wouldn't feel resentment? How cruel those people are, to boil down the continued employment of someone to the cruelty of 'do things my way or you are fired.' Everyone I have met is an expert in something and everyone I talk to has good alternative ideas that can help in any situation. Those jerks in the dinner meeting are too materialistic and measure their accomplishments only by reducing everything to monetary wealth and privilege and status – all of those things are meaningless when compared to helping a human being live fully and allowing them the economic opportunities to earn enough money to in turn enjoy following their hopes and working on achieving their dreams. It saddens me when any human being is treated as a resource, treated like a work-horse: that is an example of pure evil. Here is my final offer, my final marching orders to all of you; please go ahead and submit the merger offer at the maximum price, then please give it your top priority to get to work on drawing up an Employee stock ownership plan where I will only have complete control of the corporation for one year, then sell it all to the Employees ... I believe that they have suffered enough, so let's make it easy on them now ... they have genuinely and truly earned it. I am going to the airport, and will be flying home tonight, call me on my jet Satellite phone if you need any more questions answered." We knew that RC had enough business talk for one day, and that he was eager to get home to his family. Several of us already knew what he meant, that RC would be flying his own private jet home, serving as the pilot himself, and it would be OK to call him if we needed to, he didn't mind, since he regularly made it back to Seattle from any East Coast American city within less than four hours, flying directly ... he had one of the fastest jets in the world."

After this interview, I politely thanked him for his time and rushed to the freeway to make it home to Seattle before rush hour traffic made me suffer. I had to get home and sleep off these interview experiences ... the more I heard from these people after the funeral, the more questions I had, regarding the apparent incongruities in RC's life, and if these people could be believed, and if what they were saying were true about RC.

A couple of days later, after I was fully rested and thinking clearly again, the next person I interviewed was a physician from Seattle. We met for the interview downtown near the Pike Street Market along the water front. I chose a small restaurant that served cinnamon rolls and stoutly-caffeinated coffee. A short, white-haired physician wearing old-fashioned horn-rimmed glasses with incredibly thick lenses showed up, he appeared very much like a mad-scientist caricature from some cheap science fiction movie.

**A Doctor from Seattle** - *"At times I wondered if I was serving as a Physician to a patient who was a financial counter-terrorist for the U.S. Government...* I cannot prove what I suspected RC really was in the world or what he really did for work, but RC was my favorite patient, because he was so interesting and unique. I first met him at a military installation in Alaska after the war: I thought he was a genius with Asperger's Syndrome, but I was wrong about the medical diagnosis, yet correct about the genius part. During the 1990's, all military personnel labeled high-risk and a select few civilian contractors who were also considered high-risk, had to exit-process through a series of sociability and psychological tests before they were discharged into society. My job at the time was to clinically screen them, it was me along with a team of seven-teen other Physicians representing various medical specialties including mostly Psychiatrists. RC was the only challenging case of mine at the Alaska military installation. I will get into some more of those details later.

After my service in Alaska, I moved to the Seattle area and opened a clinic. RC was a regular patient and I agreed to look after him since already knowing the complicated details of his history and physical status after the Gulf War. I often told him that he was a specimen who could help medical research and help save lives in the future, but he laughed at me and made comments about being an unwilling lab rat.

Generally he was in good physical health, although his mental condition was a mystery to me until I referred him to a medical radiologist who used advanced imaging from Positron Emission Tomography equipment, and they detected a rare form of brain cancer. The diagnosis did help explain some of his unusual behavior. After the tumor biopsy and confirmed diagnosis results were given to me, I informed him of it the same day. He had one of the rarest and most lethal forms of brain cancer I have ever been involved with in my medical career. Because of the terminal nature of his cancer and the rapid growth of the tumor, I really was not able to offer the kind of treatment options he hoped for. I ran several times, all of the standardized clinical probability calculations, sifting through his clinical results: RC's prognosis was grim. I noticed that everything went from challenging to worse for RC in his life.

A few days after his brain cancer diagnosis, RC made an appointment for a high-tech blood draw; he wanted to have his blood sent to a specialized lab for detailed DNA analysis. Since he first found out that he was adopted, he wanted to discover the true family heritage and clear up some of the family history beyond the living memories of his adoptive relatives. He seemed intent on leaving a road-map of family genetics for his children to ponder when he was gone. When his DNA analysis came back with a specific geographic-taxonomy of his ethnicity, he brought the detailed document to me for follow-up questions. "Hey Doc, this DNA result shows some unique things on both sides of my parents' families' so I am hoping you can suggest several of the top experts in that discipline so that I can go to see about fleshing-out some more details. Ha, ha, 'fleshing-out' get it? No pun intended." I put him in contact with four different DNA Genomics experts and over the course of the next month RC got most of his answers. He had several different people confirm that he was related to Ghengis Khan. RC then traveled frequently to Ireland, Italy, Israel, Sweden, Denmark, and Kyrgyzstan and onto the Kashmir-Himalaya region, presumably to try and connect with distant relatives, before his time alive was cut short by the tumor in his brain.

After his first return trip from those regions, some government men in gray suits dropped in on me with valid search warrants and detailed questions relating to RC. Calling my Lawyers almost hourly that day, we all got into a routine that week of interviews and visits Orwellian appearing agents from Big-Brother. To me it was a dance-with-the-Devil. The government agents wanted me to know they were from the United States Government and they were trying to protect RC, not harm him. They explained why and I decided to cooperate with them. I never saw RC again. I also received more return visits from some of those gray-suited-government-men the next morning after the day RC was killed in Canada. They had more questions than I had time, so I called my Lawyer and they spoke among themselves the phone for a while, then they left. Lawyers can be so helpful.

Anecdotally, the only time I knew he was so mad at me that he was moments close to throwing me out a window, was one time at my clinic. RC was in the waiting room, it was a rough day and I had not slept for thirty-hours since I was on-call at the hospital. My staff was moving too slow for my frustration and exhaustion level, so I started yelling to speed them up and RC heard me. The first thing he said when it was his turn for a general yearly physical exam was to say to me: "hey doc, you are hurting their feelings, or put differently, you are behaving like an over-privileged, over-compensated bourgeois bastard." I got the point and I calmed down, because of anyone on the Earth I feared, it was RC: so I figured I had better show him that at least I would listen to him. I never got the chance to thank RC for helping me treat my staff better. My clinic became more profitable: it actually tripled in profits, after I treated everyone better."

This interview was worth my time, I thought, as the Physician hurriedly wrapped up answering my questions and excusing himself to get back to work. What was consistent with other interviews was the information about RC's humanitarian view of treating everyone equally well. The DNA story and RC's search for surviving relatives was fascinating. I wanted to follow-up with RC's children to see if they had knowledge of any current relatives newly discovered, that would be interested in letting me interview them in order to find out as much about RC's genetics and cultural family history as possible.

The next person I interviewed was a Hindu Priest currently living in Seattle, highly educated from attending Universities in Canada and in the United Kingdom. Among his several academic degrees he also held a PhD in Comparative Theology. We talked at his Temple in Seattle. It was an enjoyable interview, after talking with him I felt a great deal of respect for how much he cared about others and for his insights into RC's soul.

**A Religious Leader from Seattle** - *"An anguished soul, tormented by his self-made wealth and haunted by the ghosts of his unknown ancestors...* RC and I visited at least monthly on the boat trip from Seattle to Port Angeles Washington. I knew him as an acquaintance and part-time visitor to my Temple and a generous financial donor. He struck me as a rare individual; truthful, telling me at the beginning of our first few conversations that although he was no longer practicing any type of Religion, he still felt the metaphysical inertia of struggling with questions of conscience, specifically questioning whether God or Gods or other Deities existed, among several other heavy doubts. Despite his spiritual challenges, he did say that he would be happy to help me since our Temple had an active ministry effort to give food, shelter and medical care to the homeless both in Seattle and in Vancouver. I never knew exactly what his line of work was or why he traveled regularly like clockwork to Vancouver from Seattle "on business" but he seemed genuine and generous and his money and resources did not appear to be coming from illegal or immoral sources.

Most of the content of our conversations centered upon religious topics: he dissected conversational topics from a philosophical and scientific perspective. He was constantly searching for meaning in life, in his life, a life that seemed to be full of self-doubt primarily from his self-described search for answers to the questions of why was he an orphan, why would a benevolent God or Gods allow evil in the world and other similarly difficult topics.

We often discussed current world events. I thoroughly enjoyed talking with him during all of our wide-ranging discussions. He seemed to me to always be well informed about a wide range of topics, analytical without being pretentious and sincere from a heart full of humane respect for all forms of life. He had a clear sense of right and wrong. RC identified with and sympathized with the poorest people of the societies in several countries he visited often.

The only thing I noticed about him, the one thing that would provoke a streak of zero tolerance, was prevarication or deception from someone he evaluated as having evil intentions – and it didn't matter who it was. If they were being disingenuous, he would go through the roof and attack them verbally, exposing their imminent intended harm that RC perceived, as their true goal. He was open about his hatred of and opposition to evil people: those he defined as "the vain and cruel people who crave power over others in order to exercise control over those who cannot protect themselves against being exploited for profit." I had to ask him time and again about that particular view, which glaringly contradicted his respect for all forms of life. "I have several contradictory views. I am my own greatest enemy in my search for a meaningful life."

Far outweighing his negative behavior toward people he considered evil, was his very calm and kindly behavior and generosity toward those people he encountered that were having a difficult time in their life ... he was especially overprotective and worried about the welfare of families, he seemed to want to help those families I identified for him from my contact with them at the Temple, those that were poor and had experienced challenges feeding themselves with healthy food.

My favorite conversation with him was when I asked RC directly, "do you believe in some kind of a Supreme Being since you obviously have lost your motivation to participate in a systematic and societal based Religion?" He was silent for a moment then smiled at me. He began to answer the question in a dialectically logical manner, but then became embarrassingly blunt: "yes of course I believe in a Supreme-Being or Beings but it seems that our world is overseen by a passive Deity or Deities. More accurately I have respect for the forces of nature that are understood in terms of the Laws of Physics. If you hear that I have replaced my loss of Religion with a more scientific view of nature and mankind, then you understand where my struggle of conscience is leading me. The overly formalistic and hierarchical Religion from my upbringing was the only concept of a God that I had and in the Western Civilization, my young mind perceived God as perpetually angry and vengeful, as if my being alive in a human body was a punishment from birth to death. I wanted a happier existence than living in constant fear of going to Hell for the slightest questioning of my faith at the time."

RC was to me a highly developed skeptic, but not a full-fledged atheist and not an agnostic. He was scientific, but not entirely limited to empiricism and mathematics and evolutionary theory. I suspect that he avoided systematic Religion because of the insight that all Religions suffer from humanity's cultural relativism, or in high-minded terms "anthropomorphism," the fundamental attribution error of self-projection of one's values into the mystical and spiritual realms, put simply, creating Deities in your own image.

I pointed out to him that I also noticed that regarding questions of faith it seemed to ring hollow to me that he resorted to scientifically empirical rationalizations almost all of the time, instead of dealing with the feeling of spirituality directly and without referring to anything non-spiritual as its justification that it is OK to feel a spiritual connection to a God or

Gods.  He seemed to be playing a game of looking at the tension between faith and reason as nothing more than a tradeoff between humanity's emotional feelings and the sterile rational pursuit of the predictive certainty of scientific knowledge (for him), as if navigation in the spiritual world required perfect information about the destination before beginning a journey, and for him it was necessary to have perfect data to be fed into a GPS electronic guide device, before taking any steps toward a spiritual destination.  It was as if he was only willing to say that he believed in data, nothing else that was mystical and unquantifiable.  I asked RC, why would they be mutually exclusive things?  If Religion was too mystically arbitrary and unproven, then science was at the opposite extreme of being anti-human in that it is way too rigorous and overdone in its proofs to the extreme outcome of removing any wonder or mystery in his life.  At least that was the view he held and that he was struggling with.  He said is biggest problem with his own spirituality is that God or The Gods are silent toward him.  His solution to the silence was to admit only to himself that he was comfortable being a martyr, however he was unwilling to become a mystic.  I often would shake my head, realizing that it must be an ultimately tormented conscience he must have had, to try and wrestle with his unique way of living out those two worldviews in an extreme manner, while also admittedly feeling guilty for being so wealthy.  Part of his guilt was, I would surmise, from him being an orphan, and his worry over what his unknown ancestors would think of him, since he assumed they were all from a working class labor background, and would view his wealth as only the inevitable result of thievery.  He was more upbeat and optimistic when we discussed the historical patterns in most cultures that there was a need to develop Religion in order to make society function at all.  I also pointed out to RC that he should read the philosophical works of Spinoza, since they were in synch regarding some similar views about human nature and the universe.

He was happiest though, and he described with genuine joy, his experiences of getting out of the city with his family and getting back to nature, how for him a walk in the woods with his children or taking family members boating on a lake was for him a spiritually happy experience that he described as something that fed "what was left of my soul."  He shared with me that those were the few moments in his life where he felt open up to the possibility that maybe there is a Supreme Being or Beings that care for, and nurture, every living thing.  It was those moments when he was away from cities and out walking in the mountains that he felt most alive, most at peace, able to see truth and beauty everywhere. He smiled proudly, retelling stories about the sense of wonder and happiness he saw on his children's faces when they encountered wildlife for the first time while on their trips. "Dad, can we take the Caribou home as a pet?" That story made him laugh every time he retold it.

RC took me fishing with him once. We traveled in one of his helicopters inland to a lake in North Idaho. We were accompanied by three other helicopters full of body-guards. RC gave me a fishing creel, a pole and a tackle box full of everything I needed to catch fish. The fishing trip also reminded me of fishing when I was a young boy in India. The first fishing creel I saw was my Grandfather's made of thatched bamboo reeds. We would catch Snow Trout in the mountain streams near the Western Himalayas and then after we immigrated to British Columbia my Grandfather seemed to take great solace in continuing his sport fishing in the Fraser River Valleys, catching a variety of Trout and Salmon. I would stare at the fish he caught, admiring how beautiful the colored dappling prisms of scales and water droplets on the Trout would shimmer and shine in the sunlight. My Grandfather and I let all of our fish go back in the water: I couldn't bear to keep them out of water and away from their home too long. Those memories came to mind when I was fishing with RC in Idaho, and for a few moments I grew sentimental and nostalgic, holding that fishing creel in my hands, thinking of my dead relatives, thinking of how many wonderful memories they gave me during all of our family fishing trips together.

RC was the only person I encountered in my adult life who knew what I was talking about by first-hand knowledge, when I said things like, "I remember when we first emigrated to Canada, the early days of my youth growing up in a small lumber manufacturing 'timber-town' in British Columbia, over near Nelson B.C., I still remember the pleasant aroma in the air when driving into town: it was from the wood burning smoke from the old sawmill beehive burners – if you ever experienced the smell of smoke from wood cut from ancient forests; it was as if the spirits of the trees escaped to the Heavens in the smoke as the byproduct of a sawmill converting trees hundreds of years old into lumber for someone's new house." RC said that he too had similar experiences and also associated the smell of wood fire smoke with comfortable memories of being warm by a fire after a cold day spent enjoyably hiking in the mountains.

No one from the city ever wanted to try and understand RC's long stretches of time that he spent away from the city, far beyond the party crowds. RC also seemed to be a disciplined ascetic, always avoiding parties and never drinking alcohol. Instead, RC preferred whenever possible to be with his family and when they were too busy to spend time with him, he was outside, alone in the mountains and often in the summer time he was thoroughly enjoying "being off the grid and on the lake." People who lived out their entire lives in the city often misunderstood those elements of RC and mistakenly assumed it to be anti-social behavior: it really wasn't that at all. RC could only stand so much of the traffic, the vanity, greed and self-centeredness of most people that he encountered in the cities he traveled through while conducting business or working on his charitable pursuits.

RC often described to me his true love of nature on one of our final boat trips together. "I remember when I was young, the feeling, and the tangible awareness in all of my senses, of virtue, of the wonder and awe and happiness and hope and adrenaline rush of waking before dawn to go out in the wilderness to go on some fun adventures, seeing natural beauty … the most important thing to me was being out in the woods. Being outdoors communing with nature was essential to replenishing my soul. It was exhilaration over the miracle of being alive: it wasn't about cutting trees or killing animals or anything like that, instead it truly was all about life, about God's creation of beauty in nature and the outdoors. It was also a sense of being free of the burdens of society, to walk independently and in solitude, enjoying all that your senses could perceive and admire about the woods, the animals, and the beauty of *everything.* What a miracle that was. It was the closest thing I experienced to understanding and feeling what 'transcendence' means: it was connecting with the possibility of having a soul. It was balance and benevolence and a feeling of being in the right place, of a feeling of being at home … I am dwelling in tranquility where my hope drives me towards: being in the woods, in the mountains, especially on the lake."

Because I worried over the state of his health, the only unsettling thing for me about RC was a recurring insight he had about assessing the intentions and motivations of others. He asked me if I had a gift from God or the Gods that allowed me to use several senses and perceptions at one moment in time when assessing the state of someone's soul. I was perplexed by the question. "What are you talking about RC? I have to use verbal speech and visual observation of body language to figure out what is going on with people beyond their literal words." He laughed. "Of course, I do understand. What I mean is this: have you ever had a vision inspired 'insight' or an impressionistic intuition about someone's soul, someone you are talking to? The people I encounter, I can get a sense, registered to me visually, about their soul. For example, a lot of people I encounter are in business. Greed perniciously wraps itself around a business person's soul and chokes it to death, killing the humane and good light that naturally makes it to the light of day when people are younger, when they used to see the world clearly through bright sunlight. The worst cases of greed appear to me as a snarl of amber-bush bramble branches twisted in a cancerous web of tree roots around their heart and soul. I also see those frightening images wrapped around those people in the world who are in fear of everything, those who embrace mediocrity in order to find comfort in the predictability of redundant and recurring cycles of daily life." RC did apologize for the melodramatic imagery, saying that the scientific explanation was that his senses registering that type of contradictory imagery could be attributed to his medical condition, although he never divulged to me what that condition really was. I felt empathy for his condition, but he clearly did not want to worry me with too many details about his physical ailments. I assumed he was suffering from some condition similar to Kinesthesia. Strangely curious to me though, a contradiction I noticed in RC was that he was comfortable divulging to me all the various details about his spiritual turmoil, yet he was so uncomfortable and categorically secretive about most other details of his life.

Several times I encouraged RC to go see my friends at the Sikh Gurdwara in Seattle. I had to reiterate that the purpose of my suggestion was for enlightenment and that it would be a good thing based on my observation that many of RC's views on Capitalism and how RC transacted business in the complex modern world would be compatible in several ways with Sikhism. He listened intently and seemed very keen on me arranging an introduction. I made the communications for arranging a meeting and setting up the introductions in December and we were all going to get together in late January for a brief meeting in Seattle. Regrettably, RC died before that meeting took place. I had remote hopes that such a meeting would bring him towards some comfort for his spiritually tormented soul.

On what would be our last boat trip to Vancouver together, a few weeks before I received word he had died, RC gave me two presents: one was a woven basket made of Alaskan Yellow-Cedar bark, and it was full of fresh Huckleberries he had picked along the coastline of Vancouver Island, (he made the woven basket with his own hands). The second present was a Bible, but it was hollowed out inside, full of hundred dollar bills. Written on a note attached to the cash RC wrote: "God works in mysterious ways ... please use this money to help all those in need who visit your Temple." RC was a capitalist who was also a naturalist but mostly a humanist and generous man: how unique and rare he was in today's world."

I left the interview feeling like I had another brief glimpse into some of the overwhelming issues that bedeviled RC: his apparent pre-occupation with the afterlife and whether the Gods would judge him harshly. I thought that this interview was the most profound interview thus far. I was wrong.

I did not know what to expect for my next interview subject, it was with the homeless man that I saw RC give a cup of coffee to during my first chance meeting of RC in the coffee shop. His updated social status was changed recently to "formerly homeless" ever since RC had left in his will money and a Trustee's guidance to help the homeless man. For our interview, we met at the office of one of the many Attorneys RC hired. When I arrived for the meeting and was ushered into the conference room with windows overlooking downtown Seattle, I was surprised to see that the formerly homeless man was accompanied by people introduced to me as "his Lawyer, his Nurse, his Business Manager, and his Guardian." The formerly homeless man was wearing a comfortably loose-fitting tweed business suit. He seemed to be slightly sedated on drugs, yet he was coherent enough to speak in a way that expressed everything he wanted to say about RC. To make sure he said everything that was important, he was glancing at some handwritten notes on paper that looked like it had an official letterhead symbol from one of the local hospitals.

**A Formerly Homeless Man from Seattle** - *"I saw him just before he died. RC said he was going to teach me to fish someday soon: I didn't have the heart or will to tell him I was a newly converted vegan vegetarian...* I wanted to send a writing thing about RC to his funeral thing. It is my way to say sorry to his family. My lady friend at the Emergency Room, you know at the Big Blue and Plaid colored Hospital in Seattle, she is writing this for me as I talk. You don't know me, but I used to live on the street ... at least I was not in the rain gutter: I'm more of a sidewalk guy. Sometimes RC walked by and gave me fresh food and hot coffee and he stopped to talk with me. I remember him fine. We were kids together in the orphanage in Canada, so we go way, way back, in time. Our families moved to Seattle within a year of each other. I was in school with RC in America too.

Other people, my neighbors, we have all seen him, I'm not making it up, he's not a ghost ... he did stop a few times, helping me, helping my neighbors. Most people call us bums: not RC, he talked real to me, like I was still a person to respect.

He took me to the hospital a few times when I needed it. And my neighbors he took sometimes too to the hospital when they needed it, he took us all regularly to the hospital. Then and now, he somehow still pays for our medicine and my dreams are better. I don't believe his ghost pays for us, for our medical bills and pharmacy bills: I think it is the people that still work for him; they pay from his business account. That's the only way it makes sense to me. Strange thing, he's dead, but the real money from him still pays for us as we are living.

RC asked me about my life. I didn't want to tell it. He said that was OK, it was my personal and confidential business, not his to know. I told him that the street is my freedom. I don't have to answer to anyone but myself. He asked me if I wanted his help to get a paying job at the homeless shelter, I said: "I remember when I was a kid, we had a color television and hot food every day and I watched a show about a TV news story about and old wood cutter back East, in Newfoundland or New Hampshire, I think ... that guy on TV had a big truck and sharp axes and sharp saws and he would go out in the hills and find Witch-Hazel Wood, cut it and stack it high in his truck and drive slow to town and sell it for money. The town people made that clear Witch-Hazel stuff in a bottle that old guys would splash on their face after shaving with a straight razor made of special metal ... that was the type of work job for pay I wanted to do." RC was always respectable to me and I always said thank you and I really meant it as true when I said thank you to him.

I feel a crushing pain in my chest when I know now he is dead, but I want to tell his family that it is OK. RC told me often that when he dies and someday if I die too, that he will be walking by my street in the afterlife and we can if we want to, take my shopping cart down to the lake side and go fishing. He wants to take me fishing. "Come on over here my friend," he will say, "have some hot coffee, let's go fishing across the lake on the other side, we can catch some fish, then bring them here in the middle of your own street we will light a big fire and cook the fish for you and your neighbors and we will all have hot fish and hot coffee." I want his family to know that RC will be the only one who won't get mad if I still want to be a vegan vegetarian, if I go to Heaven, I hope I do, that's where he is I think. I still want to tell him thank you again.

I think that RC was the only one who didn't get mad when I told him that all the bad things in life happened in the world, because I'm a coward. He asked me why I thought that of myself, so I told him the story: you see it is because when I was fishing in Canada, in the summer, beside a mountain stream full of Trout. I was six years old: I heard a Gardener Snake eating a Tree Frog alive and the squealing sound made me cry and be scared and I ran away when I should have gone and helped save the Froggie. So I wonder if because of my cowardice from a long time ago, because I was too afraid to save the frog from the predator snake, that it was that one thing I couldn't do and that bad thing that sent out bad vibes through the skies and that somehow I had that bad energy caused RC's death. I heard news his plane fell out of the sky. I worry that I wasn't strong enough to give power to those I respected and loved ... to keep bad things from hitting RC.

My message is: don't be sad family ... RC understands ... it is not a bad thing for him to see all of you now only from far away. On my street, when the wind blows dusty air by me, it is like RC is saying "hi" to me by waving hello from far away ... his hands move the air. I will bet money that he is a good ghost now."

Wow, I was stunned ... the homeless man's story made me feel exceedingly sad. Although slightly medicated or sedated with drugs, what came through to me was that the formerly homeless man would never have to worry about being out wandering aimlessly on the unforgivingly harsh streets and starving, all thanks to RC's generosity. That interview lasted only ten minutes then I was politely ushered out of the office. Riding the elevator down forty-nine floors to ground level of the office building I had tears in my eyes.

Trying to gain my composure before going out and walking on the sidewalk to my illegally parked car, I forced myself to be objective, thinking about all of the information gained thus far about RC. Did I truly have enough data to say that I had a realistic picture of RC and that I understood his motives and thoughts?

I began to have doubts whether RC was all of those things to all of those real people. Those people who loved RC said that he was neither a renegade nor random nor a capitalist. Those who hated him muttered about him being a pragmatic humanist, too generous for his own good, ruining the capitalist system where only the shareholders of a business should have been made wealthy. Those neutral toward RC thought him to be an unfulfilled "artist," which was also an unkind euphemism in the business world at least, for someone who is unpredictable and a real pain in the backside. All admitted they did not fully understand him: "RC is too complex ... too overwrought ... a shattered soul." As it was celebrated, his life and the details of his existence seemed contradictory, dubious, murky and almost, but not quite, mystically enigmatic.

Among those who knew the flesh and blood RC, there was also in their speech an over-use of terms like "genius" which to me seemed to be stretching reality. Although I would concede the point that RC was capable of multi-step thinking at more levels and in more ways than most normal people, yet it was a practiced skill, nothing super-human. There seemed to be nothing spiritually mysterious or alien about RC's way of mentally processing information about the world, at least the way I saw it transpire in front of me when I spoke directly with him. I am not convinced he was solely responsible for all of the accomplishments attributed to him. There seems to be a benign conspiracy to portray RC as the most over-accomplished person on Earth.

My vocation in life as a journalist is to investigate human actions, thoughts and motivations that drive events in our world, so as to get at the true cause and effect of what is going on in society. When I am confronted with deceptive people that try to hinder, delay, diminish or deceive me in my effort to bring the truth to light for everyone to read, I usually feel intense disgust and revulsion. I feel the greatest amount of intense disgust for hypocrites and game players seemingly getting perverse enjoyment out of their efforts to divert me and try to manipulate me into areas where they want my story to go. It may work with their reluctantly compliant Employees who need to comply with a tyrant's whim only in order to keep their jobs and survive financially, but those bosses of the downtrodden are mostly psychos and pathological egomaniacs who cannot begin to accept or realize that their efforts at deception always fail to work on me. I know how to defend myself. Independently verifiable facts flowing from what is truly going on in the real-world are more important to me than currying favor with evil overachievers by mindlessly believing what they say, without empirically testing the information on my own.

Trying to use self-awareness to relate and integrate all of my mental efforts to understand all of the truth, in its complex entirety, and connect all of the true data points and facts of RC's life story, it still continued to bother me that my questions regarding RC would likely go unanswered because the dead cannot answer me truthfully or at all. Pursuing the story, I encountered several issues of self-doubt. It was a feeling of heaviness in my heart worse than missing a major deadline: it was more of a feeling that life had passed me by and I had missed winning the lottery because I used the winning ticket in my hands to blow my nose instead of cashing it in. Irreversible loss of not seizing a one-time opportunity, felt to me like the feeling I had in the past when at a funeral the coffin containing a favorite relative is closed permanently and we place them in the ground to rest in peace forever. The one-way direction of the arrow of time and the irreversibility of life events that already happened, seem to me to be a plate of scrambled eggs that I cannot unscramble. Too much is lost ... too many things I wanted to discover for information sources about this story, are permanently gone, forever. That is my experience of getting at the story of RC's life and death, thus far.

Before pursuing any major story requiring award-winning and super human effort on my part, I had with great success involved my ever-changing series of Analysts, Psychiatrists, Psychologists, and Faith-Healers, to make sure I wasn't projecting imaginary elements of RC's story, and that I wasn't losing touch with reality, like I did on my first documentary story about another public person, several years ago. Although I change Therapists like most people change their favorite ring-tones on their cell phones, my Therapist at the time made me promise that my first step before working-my-heart-out, would be to empirically verify that I had a story to pursue in the real-world, so that it would not only be something pursued by, for, from and to, my imagination. She cautioned me against pursuing something totally fictional, something that was a result only of the imaginings of my psyche working overtime to invent and project a psychological-double of my wishfully-conjured-musings instead of dealing with the idiosyncratic conflicts of real people that were the focus of my journalism. She said something about being aware of "rapid cycling" of my thoughts, that to her appeared "unhealthily-frenetic." I thought she was treating me like a crazy person, so I dumped her in favor of a more modern, progressive and enlightened Therapist. Therapists, what can you do with them...except, maybe, throw lots of money at them and get in exchange, well, nothing!

Seven Therapists later, the most recent session with my new Jungian Psychiatrist took place the day before RC's funeral. This Therapist also got exceedingly furious at me when I corrected her "don't you mean my mental ghosts are doppelgangers?" I really was just trying to jokingly congratulate her, since she was able to help me distinguish the imaginary world from the real-world, much more efficiently in terms of reality being a source of tangible monetary benefit to me. Maybe she wanted to make sure I was rich as a way for her to ensure that I could pay her fees. I suspected she was someone who had a class in college economics regarding the theories of Malthus, because her approach was to encourage patients to be aggressive and acquisitive by making all of the money in the world that they possibly could. She didn't seem too worried about being humane. Her concern was doing the minimum according to the standard of only what was legally required, apparently acting on the assumption that, if only to keep your freedoms, do what is legally required so as to allow you to live on at least one more day for the sole purpose of making more money for yourself. That seemed to be the short-term time horizon of a hungry reptile, not a human being. I had to explain to her, that since I was able to get an emotional reaction from her and since she was in the real-world, my priorities were in order in an effort to be more healthy by focusing more on the real-world: "it is better to express my emotions to real people, not imaginary fictional characters, so good job Doctor. I'm cured! Can I get a discount for early healing ahead of schedule?" She threw me out of her office, shouting that I was wasting her time and that her time was more valuable than mine. After that point in my course of therapy, I concluded that my present Therapist was unlikely to be of further positive help to me, so I quickly switched to another Psychiatrist who was willing to charge me more money per hour. The cliché that "you get what you pay for" has not yet rung true for me in my experience with Psychiatrists. The Psychiatrists say it is my fault and then they want to get paid, for insulting me.

When I was a kid, I got the same treatment at elementary school for free: why should I have to pay outrageously high fees for it now? Psychiatrists to me are problematic. With my experience from all of my Therapists, I astoundingly wondered what happened in the world to make the Hippocratic Oath of "doing no harm" disappear when it came to physicians charging exorbitant amounts of money from their patients? Why was it that no physician I encountered, applied the Hippocratic Oath when it was time for them to get paid? All Therapists harmed my wallet by diminishing its full cash contents down to emptiness. Ironical, I thought, that for all their talk of helping you, if you could not pay, then they were not the slightest bit interested in you, at all. I would fire a Therapist when I reached the conclusion that there was no restraint to the limits of their greed and that I was only a shadowy simulacrum of a transaction, not a person to them, and not someone they cared about, independent of how they could use me to get money. They seemed willfully oblivious to how cruelly they treated their staff and patients, as a way to brag to their colleagues about what an astute business person they were. I wish they would come out and admit that for them, money is more important than people and their patients. In America, most Physicians I encountered were fiercely self-centered capitalists, predominantly concerned with profits and hustling patients through their offices in the most efficient manner "patient through-put equals larger billable revenue: push the patients through faster!" Doctors that bothered me the most were those few who were indifferently focusing only on profits when treating fragile and vulnerable patients like they were transactions or commodities, instead of treating human patients with care and genuine concern for their well-being. It made me feel disgust toward most Psychiatrists and Mental Health Therapists. If only I could persuade more politicians in America that healthcare should be free for all, to take the profit out of it for Physicians ... that would likely solve all of our healthcare problems! However, I know with certainty that RC would have laughed at my naïve views. He often laughed at me during our interviews.

I wanted to talk with my most recent Therapist about the mental bias involved when people try to make sense of a tragically accidental death of someone close to them and very important to them. The Therapist thought it exceedingly off-topic, but was interested in pursuing the theme of the question since it was the first time she had seen me focus on something other than myself during our sessions.

We talked for over half of the session about the stages of grieving that most humans in America go through. She did not have any education or experience in dealing with other nationalities and countries' cultural traditions of grieving, so she couldn't help me, not in the real sense that I defined as being helpful...that did not stop her at all, from billing me extra fees for being off-topic. She was sending me the message that her time was more valuable than mine. What a witch.

I was hoping she could help me sort through the psychological things that I knew were the main factors driving some of the comments that people shared with me at the funeral, volunteering their theories of who or what killed RC. You should hear what unbelievable things some people told me! It was not a fun experience to try and take the outlandish theories seriously.

My serious questions boiled down to this: for the person or persons who could take over a Drone as an instrument of assassination, how and why did RC get onto their kill list?

## Chapter 2

## A Veritable Cornucopia of Theories:
*Conjectures of why a Drone killed an innocent man...*

Beginning the investigation and writing the story of RC's life and death, my mind danced and conjured and buzzed through the several possible causes that would answer specific details of how it happened and why it happened: I had so many thoughts and so many ideas! That type of mental exercise was all admittedly phantasmagorical and imaginary. Originating from a surging mental state of reverie I would cling to the entertainment value of this story's unexpected turns, surprises and my counter-productive yet hopeful searching of elusive information for answers. I liked achieving a tantric state of reverie since it helped me in the past solve riddles. But this story was one-of-a-kind. As I gathered more information, the facts were brutal.

Pushing myself past exhaustion with no sleep, my headaches increased in frequency and duration and were diagnosed as Hemiplegic Migraine headaches. I asked my physicians if my propensity for Migraines were caused by my birth delivery with forceps. The physicians did not really know how to respond to my question, except by giving me more medications. The medications administered by my doctors to help manage my condition, slowed the speed of my more rational mental abilities. In my brain, the swirling vortex of images and thoughts were still there, which kept me pursuing the story, no matter how much pain I experienced along the way.

In my mind, the vast landscape of possibilities narrowed painfully and rapidly with an ever shrinking breadth and height: large pieces of theories became images in my mind that spun up mightily during my reverie then abruptly they would disappear, chewed up by the incongruities in the real-world data. Several of my conjectures were destroyed by the data I could empirically verify. Information storms overtook my mind. Darkening answers from actual facts were dragging my mental perspective on this story down into a chilling and dark oblivion.

Was RC's death accidental or deliberate planned and executed? If it was accidental, what were the chain of events and forces that led up to the accident? If it was a deliberate death, which was a very unlikely thing then who was involved in the planning and logistics and final strike operations? If it was planned, was it a private or public entity that was out to get RC? Who was the engineering genius behind the malicious software code that took over the Drone and made it behave as the weapon? Why were the decisions that finally settled upon a specific time and why was it a good idea to use that particular strike-point in time? I had to stop myself from postulating too many "what-if" questions in order to forestall the occurrence of another mind-splitting painful experience from a migraine-headache.

That series of marathon-like mental exercise left me exhausted from an overabundance of adrenaline, over the course of a week. It was a strange sensation to be slowed a bit by the migraine medications, yet still feeling a rush of adrenaline for a long period of time. If ever someone could feel their internal energy level act is if it was a car engine and you pushed your feet on the accelerator and brakes at the same time, then that was what it was for me: I was going nowhere fast but making lots of noise and burning fuel with no movement. After seven days and nights, things slowly started to return to normal for me...it was late at night on a Sunday and I was beyond exhausted. The medications faded away, I knew this for certain because I looked out my window, and could look directly at the sunset light and soft gray clouds and not feel pain from the light. To recuperate and get back to researching RC's story, I had to calm myself enough to try and get to sleep. To force myself to relax, I had to write down a summary list of remaining open questions I had, from re-running in my mind all of the several discussions at the funeral ... I titled it 'A Brief Litany of Prevailing Theories, Rumors and Opinions Relating to the Possible Probable and Actual Causes of the Death of RC, Including Some Conspiracy Theories.' With a blood-red ink-pen on yellow legal paper I scratched out the information I gleaned at the funeral luncheon in decreasing priority.

Here is my summary of other's answers to my questions: "how is it possible that a U.S. Drone could accidentally kill RC, and if it wasn't an accident, then who or what group was behind the assassination and why was RC's death a necessary solution to fix some problem?"

"A foreign government assassinated RC and it was carried out by that country's intelligence services." To my way of thinking this was unexpectedly and surprisingly the most popular theory. Several people at RC's funeral I talked to thought this was the most likely explanation. In a follow-up effort, I raised the basic issues and questions: "which country had the means, motive and opportunity to kill RC by taking over an American Drone?" The responses were that almost 90% agreed that the 'means' to kill RC was a non-issue, because it was reported on CNN a year or so ago, that anyone with basic Wi-Fi equipment could hack into the video signal of a Drone within radio range of the hackers and it would allow you to see what the Drone was registering on its video camera in real-time. My response to their point was, "OK, but there is quite a difference between passively watching a broadcast video, versus taking over all of the complex systems in modern Drones." Yes, most people agreed with my counter-point, but they said that the public perception used to be that there was nothing on any hi-tech Drone that could be hacked into, however since the video system could now be hacked, that meant there were enough weak spots to hack into anything else on the Drone, provided that you had the equipment that is correctly sophisticated and powerful enough. I asked these same people to kindly share with me their guesses on which country or countries it could have been, to identify which person, entity or organizations had the 'motive' to kill RC in such an elaborately high-tech manner?

Everyone had widely divergent theories about which foreign country that was primarily responsible; interestingly several people thought it was a consortium of countries. There were divergent views on the motive being based on who had the most to gain from RC's death. I reiterated several times that at the time of RC's death, he had "given away or sold almost all of his ownership property interests in every one of his businesses, so that he had been taking himself off of the world stage voluntarily for quite some time." Yes everyone agreed that was true, but they highlighted for me that my point "forgets the powerful motive of revenge." The people in the camp of revenge as the motive, encouraged me to do some investigative journalist research into RC's enemies were from his past, especially far back in his younger days of first getting on the world stage of capitalist business transactions and multi-national banking, and especially the early days of RC's then newly launched commercial Satellite business.

They seemed to be leading me toward his pioneering work on Satellite and software based communications involving banking transactions. "Imagine how sensitive it would be to mess with someone's bank accounts and life savings!" Despite the lack of empirical evidence that I could verify, there were enough people at RC's funeral that I talked to that mentioned this theory, so I had to put this one theory as first on my list. My guess was that this theory would be scored at 80% likelihood as the true cause of RC's death.

"Someone hacked into the Drone's remote radio controlled signal and took over the Drone, specifically targeting RC to make it look like an accident." This theory, in my mind, was an evil-identical-twin to the first theory, since there was plenty of information from the crash site and the Drone's mission data bank records that there was an unauthorized takeover of the Drone by a radio signal that carried and injected a fatal dose of malicious software code. This theory I categorized as a subset of the first theory listed above and I too gave this one an 80% likelihood of explaining what really happened to RC.

"The Drone had a software glitch and it was a one-in-a-trillion accidental event." This theory was offered by people who had not heard that there was proof that malicious code was injected into the Drone on the back of a hacked radio signal that took over the Drone sometime when it was airborne. The sheer number of permutations and combinations of variables of all the possible data-variables operating and actively controlling the flight operations of the Drone's systems and step-wise software operations altogether makes the spontaneous-cascading-failure-internal-accident-theory, highly unlikely. I place a score of 5% likelihood on this theory.

"The Drone was flying a war-fighting-counter-electronics test mission and the electronic warfare systems went haywire because of a power failure caused by a disruptive lightning strike on the Drone's central computer control system." This theory was held by only three people at RC's funeral and it seemed anecdotal. Because validated weather reports at the time of the accident showed no lightning within five-hundred miles of the accident site, I placed a "does not apply" tag on this theory and discarded it. The weather was not to blame.

I reached speculatively for a justification about something in the sky zapping RC out of thin air, but it was just too bizarre, since I would have to appeal to the space-based laser dreams of the 1980's Strategic Defense Initiative. There was no time for that.

"Some powerful business person hated RC and wanted him dead." This theory was popular among people in the defense contracting industry, but there was no evidence to find identities of the people that ordered a killing, so it was difficult to prove. Of RC's publicly known enemies, disputes were on philosophical bases of how to conduct capitalist business transactions in a free-market economy. There was no evidence of something that would provoke a blood feud among business people. I thought it very likely that if RC had private enemies, they would be incredibly astute at spy-game tradecraft and would never allow into the public realm anything I could discover and verify about their identities and actions against RC, if there was such a thing going on, it would likely be hidden from me forever. Also, RC was scrupulously careful to avoid anything illegal in his businesses, so it was unlikely an organized-crime sponsored hit that killed him. I pondered the remotely successful effort to quantify any hatred toward RC from his competitors in the business community: however I would be reduced to using linguistic word-counts of public news articles...not a fruitful endeavor, since those articles were childish-spats based on differing views of the pure theory of capitalism and whether people or profits are more important, and whether RC should be condemned to a capitalist's hell for violating the efficiency doctrine of a for-profit economic entity, whenever RC was generous instead of greedy. I could find no evidence that the trigger person or the money person behind the killing of RC, was from the business community, so I scored this theory a zero on the likelihood of being the explanation of RC's death.

"RC was unfortunately in the wrong place at the wrong time: he should not have flown through a "No-Fly-Zone" test mission area of airspace." This was a theory that was believed by over a third of the people that I talked to at RC's funeral. I noticed that people who said they held this theory were trying to not think too much about how RC died, they were consumed by grief and sadness and likely picked this theory so as to minimize the time that they spent talking about it with me. The Physics of the accident show that RC was targeted, so it was a situation of the Drone being in a precise place at a precise time and since RC's jet was the one target, anywhere RC could have flown would have been the wrong place.

This theory was not realistically quantifiable, so I gave it a "does not apply" score on my empirical analysis data table of theory scores and rankings.

"It was an Electro-Magnetic Pulse Weapon fired in RC's general direction from the Drone caused by a Software Hack Team or Teams, something that was a pre-programmed and deliberately exploitable vulnerability of the software that would allow it to be taken over, for exclusive control of the Drone." The pulse weapon theory also seems unlikely, since all available reports from other aircraft within two-hundred miles of RCs jet disprove this theory. None of the other five escort jets suffered anything like what hit RC's jet and no other aircraft lost their entire electronic systems functions (or power supply) before, during, or after, RC was shot down. A lightning strike on RC's jet would have been more plausible, yet the skies at sunset were clear for five-hundred miles in any direction around RC's jet at the time of the accident. I gave this theory a zero percent chance of being true. I had read an article published in several of the British Columbia Newspapers highlighting that the most scientifically popular story about how RC was accidentally killed, was a theoretical scenario advanced by a group of credible scientists. Without my effort, it was they who contacted me and offered to visit for a group interview after RC's death. During a telephone conference-call interview with me, they told me bluntly that the Drone strike and the damage and debris pattern I described to them was most likely "caused by a focal electromagnetic pulse weapon" which I presumed was only something that was possible in a science fiction story of futuristic weapons. They countered that it is a system in use in the real-world already. In sum, it is a coordinated weapons system, where an orbiting Satellite and a series of airborne Drones all launch a coordinated attack at one target by shooting beams of electromagnetic pulse energy into one focal point on a target. My reactions were based on solid skepticism: "OK, but why select RC and make it look like an accident?" They couldn't make a plausible conjecture that would answer my question. Their opinions would be considered hearsay in a courtroom. None of them wanted me to use their real names. I couldn't do much with what they told me. I suggested that they contact the Attorneys leading the class action lawsuit on behalf of RC's widow and ex-spouses, to see if their information could do some good. I still scored this theory as zero: no other aircraft including the five chase jets closest to RC suffered any electromagnetic anomalies before or during the accident. The only way I could imagine this explanation as the true cause of RC's death, is to consider the detailed physics involved, and only then could I see this theory as a plausible explanation, would be if one of the missiles fired by the Drone had a capability to emit an electromagnetic pulse toward RC's jet while the missile was flying away from the Drone so as not to damage it, and toward RC's jet so as to focus the electromagnetic pulse in a narrow beam and only at its target.

"RC engineered and carried out the whole thing as a cover story in order to escape and have some quiet days alone before the brain-tumor killed him." This theory was suggested by some of his closest and longest lived friends, so I couldn't dismiss it outright. Their supposition was that RC needed a public death that could be official, so that he could live a private life, supposedly with loved ones, perhaps some quiet days with his current wife in Bangladesh. I considered this in detail, but based on RC's personality and pre-occupation with the truth and adding into that mix his great efforts to be considerate of his family member's feelings, I give this theory a half of one percent likelihood of being true.

"RC was an alien and he left Earth to return to his original home somewhere else in the Universe." This theory was advanced by a middle-school student who was with her parents when I interviewed them about their memories of RC (the parents were former classmates of RC during their teenage high-school years in Seattle). The parents tried not to roll their eyes in mockery, so I did play along cooperatively and considered it worth writing down. I respectfully asked the student "if there might be some evidence to support that theory in case some skeptical person wanted to see a convincing proof, so that others could take it seriously?" The response was "no, nothing solid; I had a dream about that pilot that got killed. Mom and Dad were talking about it all day. My dream was that he recently decided to leave Earth since he accomplished so much and he teleported home seconds before his jet crashed to avoid being assassinated." I wrote down the details of her dream based explanation, not wanting to exclude anything in my journalistic investigation. Privately, I did wonder what new designer drugs the teenager was on, to cause such hallucinations at dream time. The other child in that family was a middle school age brother, very much enamored with video games. His theory was more plausible than his sister's theory: "it is easy to hack into the video signal of Drones; that has already been proven and the specifications and equipment list is easily found on the internet and it only costs about $45.00 U.S. Dollars to buy and get a decent Wi-Fi transceiver, hook it to a powerful laptop computer and then write some simple code in order to pull it off."

That comment definitely interested me and I passed it onto the Drone engineers I had interviewed, which they said was possible, however new encryption systems had made that unlikely. Another dead-end: this theory is another one I calculate at being less than one percent true or likely. Only seven people at RC's funeral held this view, they phrased it as: "Computer hackers intercepted the flight control signal of the Drone, thought it was a video game: misunderstood it was real and guided the Drone to the kill-shot." The engineers I spoke with in the field, explained to me that the Drone's encryption key character sets used several long digits and several layers of encryption firewalls, so they suggested that there would be zero chance of that outcome: "infinitesimally possible but not likely."

"A Sasquatch was throwing rocks at the stars and accidentally hit RC's jet." This theory was sincerely put forth by a formerly homeless man. Because he seemed like he needed to be heard and taken seriously, I listened carefully and wrote notes of what he was describing to me. I thanked him for his thoughts and to show appreciation I gave him a cup of hot fresh coffee, which he greatly appreciated. I don't have much to say about this theory. It seems the probability of this explanation being true is less than zero. I assume every sane person would agree with me that it is less likely to be the cause of RC's death than the most remote thing I can think of, let's say this theory is more unlikely than the mathematical odds of a 'quantum barrier tunneling event' causing a sliver of anti-matter to pass through our Universe and strike RC's jet. Neither are likely explanations of what happened in the real-world to RC's jet...not in this world of predictable realities.

After listening to what RC's fans thought was the explanation of the cause of his death through descriptions of what is possible, probable and actual and unexpectedly encountering a higher degree of kooks and crack-pots and conspiracy theorists during those discussions, mental health required that I truly needed something a bit more 'real-world' to get me back to an investigation of the story that made sense.

To compose myself and allow the surge of the detailed images dancing in my memories to coalesce into a retrospective, I leaned heavily upon a stoutly caffeinated cup of coffee to see if it would lift me up for a higher mental perspective on the whole thing. I was trying to force my mind to imagine a story-board that is congruent, sequential, explanatory, clear and concise: once I had that, then I could sit and write it all down on paper.   The comfort from slurping a cup of hot coffee while I type everything helps me remember RC's words: his speech patterns, the real meaning behind what he said to me before his death.  We shared several conversations in the coffee shop during the year before he died.  I recorded several of our conversations and I'm glad that I have preserved digitally the sound of his real voice.  As I type his recorded words on my old typewriter machine I can smell the black ink on my white typing paper as the words come to life.  The old inky smell combined with the steamy aroma of hot coffee altogether seems to help jog my memory.  It helps me to type things the old-fashioned way before I re-type them into the computer.   There are so many important details to commit to paper.

My next step as an investigative journalist was to focus all of my time and effort upon the major lawsuit filed by the ex-wives and widow of RC.  Maybe their Lawyers will already have dredged up more answers than I discovered thus far.

## Chapter 3

### A Class Action Lawsuit:
*Wives versus the Military Industrial Complex of Drone Creators, Purveyors, Pilots and Dark Forces yet unnamed...*

Three months after RC's funeral, a class-action lawsuit was filed in U.S. Federal Court in Washington State by all of the former wives and the widow of RC. They voluntarily got together as plaintiffs, cooperating for the first time in their lives instead of avoiding each other.

Suing on the basis of wrongful-death, they altogether seek 46 Billion U.S. Dollars for punitive and compensatory damages. The named defendants are the U.S. Government Executive Branch, NORAD, the U.S. Air Force, the U.S. Department of Defense, the Canadian Air Defense Electronic Control Network, the military commanders and personnel of the recovery team at the crash site from both the U.S. and Canadian Military Branches and the several engineering contractors and their Employees and project directors and mostly everyone else who could plausibly be connected to the research, development and testing of the Drone that was used as a weapon to kill RC, and as an homage to the Gods of perfect information, they had a collectively exhaustive list of named defendants "...persons unknown, intelligence agencies unknown, organized crime entities unknown, terror groups unknown..." to include addresses of entities scattered across thirty-seven different countries.

The plaintiff's legal theory of the case is that the human Drone Pilot and his employer are primarily responsible for dereliction of duty caused by willful negligence when choosing to be away from the Drone's flight control remote console during the attack. Everyone else named in the lawsuit is negligent because of an alleged systemic lack of failsafe features that were negligently omitted during the design, testing and operational maiden-voyage phase of the Drone project. The plaintiffs are asking the Court to hold each of the defendants "jointly and severally liable especially since the wrongdoer(s) cannot profit from their crime."

The Known-or-Knowable-Defendants are strenuously denying all allegations and counter-suing each of the ex-wives and the widow of RC, pointing to the responsible party as "an unnamed defendant who acting alone or in concert with others, carried out an illegal computer electronics hack into the Drone without our knowledge, control or cooperation."

The case was originally filed in the U.S. Federal Court for the Eastern District of Washington State however it was moved to Seattle because of the international nature of the case and the sheer quantity of "International and National Security Issues important to both the United States and Canada." The Attorneys reasoned that the case should proceed in American Courts since the Drone was flying 100% within U.S. airspace when it committed the wrongful act. Unofficially, it seemed that the parties involved all agreed on one thing at the beginning of the legal process: they all preferred Seattle instead of Spokane Washington, as the proper venue for arguing the dispute in the U.S. Courts.

I requested access to attend the Court proceedings, but was denied, on the basis that the "matters heard before this Court require disclosure and discussion of flight capabilities and weapons systems that raise several national security issues, so therefore we must exclude from attendance the journalist in question since he does not presently have any U.S. Government security clearances of any kind that would normally be expected of participants in this case in order to safeguard the National Security Interests of the U.S. Government." In response, my Lawyers dealt with that rejection by formally requesting that the proceedings be videotaped under the new pilot program offered by the Court, yet that request was also denied on the same justification of national security interests and the prevention of any disclosure of vital secret information. So much for freedom of the press: how awfully frustrating!

Perhaps to avoid the appearance of being completely closed to media interest in the proceedings and possibly to throw me some bread crumbs, the Court did allow me to get a complete copy of the initial lawsuit documents as they were filed by the plaintiffs with the Court, including the detailed pre-trial discovery requests involving several defendant's names (corporations and individuals). Of particular interest to me are the following documents and related information and testimony requests for "hard copy documents and electronically stored information in the party's possession, custody or control: including but not limited to:

1. RC's jet flight data recorders gathered at the accident site by the Rapid Response Recovery Teams sent by the U.S. and Canadian Military Authorities.

2. The electronic data recorders at the U.S. Federal Aviation Administration ("FAA") and interviews with administrative personnel responsible for air traffic control operations and other front-line personnel who were responsible for of all air traffic control flight information for all the aircraft within 500 miles of RC and including RC's air traffic flight plan, at the time of the crash.

3. Interviews with all air-traffic controllers, pilots, co-pilots, flight crew and any other responsible personnel involving any and all of the aircraft mentioned in item #2 above.

4. The flight data recorder of the Drone, including all of its recorded video, telematics information, navionics information, flight logs, software code, flight and weapons commands that were sent to and received from the Drone, before during and after the accident and all after-mission reports and documents and electronic files of all imagery gathered and stored by the Drone, before during and after the accident.

5. The testimony of the remote Drone pilot; specifically whether he was listening to music through his head-phones instead of listening to the Drone alert warning signals during his un-authorized coffee break and a description of his actions leading up to the accident, during the accident and after the accident: including the results of any drug and alcohol tests required of the Drone's remote human pilot after the accident and a copy of all of his mission checklists and mandated electronic protocol checklists used during the Drone flight.

6. All computer server files, email messages, recorded phone calls and all information relating to the Drone command center's actions in response to the Drone accident, including all data logs, flight plans, voice and electronic transmissions of any kind, to and from or within, the U.S. Air Force E-3 Sentry "AWACS" jet that was flying in the air above Priest Lake Idaho at the time of the accident. If the AWACS was not a United States Aircraft, then disclose in detail the name of the Sponsoring Country who owned the AWACS and describe the

equipment and electronic capabilities of that aircraft and disclose the specific mission it was carrying out.

7.   A complete copy of the old and new systems integration software program(s) and database that was uploaded into the Drone on the day of the accident and downloaded from the Drone when it returned to base in Nevada, after the accident, including its encryption algorithms and radio communication frequencies used during the mission in question.

8.   Testimony of each of the flight ground-crew technicians that prepared the Drone in Nevada before its flight: specifically and including the technicians that loaded the missile(s) onto the Drone, those persons who calibrated the GPS atomic clock synchronization for the Drone's onboard atomic clock and the persons responsible for the pre-flight systems response checklist and tests and disclose any and all information that documented the results of those pre-flight tests.

9.   Testimony from the Flight Director of the Drone Flight Operations Base in Nevada on the day of the accident and all of his emails and recorded phone calls on that day, before, during and after the accident, including an official transcription of his conversations with the remote Drone pilot that day.

10.  Copies of all imagery, electronic and/or video films and digital files of the Drone's entire flight leading up to and after the accident.

11.  Copies of all planning documents and tasking orders that were submitted to the U.S. National Command Authority for pre-approval before the Drone flight.

12.  Testimony from and all relevant documents from the Department of Defense liaison officer at the Northwest NORAD Airport Regional Radar Operations Center who was on duty the night of RC's death: including all official and un-official back-channel coordination communications of shared intelligence information with and consultations with, the U.S. and Canadian Homeland Security Officer(s) on duty the night of the accident and any responses to or from the U.S. White House Situation Room.

13.  The complete set of documents from the contractor(s) who developed the firewall security encryption system(s) of the

Drone involved with radio signal communications, command and control, complete with master encryption key lists of people who had access to the master encryption key list for the Drone's mission at the time of the accident.

14. The complete set of documents and all computer software code from the software vendor and related contractor(s) who developed the "Flight Plan Correlation" program that checked all flight plans both military and civilian, when the Drone tried to determine whether aircraft flying within its designated airspace were friendly, or not.

15. All encryption cipher code setup and randomization sequence records, data, checklists and testimony of the technical people who performed the pre-flight calibration and testing of the Drone's atomic clock and GPS clock and navigation flight data recorder, that were used to start the random number seeding sequence for encryption purposes, including the synchronization of the frequency harmonic control sequencer for encrypted real-time navigation position reporting of the Drone.

16. Testimony of all pilots (U.S. and Canadian Military) who piloted jets, planes, helicopters and any other airborne vehicles that were dispatched to respond to the crash site for any purpose whatsoever.

17. Testimony of medical rescue personnel, to determine whether there was a body or body parts recovered at the crash site.

18. Whether at the time of the accident, RC was (or several of his business entities were) in any way contracting to work with the U.S. Government, The Central Intelligence Agency, The National Security Agency, The Department of Defense, The Defense Information Systems Agency, The Department of Homeland Security, The Office of the National Counterintelligence Executive, The National Reconnaissance Office, or any other Governmental Entity, Department or Agency.

19. Copies of all Top Secret reports, including but not limited to the National Security Finding that was written in response to the President of the U.S.'s request for an investigation into this incident to determine the presence or absence of any terrorist sponsored activities against RC.

20. A complete accounting of all Satellites owned, leased, used or borrowed, and under the control and command and communications of either the N.S.A., D.O.D., C.I.A., D.I.A., F.A.A., U.S.A.F. or any other Satellite and entity that had radio communications with the Drone, The A.W.A.C.S. or RC's jet.

21. A full disclosure of the impact missile(s)' complete mechanical, electrical, hardware and software capabilities as configured and operating at the time of the incident, especially a description and explanation of the structure, activities and functions of any and all Electro-Magnetic-Pulse ("E.M.P.") weapons within or through the missile(s).

22. A computer engineering assessment and a physics analysis, of the vulnerability of any of the missile(s) and the drone, combined or individually, to be open to being hacked, decrypted, intercepted involuntarily, or otherwise compromised electronically."

The case started four years ago and is still ongoing. At the time it was first filed in Court, I anticipated it would go on forever in time. I certainly did not and could not wait for information to be brought out in open Court, especially since it was entirely closed to the press.

I decided it would be a productive strategy for me to approach the Lawyers for the plaintiff, request interviews and for each interview granted, I could offer to trade in return, copies of everything I had including the full disclosure of all electronic information I gathered on my own, or had in my possession from others, up to that point in time. I did get some information and some names of persons that would be called to testify at trial, yet I had to agree to communicate with and totally let the Presiding Judge of the Federal Court in Seattle become the sole and exclusive gatekeeper of a great deal of my investigative journalist's information. Of course I also had to agree to make myself available to testify in front of the Federal Judge, regarding any interrogatories from the Lawyers on the case, and to explain any new information I uncovered.

This time around I needed to use newer and more aggressive Lawyers, ones who were still early on in their career, for my new planned requests for documents, submitted to the appropriate U.S. Federal Government Agencies, pursuant to the Freedom of Information Act. The Lawyers I had already used were in the latter part of their working careers and it seemed they were interested only in maximizing their billable hours and really didn't have much tolerance for me and my detailed questions. "You are too detailed! Knock it off!" Those type of Lawyers (there were a few) that had given up on getting perfect truthful information and instead focused upon avoiding being disadvantaged because they would tell you that their time is worth more than yours, since you did not go to law school, pass the bar, and be entitled to behave as if everyone else in the world should be lucky and throw down money to be so fortunate as to get legal help from such an eminent lawyer.

I was amused, since many lawyers to me as though they thought of themselves as if they were Gods walking superiorly among idiots. I called them coasting capitalists, those few who decided to not really put forth genuine effort to find the truth and those that were not really interested in a client's case unless they would be paid handsomely, cash up front preferably.

I know it sounds naïve, but it would be nice to meet more people in both the U.S. legal community and more people in the business world of the market based economy, that could stop for a few moments in their pursuit of money and personal gain and for a moment agree with me that sometimes it should be that our efforts should be primarily expended for the goal of searching for the truth, instead of a single-minded search for profit and pleasure, where others would be ruined along the way. One of the cruelest things I have overheard successful people in America say, is "...wow, that's too bad, I guess it sucks to be you. Glad that it's not my problem. Stay away from me."

Pursuing the truth was considered by leaders in almost all areas of the successful business community as a certain money loosing drain on the economy, unless you were doing potentially profitable basic scientific or applied scientific efforts and patentable processes within the confines of some well-funded academic research and development effort ... at least that was the view that had been communicated to me during interviews I conducted with the more curmudgeonly capitalists that believed in a harshly pro-competitive form of capitalistic free-market economics. Anyone who disagreed with them or wasted their time with discussions of treating humans better, was considered immediately guilty of the unforgivable sin of committing economic inefficiency and losing money somewhere in the system. If such a situation caused them to lose even pennies on a transaction, then the people involved would be immediately have their jobs terminated with harsh notice: "I can't use you anymore...you are fired. Pack your stuff and get out now."

That one noticeable spark of my spirit that exudes an indomitable and undaunted drive to pursue the truth, no matter how much that isolates me from popular society, perhaps *that* is what RC recognized in me as a quality that was worth his time. Maybe that is why he was willing to visit with me again after our first interview.

I couldn't stop pursuing the story. So I plodded along for two years on my journalist's meager pay, money scraped together from small scale technical writing work, scant book royalties and limited bank borrowing ability and resorting to the extreme step of maxing-out all of my credit cards.

My fund raising money was used all in order to pay for trips to interview all of the plaintiff's Lawyers and their witnesses, who resided in the United States and Canada and also to pay for "copies of or press access to the official R.C.M.P. reports and/or U.S. F.A.A. transcribed radio traffic and/or any other military discussions and/or law enforcement or rescue assistance information" relating to the events at RC's death site and crime scene, including any local police files and any autopsy and inquest documents and a long list of electronically stored information and hardcopy data.

I worried every day and night, that my expense and time spent on this, might never be compensated, recognized, rewarded, or even mean something good, to anyone.

I was not suffering alone in silence during this time. All of my requests were obviously reported to the Presiding Judge at the U.S. Federal Court in Seattle. As expected, I routinely received phone calls from the U.S. Department of State and the Department of Defense and the F.B.I. inquiring as to what I was working on any particular day and re-iterating to me that they had a valid perpetual search-warrant and further that they wanted to be copied on everything I was gathering and that further they reminded me that I had a legal duty to submit everything to the Federal Court in Seattle ... but they wanted to see everything first.

Though there were some agents that seemed less than fully-human and more like dark minions or robotic bureaucrats from the U.S.

Government that checked the validity and current legal status of my press credentials several times through detailed background investigations of my past, there were some governmental agents who predictably interfered in my data requests from the government and at every opportunity it seemed that their job was to slow-roll and obfuscate, hinder and delay the government response of producing documents, for each and every one of my requests. I was undaunted. My own Lawyers regularly returned to Court several times on both sides of the border, pleading for more access to information I needed in a spirit of 'freedom of the press.'

Pursuing the truth was costing me countless hours and getting me confined inside buildings, libraries, cubicles and airplanes, which led to a feeling of global claustrophobia. I needed fresh air. Perhaps I could walk the ground of the crash site, as part of my journalistic investigation.

The first stop I made was at a private airport in North Bend Washington, a pleasant drive north east of Seattle, to charter a helicopter to fly me to the crash site in British Columbia Canada. We flew for about two hours heading north east and up the South Salmo River Valley, staying on the U.S. side of the Border.

Seeing it for myself the first time that next summer after it happened, it was a June Summer's day. There I was at the crash site where they located RC's remains. It seemed surreal, because this place seemed like paradise, not a grave site. I felt like the wild animals were watching me from the shadows, as I was noticing the surroundings of a beautiful alpine scene of granite gray mountains, blue sky, and green trees: the whole panorama appeared as if it was from some eye-catching and inviting tourist video commercial.

Remarkably, again only for those times in my life that are connected to RC's story, I was keenly aware that the mountain air was cool and clear because my lungs felt happy in response to getting pure oxygen from truly alpine air ... it was pleasantly full of the smell of aromatic Sitka Spruce Trees. Sunlight, golden and warm, shone brightly on my face: my eyes were straining in the brightness to see the impact sites and debris field where RC's jet slammed into Earth. Only the ground was damaged. There were noticeable scars and overturned rocks and shallow craters of blackened soil. Near the disturbed Earth an aroma lingered that was akin to smoke, or smelled more specifically similar to the aftermath of what a brick-chimney smells like after a creosote-fueled-chimney-fire burns all of the soot away, there is nothing left but a film of black goo and a terribly acrid smell. About every ten steps along the impact pathway I would also occasionally sense a brief aroma left behind from burnt plastics and other aromas like the smell when you first open a container of freshly ground coffee.

At the highest elevation of the crash site, there was a natural rock-slide pattern of granite, dumped by a melting glacier 10,000 years ago, that was in the shape of a heart: how ironic – RC could not have scripted his own death any more poetically. I could see some artificial landscaping was done to repair several small scale impact sites on the ground, craters made from the crash debris were now covered with Blue-Spruce trees and Kentucky Blue-Grass, both not indigenous to this area. They could have used Bear Grass and Engleman Spruce Trees, to be more environmentally friendly. Anyway, the damage was covered by Both American and Canadian military personnel when they did the chemical clean up the debris fields and crash site.

I brought with me the printed Canadian – U.S. Joint Operations Official Reports of the 'Environmentally Sensitive Cleanup Effort of the accident site debris field which began south west of Bridal Lake British Columbia and continued for 9.17236 kilometers or 5.7 miles to the South Salmo River Valley in the U.S. The subsequent environmental assessment reports from Environment Canada and the U.S. Environmental Protection Agency listed a variety of impact sites and hazardous material abatement and cleanup efforts. This was a combined cooperative effort since about one-third of RC's jet parts also crashed onto U.S. Soil. Those reports I too had to get through the Freedom of Information Act. Because of the high profile and public interest of the crash and the possible environmental damage, both governments decided they would expedite their disclosure of the documents on the crash site cleanup I had requested. From what I read, I knew that their methods of site sifting were so thorough that there would be nothing left that was metal or technological or human for me to discover.

Not that I wanted to find anything, but my curiosity to find out "who, how, and why" was always more powerful than my sense of reverence for blood soaked soil and hallowed ground after the crime was committed.

It wasn't that I was incapable of feeling sadness, humility and a sense of loss over RC as those feelings would be provoked while I stood over this plot of land as if it was a gravesite ... I did feel those things. However it was also true that my feelings provoked by my imagining what RC would say to me, what his ghost might say at this moment, included the reality of a specter that would be scolding me that I should view the moments of his death as a small piece of a larger reality, and stop wasting time on emotional indulgence for the sake of skulking. I wondered if his ghost would lapse into his nature-loving monologues by intensely comparing his own death to the history of this whole region, with an attempt to make the point that in the large scale of Earthly time, his life and death was mostly insignificant, when compared to the ancient age of the rocks and plants that have been living here at least since the last ice age. I also suspected at that moment, that the ghost of RC would have laughed that I was here at all, and he would have been bemused by my wrestling to separate a chaotic mash-up of thoughts and emotions. What bothered me most about my visit to the crash site was that RC would *not* have liked my presence there. "Do not waste time with the past – it is done, I am gone. Spend time helping people and do not chase ghosts asking questions that begin with the phrase: *Why did it happen?*

Instead of relying on ghosts for revelations that might answer my questions, my plan was to use an empirical approach to analyzing the available evidence and then of course using modern statistical methods to fill in any and all gaps in the data streams, and there were several. The data was admittedly fragmentary information and in disarray like a thousand piece puzzle recently dumped out of its box: all of it quite a challenge for me to try and reassemble and interpolate through the gaps, in order to get to the truth. I read all of the documents, but especially the military reports, several times: it paints a bizarre and unlikely scene. I finally received enough information to reach a minimum level of what was necessary to begin publishing the story of RC chapter by chapter in the local newspapers.

What follows is my best truthful summary of the real crash events from the available facts of everything I gathered up to that point in time.

Christmas Day, afternoon, RC and his five escort jets were all airborne, hovering in a circular pattern 4.4 miles north of the Canadian border at an altitude of approximately 37,000 feet, awaiting border-crossing authority that was requested over the radio, following a custom of being deliberately and conspicuously noticeable to radar.

The U.S. Government was running a first-time test flight of some sophisticated experimental airborne surveillance technology over the area, in the form of a new Drone that had a new technology described as a 'multiple target strike mission capability' and it had onboard the Drone all of the latest generation of surveillance technology that could for several hundred miles in all directions "see" both sides of the U.S. and Canadian border with a new lateral side viewing look-down angular synthetic aperture light detection and radar technology or "LIDAR" built right into the Drone. LIDAR was not unique, but in this test it was used as a multi-dimensional layering imagery and what was a first of its kind, was that it would be combined in real-time with ultraviolet, infra-red, and radar spectrums all simultaneously into one coherent image. It was linked in real-time to several orbiting Satellites and had a vastly high speed integrated command and control network that was executed by the Drone autonomously (or more precisely executable as pre-programmed to be autonomous). This war machine would still be fulfilling its mission if the headquarters was obliterated in a nuclear blast.

The flight plan and tasking order from the National Command Authority was to have the Drone patrol the border along an elliptical route dissecting areas of Washington and Idaho and Montana, close to but near and South of the Canadian and U.S. Borders. While aloft, it was supposed to be a routine run-through-practice-drill of all systems tests, with multiple electronic recording devices, in order to establish a precise baseline for performance benchmarking of the design and function of the new Drone.

To minimize any conceivable risks to civilians, the Drone was to be flown on an initial "test only" flight during the afternoon of Christmas Day. The flight planning officers selected Christmas Day on the assumption that if anything went wrong and the Drone had to self-destruct, there would be almost no one near or below the Drone's remote flight path, so human life on the ground beneath the airspace would not be a planning risk worth worrying about. The Drone's pilot would be able to pilot the Drone at all times and literally run everything the Drone did by computer control inputs signaled from the Drone's home base in Nevada through an encrypted Satellite Communication ("SATCOM") radio signal downlinked directly to the Drone from the web of orbiting Satellites arcing across the heavens. The tests to be run included a long list of flight capabilities, communications, electronic target recognition and response and weapons escalation and offensive and defensive protocols. The remote human pilot would be able to see on his computer screen in Nevada, everything in true real-time that was captured by the Drone's forward-looking infrared, ultra-violet and visible light cameras. The Drone was programmed to follow a specific flight path controlled exclusively by pre-programmed auto-pilot inputs during the entire test flight. Everything the Drone did would be recorded every 100-milliseconds for follow-up engineering analysis and be available for any design modifications of the present and future generation of Drones.

No one was able to explain why the Drone took itself off of its autopilot program, yet several people were ready to testify based on verified evidence, that an unknown radio signal had breached several firewall communication barriers within the Drone and had somehow opened up the Drone to following a new set of program instructions, including the nightmare scenario that it had stopped responding to positive control inputs from the Nevada home base human remote test pilot.

However, had the remote pilot in Nevada been at his flight control console instead of taking an un-authorized coffee break, he would have been able to start the fail-safe procedures declaring an emergency and that the Drone was out of control and to send to it an emergency and immediate self-destruct signal. It is doubtful that this would have made it through to the Drone since there was some kind of "unauthorized hacking and takeover." Seconds after returning from the unauthorized coffee-break, the remote Drone pilot notified the Nevada Drone base commander of the problem and the commander then radioed an emergency and immediate order of "kill the Drone" to any available airborne military aircraft closest to the Drone. The airborne Drone going off of positive control sent the military into panic response mode.

In Seattle and in Canada too, military commanders hurriedly issued a "frag" search and destroy mission for immediate execution of an imminent threat. For the Drone's test mission, there were on the ground a few military assets in the area with pilots ready to run to their jets and get airborne in case something like this happened during an un-manned test flight. Four U.S. military pilots flying F-16 jets were scrambled to respond with emergency speed to fulfill the Kill Drone Order. As the out of control Drone was turning north toward the Canadian Border, aiming for the highway cutting through Kootenay Pass and Bridal Lake in British Columbia Canada, the Drone was targeted for termination by the four U.S. pilots taking off from two-hundred-ninety-six miles away. Although they were flying super-sonic for most of the way there, it still took two minutes to get airborne, eleven minutes going supersonic to get to the Drone and get a missile lock, so the time lag between the moment when the jets were scrambled to shoot down the Drone and when the Drone turned itself back onto autopilot was about thirteen minutes.

At the very last moment, as the Drone apparently returned to positive control of the remote Drone base, all four of the F-16 intercept pilots were ordered to abort the kill mission and to fly alongside and escort the Drone back to its Nevada base. I have requested several times official legal disclosure to me of the identities of the F-16 pilots in order to interview them, yet the U.S. Air Force is not cooperating with me at all, and the Presiding Judge is not interested in giving me access to those pilots.

Around midnight on Christmas, the engineers were grateful that their Drone had returned to home base in Nevada and they began to take it apart for a root-cause analysis so that they could analyze what went wrong. I interviewed three of the engineers that performed the deconstruction analysis of the Drone: all were non-committal when asked for their conjectures as to how the Drone could have been taken over and why civilian air traffic would have been targeted and actually attacked. The company had two Lawyers present alongside the engineers, which was troublesome and impeded full disclosure since the engineers would look to the Lawyers for a head nod of yes or no to go ahead and speak an answer to each of my questions. I did ask the engineers that since the Drone was designed for multiple target engagement, then why did it not launch missiles to kill the other five chase jets as well? *"No comment."* They also were evasive when I asked what happened with the flight-plan-correlation software: shouldn't the Drone have recognized RC's jet as matching the flight plan that RC had already by that time pre-filed with the F.A.A. and categorized RC as friendly? *"No comment."* Finally, and as I expected, the lead lawyer standing beside the engineers angrily terminated the interview, when I asked "how could a Drone on a test flight be fitted with live missiles active in a weapons-hot status that included an electromagnetic pulse weapon capability without direct authorization from the National Command Authority? Is it not true that the only way that could happen is if the weapons were going to be carried secretly to somewhere they should not be in the first place, all for the purpose of spinning a web story of plausible denial?"

Reviewing available data, it took me a few days to distill all of the aircraft movements.  I tried to get a sense of the scale of the military response to the accident.  The Nevada Drone Mission Base Commander issued the emergency call to the U.S.A.F. test program General from McChord A.F.B. near Seattle.  The General gave the orders to immediately scramble-launch a C-17 Globemaster cargo jet full of Air Force Rapid Response Recovery Personnel and Equipment, then he notified the Canadian Air Forces intercept squadron already airborne on a training mission along the border to divert their CF-18s which they did immediately; six CF-18 jets based out of Comox Air Base north of Vancouver were joined within minutes by their brothers flying four additional CF-18s from Calgary Air Force Base.  All of the U.S. and Canadian Fighter jets were called off from killing the Drone at the last minute when the Drone switched itself back onto weapons-safe status and reset itself onto auto-pilot and headed to its home base in Nevada.  The abort mission order was not heard at first by the fighter pilots since they were arguing which one should have the first launch honors to get the official record for splashing the Drone.  Within four minutes of receiving the flash emergency recovery alarm message from Seattle the General ordered from Fairchild A.F.B. near Spokane Washington an emergency launch of three Chinook Helicopters and one Sea Stallion Helicopter, all carrying soldiers and equipment from a special civil engineering hazardous response management team.  All of these airborne "assets" received additional detailed information about their mission and the updated real-time data as soon as they were airborne above 10,000 feet altitude, heading North East from Spokane towards the accident site.  Only the Canadian CF-18 pilots were familiar with the Kootenay Pass area: it was in any season windy from the mountains and valleys and always meant dangerous flying conditions, which was true also during a normal temperate summer's day.

Both U.S. and Canadian emergency phone call conversations were transcribed and handed over to the military and the U.S. State Department. In British Columbia, the Nelson R.C.M.P. Station received an urgent call from the U.S. Consular Officer on Duty in Vancouver who was also on speaker-phone with his counterpart in Washington D.C., at 5:28 pm Pacific Time on Christmas afternoon.  The officer called to report a ground crash non-vehicle airborne military accident.  The Consular officer also simultaneously conferenced in his cell phone call to the Nelson Provincial Fire Rescue Emergency Response Center so that he did not have to make two calls. The Consular Officer asked the local emergency dispatcher to hold one moment for a third and fourth call from the Consular communications emergency center switchboard. All of those calls also joined the teleconference. The final voice joining the teleconference was listed in the transcribed documents as a military emergency airborne call from an unnamed U.S. Official claiming to be in an AWACS jet flying over the accident scene: "sir please dispatch a medical evacuation helicopter to the following coordinates" but from the official report I have, the precise location is marked out and un-readable, although I could read clearly that the crash site coordinates were described as 9 KM south by southwest of "Bridal Lake, and east by southeast of Ripple Mountain, B.C. Canada, terminating in the U.S. approximately 3.4 KM north of Salmo Mtn." As transcribed in the R.C.M.P. report the panoply of voices from the jointly teleconferenced calls trying to manage the response to the accident were silenced voluntarily when an authoritative newly added voice finally joined the teleconference of government guys. The transcript shows that the caller did not make any additional requests for accident response but was instead determinedly and with a voice of authority making commands and trying to coordinate a joint response effort for everyone and everything rushing to get to the accident site. "Gentlemen I represent the President of the United States and I have been given National Command Authority to lead this recovery and response mission. I have the U.S. Federal Aviation Administration Sector Boss with us now on the call from the Regional Operations Command Center and also joining me in real-time is the Canadian Air Control Command Air General who is also on this call. Everyone please be silent and listen to my coordination orders. We have recovery choppers and Med-Evacuation teams airborne now northbound out of Fairchild Air Force Base. We are approaching the accident site. Estimated Time of Arrival is nine minutes inbound now. Presently my rescue assets are airborne transiting northeasterly at altitude 10,000 feet now crossing above the Pend Oreille River. At 5:45 pm Pacific Time the helo-flights will keep a static airborne post holding five miles South of the Nelway Border Station ... we are a combined flight of three Chinooks and one Sea Stallion: the four birds are squawking transponder codes 57911, 57912, 57913 and 57999, all have pre-approved Border Crossing Authority. We will handle right now all emergency humanitarian assistance and recovery of personnel and government property. Immediately cancel all of your open requests for land based ambulance and air medical assistance to that location. Clear the airspace within a ten mile radius and make it a no-fly zone immediately, divert all air-traffic away for a fifty mile buffer-zone. The U.S. troops will have exclusive ingress, and landing authority and egress authority as the on-scene-commander sees fit to exercise, until further notice. Have your Canadian ground forces seal the area within five miles of the ground impact site. Start a complete news media black-out until further notice."

In this messed up puzzle of a million pieces, the AWACS jet was the piece of information that seemed the most quizzical and curiosity provoking thing to me; why was the Drug Enforcement Agency conducting airborne interception drills under the guidance and control of an AWACS jet, when all of that took place in the same airspace as the Drone test? How were they connected? No one would directly answer me, although I have asked every U.S. Government official I met during this story that question, most of them break eye-contact with me, look at the ground, and say that they cannot comment on that question. I am interpreting that posture as a sign that the AWACS is incredibly important when figuring out the factors that were involved in RC's death, although I cannot exactly explain how, at least not just yet. I felt a clear intuitive sensation that the two most important war machines were the AWACS and the missiles with exotic weapons capabilities.

Witness statements from the crash site describe quite a serious government response. An older couple driving their dilapidated Recreational Vehicle through British Columbia from Calgary toward the border and onto Spokane Washington saw it all happen within a mile of the accident scene. According to civilians' official statements to the R.C.M.P. officer onsite "...at 4:23 p.m. we saw a brilliant blue flash of light from a distance ... It looked like a missile to me. It shot straight toward six jets: we could see their red strobe lights blinking. Five of the jets took off in different directions ... it looked like evasive maneuvers. The first jet was the lead jet. We could see its strobe lights flashing, but then another red-pulse light hit the lead jet and then all of its flashing lights went dark for about two seconds. We both could still see the dark outline silhouette of the jet against the sunset skyline. Then right after that jet went dark a missile hit it, there was orange light and sparks then you could hear a screeching sound and the jet engine blew up. The shot down jet literally fell from high in the sky down to somewhere south-west of Bridal Lake. After the crash and after a few minutes passed in silence, I thought I heard helicopters toward the

South, but I figured it was my wife using the restroom in the RV. So we drove on westerly along the Crows' Nest Highway and arrived on their recovery scene slowly, it took about 30 minutes after I first heard the helicopters. Funny thing, our cell phones and our FM radio did not work at the accident site: we saw quite a commotion of military folks and I figured that a courtesy stop would be a good idea to get the hell out of the way of what I thought was an accident and wanted to get off of the highway. There were emergency vehicles speeding by with sirens blaring loudly and coming from both directions to the site. We were all ordered off the road and to stay in our vehicles. I could see that already landed and sitting right on the centerline of the highway were four huge helicopters, surrounded by soldiers with machine guns at the ready. I had not seen a set of big helicopters like that, since the International Air Show in Vancouver last year. Damn those Kielbasa sausages were good and spicy at the Air Show. Anyway, I counted; forty-eight fellas in greenish-gray camouflage, about five Royal Canadian Mounted Policemen, a local ambulance crew of three, a local Canadian Air Emergency Air Force Helicopter: you know, those fluorescent green things with a Red Cross Painted on the sides and three medics arguing and shouting and taking the Good Lord's name in vain several times. Suddenly it occurred to me, that I realized, that this was probably not a joint military practice drill session, and it was not a routine accident since there was a white sheet draped over what must have been pieces of a body, placed near the edge of the highway pavement, all in a row. A smaller helicopter with a cable, brought onto the highway what was in the shape of a burnt piece of metal, it looked kind of like a pilot's ejection seat. They placed that right next to the body parts covered with white sheets. From how extremely enraged the Americans seemed to be, most of them were young looking kids it must have been an American under that white sheet. They took the body away on a stretcher then used a jeep with a cable to get the pilot's ejection seat into a crate, then they hooked up the crate to the back of a jeep and drove it right into the back ramp of the largest helicopter. And then the troops all loaded up: it was up, up and away, all done in about less than half an hour." The R.C.M.P. that told us to go ahead said that we might not want to worry too much about what we saw, but "of course it's up to you folks to speak up or not. Thank you for your cooperation and please have a pleasant evening." From the confused and disgusted expression on the R.C.M.P.'s face, I could tell he was bothered by the event, but he seemed to be dutifully following orders to wrap it up quietly. I used to be in the military, I know what that look on a guy's face means, I know how that feels. I felt bad for him. Anyway, my wife and I kept driving toward the Nelway Border Crossing Station on our way to the States for our vacation. I kept reading the newspapers later that week to see if any obituaries might mention more information about what we saw and who died, but what I read seemed more fiction than the facts I saw firsthand. I saw some of the facts printed in the papers, but what I saw in-person was not fully mentioned in the papers."

RC's cause of death is listed as "most probably a lightning strike" in listed in both the U.S. and Canadian joint military report. I wonder if anyone in addition to me thought this was absurd, since the sky was clear of all clouds that day and the sunset sky was clear for hundreds of miles around the accident site. Several other witness statements of civilians in the area also described the same images and sounds: "a blue flash of light like a rocket heading toward some jets, then one lead jet lost its lights and exploded and it fell down to the ground near a south-west direction away from Bridal Lake but south-east of Ripple Mountain." All witnesses heard helicopter sounds less than an hour after the brilliant blue light and explosion (which could have been innocently mistaken for thunder sounds). Nothing in their descriptions suggested lightning, at all. The military report's cause of death was ridiculous to me: I sarcastically named this report the *"lightning-strike-from-the-Gods-and-Goddesses"* theory.

Before the largest part of the jet fuselage was taken away by the military, a young R.C.M.P. Officer searched its contents and found a cargo box presumably from the bomb-bay of the crashed jet: it was made of thick steel and painted fluorescent green. The R.C.M.P. Officer began an inventory of the items within the cargo box. He found a bunch of Christmas presents from RC's family, a heavy duffel bag containing cash in the total amount of $157,000 U.S. Dollars, three Satellite phones, electronic communication encryption scrambler boxes marked 'top-secret,' a portable Satellite burst transmitter, seven laptop computers, a custom made laser targeting device and what was remaining of two picnic-baskets of Huckleberry muffins, still warm and steamy in the cold air.

Reading the final pages of the official documents, the last entry in the bizarre official accident record, that I can only presume was transcribed from intercepted radio traffic and released to me, was from an R.C.M.P. recorded radio transmission. The transcribing R.C.M.P. officials signing off on the report, attributed the final radio transmission to RC, caught on a police radio frequency monitoring device, before the blue light of a rocket streaked toward RC, and so it was assumed to be RC's voice cryptically saying calmly and clearly: *"Alpha-Mike-Foxtrot,"* and then a loud boom sound and then static from RC's radio transmission and then nothing. I guess it was a cryptic code borrowed from RC's military days, meaning "adios my friends." When I mention this acronym and my interpretation of its meaning to military people during my interviews, they hilariously laugh in my face and say, "yeah, sure, go with that interpretation, ha-ha-ha!" I guess I will never know the inside joke. No one seems to want to help me understand what it really means.

Taking none of the official governmental documents as the definite, truthful and complete account of what really happened, I had to put everything to a scientific test and hire a team of Engineers, Physicists, Material Scientists and Ex-Military Crash Investigation Experts and of course Lawyers, to help me try once again to request more detailed information about the new Drone and to try and perform a detailed accident reconstruction and finally determine what really caused the Drone to attack RC. The people I hired for document and evidence research in order to re-create the root-causes of the crash gave me as "the most probable scenario" a slightly different version of what I already knew. It cost me $400,000 to get their scientific account of the events, as they could reconstruct it from the available information.

Here is their version of everything they thought *"essential and relevant"*... I had hoped their report would be less cryptic, but no luck:

**Home Base -** The new Drone departed from a remote test base located in the Nevada desert precisely at 38 degrees 31 minutes 43.60 seconds North Latitude and 115 degrees 42 minutes 20.25 seconds West Longitude, the runway was at an elevation of 4,715 feet.

**Flight Path -** Its flight plan traced a circular pattern along alpine lakes of the Canadian and U.S. border.

**Test Goal -** The purpose of the test flight was to calibrate the hypersensitive imagery equipment and onboard computer systems and run a systems integration test.

**Risk Management -** Because of the insurance risk of a new test Drone possibly crashing or blowing up in an explosion, the test engineers and the Air Forces of both Countries selected the tests to begin at sunset on Christmas Day: their goal of making the entire test flight risk-free, was predicated entirely on the holiday assumption that most people would be home safe and far away from the test flight path.

**Targeting Imagery Tests -** To challenge the hypersensitive war-fighting and imagery features of the new Drone for multiple target detection, the engineers conjured a series of bizarre test targets that would be located upon the surface of four alpine lakes near the border and along a parallel flight path to the border. The presumption to test-out, was whether a Drone flying supersonic speeds at almost 60,000 feet could, or could not, distinguish and detect 'ground clutter' from the targets they placed on the frozen lakes and lock the weapon systems onto each ground target simultaneously. That test would prove whether the multi-targeting capabilities were functional in the real-world. The Drone's project team decided that the targets would be a block of white chalk with the dimensions one meter by four meters by nine meters, placed by helicopters onto the frozen ice of the surfaces of Sullivan Lake in Washington State, Boundary Lake in British Columbia Canada, and Continental Lake in Idaho and Kintla Lake in Montana. When the chalk targets were in place Christmas morning, then the signal would be sent to begin the Drone's test flight. If the project team had an opportunity to fly the Drone close to the ground to test its terrain following radar, and to try and confuse the Drone, the project team selected the targets for the steep angles of the surrounding mountains. To test whether unexpected aberrations in the ground soils could be detected by the Drone so as to find hidden metal bombs and weapons caches the project team in particular selected Continental Lake. The idea was to test the Drone's high definition detailed information gathering sensors in response to the Lead-Metal waste in the creeks that would give a metallic resonance return signal to the Drone's radars and give it a chance to show it could differentiate specific types of different metals from the granitic rocks in the surrounding mountains. The Lead-Metal waste in the creeks was from the decades of mining waste pollution on the north-eastern slope of the Continental Mountain and all of that would make it difficult to accurately detect and capture for imagery recording and analysis, since at that time of the year it was buried under eight feet of snow and ice. Kintla Lake in Montana was also chosen for its water having a high degree of glacial silt and soda deposits that would appear to the Drone's sensory equipment as background noise. The Drone was airborne at 3:00 pm Pacific Time on Christmas Day and traveling at an average airspeed of Mach-1 it was onsite at Kintla Lake Montana at 4:07 pm. The plan was to, after the remote pilots controlling the Drone could successfully detect the first chalk target against the background using thermal imagery looking down onto the frozen lakes, then the controllers at the Nevada test-sight then turned the Drone west toward its next targets, and activated its auto-pilot.

**Unauthorized Software Breach** - Minutes before sunset RC radioed the U.S. F.A.A. asking for border crossing authority, while flying in a holding pattern on the Canadian side of the border. Three seconds after RC's radio request was transmitted and acknowledged by the Seattle F.A.A. tower, and confirmed by the Air Sector Boss at Vancouver Canada Radar Operations...that radio signal seemed to be the most likely triggering event, to begin the precise moment when the Drone was hacked by an unknown person or persons, their aim seemed to be to turn the Drone directly north toward RC's jet on an intercept course and takeover control of any onboard weapons.

**Hacking Method(s) and Tactic(s)** - The engineers deconstructing the Drone for an official root-cause analysis of all of the accident data as it was recorded in the onboard flight recording devices, found several records proving a sophisticated seven-step hacking method was applied to take over the Drone.

**( 1 ).** The hardware point of vulnerability used in the hacking exploit was a Gigabit Wi-Fi antennae temporarily installed on the aft-underbelly of the Drone, and connected to the Drone's central computer. The Wi-Fi antennae was used at the last minute before live flight, to allow the computer software engineers a port and path to rapidly upload the last few lines of software program code, completed hours before the Drone's first flight. The latest code would allow the Drone to execute its command and control operations at a faster speed with several parallel processes being executed all at the same moment in time, instead of sequentially, all done while in auto-pilot flight test mode. The code was prepared hastily, it was not tested, and it was rife with flaws. Haste makes waste, and in this case, haste makes death very possible. Normal pre-flight Drone preparation procedures demand the removal of any temporary devices attached to the Drone, including the temporary Gigabit Wi-Fi antennae. In this case, it was not removed, and was still attached before, during and after the missile attack.

( **2** ). The specific software code point of vulnerability was a startup booting process step, contained in the file titled: *"bootup_packet_chatter_latency_test.\*"* instructing the Drone to test its communication links to headquarters, by broadcasting its radio frequency used only for an emergency, which changes with each specific mission. The packet is an electronic message container, in this case a bundle of message information sent atop a radio frequency, like Santa Claus delivering a present in a box carried by his sleigh pulled by flying Reindeer. The test signal bounces off of mission-critical satellites on its destination to home base headquarters, sending a positive-acknowledgment packet test communication, and fulfilling its design goal of validating and correcting for slight packet losses and transmission latencies or chatter in the communication stream. All of this stuff is done as a *tuning-in-test* to get a clear communication channel open and active. This is a basic and often considered low-level low-tech test, like turning on your car radio and tuning in your favorite radio station in order to hear music clearly with no static or bleed-over signal from a nearby radio station.

( **3** ). During its entire flight he Drone used the Gigabit Wi-Fi antennae in its powered up mode, transmitting continuously a ping broadcast of at least one frequency every two-seconds. The specific frequency transmitted through the Gigabit Wi-Fi antennae was most likely a publicly used frequency such as the commonly used 5 GHZ Band. This frequency is easily monitored by a wide variety of digital radio enabled devices within transmission range of several miles of the Drone. This vulnerability is one of the most serious of the Drone's flaws that left it wide open and vulnerable to unauthorized radio communication hacking traffic being received and processed: it was as if a loudly announced opening of a new freeway on-ramp was shouted to an entire city.

( **4** ). The Drone's weapons systems' firewalls, protected with Military Grade Encryption Cipher Codes, were circumvented entirely by this open communication channel, by someone recognizing there was a simple opening through an unlocked doorway into the Drone's main movie theater.

( **5** ). Since the Gigabit Wi-Fi antennae was located on the aft-underbelly of the Drone, the most likely source of the hacker(s) radio monitoring and transmission equipment was at an elevation below the elevation of the Drone, which at the time of the attack was flying at least

60,000 feet or less. Given the remote mountainous location of the attack, it is unlikely that winter sports enthusiasts were carrying sophisticated electronic equipment with them during their ground based sports activities. It is more likely that an aircraft of some kind was the source(s) of the hacker(s) electronic attack on the Drone.

**( 6 ).** A hostile radio signal was beamed up to the Drone, carrying an electronic file with the same name as the packet test file mentioned above, but this new file appended additional information to the already existing file, telling the Drone to follow the newly installed flight orders. This step deliberately circumvented the Drone's encrypted firewalls and injected twelve lines of targeting program code with an immediate execution priority.

**( 7 ).** The malicious code instructed the Drone to shut off its autopilot, activate its weapons systems, speed up and change direction to intercept and lock onto the GPS real time location of a transponder code that matched exactly the transponder code in RC's jet and when the Drone was within nine miles of the target then it should launch all weapons.

**( 8 ).** The final step of the newly injected program code told the Drone to reboot its entire systems and place itself back onto autopilot mode, and erase the IP address and MAC address of the digital device that sent the hostile radio signal and instructions in the first place, and to wipe clean the Drone's onboard computer record of IP configuration files, that too held a record of IP addresses for communications devices transmitting information to the Drone. It left the Drone with a record of what happened and how, but not with a remaining record of the tracks of the assassin(s). *Who did it* is undeterminable from the empirical evidence available.

**Response and Recovery -** Pieces of RC's jet were on fire and scattered on both sides of the border. Recovery rapid-response teams from both countries were scrambled immediately to deal with containment and cleanup of the situation.

Their report concluded that it was an attack too sophisticated to be carried out by one person. There were too many logistics and real-time coordination steps involved to make it happen. A single hacker with some equipment bought at a local hobby store, could not possibly pull that off.

Well, well, well, the technology part of this puzzle was falling into place, except for the great big unknown of *who did it?*

I was disappointed that the team of experts did miss some crucial facts, and did not fully spend more detailed time on the AWACS jet.

The first set of crucial facts that the team of experts missed, was detailing how RC's private medics had been following alongside his flight in one of the Harrier escort jets. They had beaten the military recovery teams of both countries to the wreckage and were ready to whisk what was left of RC away to the nearest hospital in the U.S., however the first rescuer on scene reached the pilot ejection seat and saw that there what was left of RC was melted into the pilot seat from the missile explosion. Radioing the message *"Boss is K.I.A."* he was pronounced dead on scene. Within a few minutes, the first R.C.M.P.'s showed up in a helicopter and had "arrested" all of the aircraft and vehicles at the accident scene until they sorted everything out. Then when the American Military showed up, with what must have looked like an invasion force, eyewitness reports by civilians near the highway and R.C.M.P. Officers, all consistently describe that "the five pilots from the escort jets were taken away by the U.S. Military guys ... they put them hurriedly into the first large Chinook Helicopter and flew away." It seemed exceedingly strange to me that the chase planes for this trip were Harrier jets that could land with no runway near the crash site, instead of the oft-used and RC's favorite A-10 jets used in almost every other flight RC made within the last decade. None of the pilots in the escort chase jets were allowed to speak to me, as mentioned, I am still trying to discover their identities and request interviews.

The second set of crucial facts not covered in detail by the team of experts, was that the closest military Airborne Warning and Control System ("AWACS") jet was fifty miles away from the crash site, it was conducting airborne flight-follow interception drills with the Drug Enforcement Agency in dedicated and exclusive U.S. airspace high above Priest Lake Idaho. The AWACS recorded data and electronic signals were evaluated for interference with the Drone. Not surprising to me, and according to information released officially by the U.S. Air Force Inspector General, the *"AWACS in question was on a totally different set of frequencies than either the Drone, or the civilian pilot's jet radio signals"* at the time of the accident. According to the U.S. Government, no other aircraft were on the same frequency as the Drone, so it was their conclusion that it was highly likely and very possible that the hacking radio signal was either from a ground based source in the area or an airborne craft flying at or near the same altitude of the Drone, and the identity of the suspect aircraft is unknown.

The U.S. Government ruled out the AWACS jet and its crewpersons as possible interfering agents in the accident. But I didn't rule out the AWACS, even if it may only be the platform used to bounce off the hostile radio signal, like a trampoline, even though its crew may not have known anything about it. The more questions I asked about the AWACS, the more evasive and non-committal the government personnel became towards me. The AWACS must be a very significant piece of this puzzle.

I found it one of the most ironic situations in Western Civilization, that a popular humanitarian who in his own right respected technology so much and trusted human nature to a high degree and spent his life to improve the world for all, was killed 'accidentally' by hi-tech military technology in a supposed accident.

At this point in my investigation, nothing seemed accidental at all to me. My most intense curiosity was spent in trying to discover who used the Drone to kill RC and why? My leading questions were the same ones I raised to those people who visited with me after RC's funeral at the luncheon. *Who had the means, motive and opportunity to carry out that sophisticated hack and hit? And why was RC specifically targeted for assassination?*

Maybe following RC's money trails would lead me to the responsible person(s). Who was involved with the sources of all that money of RC's?

This story had to make sense, somehow...

# Chapter 4

## Following the Money:
*Transactions from Vanuatu to everywhere...*

RC's electronic money transactions were an imminent risk to the U.S. Monetary Supply. The magnitude and quantity of the money transactions worried the Federal Reserve's watchers of monetary supply. They immediately called their cousins to have a look at the possible de-stabilizing impacts from RC's transactions. The call went out seven days after RC's death. The U.S. Office of the Comptroller for the Currency requested Presidential approval to assemble a U.S. Special Project Task Force to audit and report back to the President on RC's financial transactions that percolated through the U.S. and International Banking Systems at high speed after his death. The U.S. President approved the request that same day.

The U.S. Special Project Task Force team journeyed to RC's floating banking headquarters on the beautiful waters of Vanuatu, located North East of Australia. RC owned a decommissioned U.S. Aircraft Carrier which at the time of his death was anchored close offshore of the perfect sandy beaches of one of the islands of Vanuatu. RC had purchased the ship and then re-furbished it with hi-tech equipment so it could be used as his mobile business headquarters. I doubt the project team members grasped the irony of what RC was doing. His offshore banking was conducted in a ship which itself was anchored offshore. RC was highly amused by puns, this one too must have made him chuckle. RC had hired several people to staff it and run all banking operations from his various businesses through this single point of management, according to his specific instructions. Most of RC's Employee-Owners were skeptical about the real purpose behind why U.S. Federal Government agents were onboard, yet they were still cooperative: that was one of RC's directives regarding the morally and ethically correct way to do business. RC had required anyone working with him to respect the rule of law and to be completely open when conducting business. RC thought that specific method would deter corruption and illegal activities. The project team from the U.S. Government was given every courtesy and access to information by RC's staff on the ship.

The U.S. Government Computer Forensics experts were baffled. "No one in the private sector should have this technology!" Locating the main computer server onboard was easy. Unfortunately it took quite a while to isolate the master program running all of the financial transactions. After four days of concerted effort they found it. The project team had to bring in a Latin Translator. "Quattrini Extraho Hilarito" is the name of the software program RC built to handle his money. That file name is translated from Latin quite literally as "the money should be extracted mirthfully." The translator was also shown several computer screens full of and scrolling through RC's program code, which was also written entirely in Latin. The translator was asked to decipher all seventeen million lines of code. After laughing at the absurdity of the request, the translator explained patiently that he would need to request a team of over one-hundred persons to help him accomplish that, since it was estimated that such a specific translation task would take a minimum of two years of full-time effort to decode it all and put it into English and phrase it in terms that computer programmers could decompile and figure out. I would guess that RC's specific choice of that title was for the sake of humor, something quirky that was to me another example of RC's several inside jokes known only to him. Writing a custom program in the Latin Language, that was serious; it was typical of RC, to do something no one else would ever attempt: to use a dead language from long ago in a modern piece of technology. It was a one-of-a-kind computer program with its own serpentine logical gates and mathematical nuances. The government report refers to that program name by the abbreviation ("Q.E.H."). The Q.E.H. Program worked at high speed after RC died: it is still working to this day.

RC's business staff on-board was never given passwords to get close to or into the server. RC had taken care of all of the creation, updating and maintenance and daily use of the program and its output, during his entire life by dialing in remotely through an encrypted Satellite Communication downlink channel early every morning. RC had not instructed any of his business staff with what they should do in case of his death. I took that fact as proof that RC was not planning to die anytime soon and therefore the theory of RC committing suicide could be disproven.

Everyone on the ship was still faithfully working away, with dim hopes of possibly expecting RC to magically sign into the computer servers from some remote location, although secretly they knew it would never happen again. They were not aware that soon they would receive news that upon RC's death, that they were to become owners of this particular business. RC had several Trustees and Attorneys and Accountants carrying out the stock purchase agreements for the Employees' benefit, making them instantly wealthy, yet instantly more responsible for their own working future.

The U.S. Special Project Task Force Team left after nine days onboard RC's floating bank headquarters. Their report was delivered by F.B.I. courier to: The Chairman of the Federal Reserve Bank, The Comptroller of the Currency and most importantly the President of the United States. The report was initially classified as Top-Secret.

My requests to the U.S. Government were initially denied, but after three and a half years of filing multiple Court cases and appeals, by using the Freedom of Information Act, I was given an opportunity to view the report at the Washington D.C. Headquarters office of the F.B.I. and take notes. I would not be able to take any government documents with me when I was done, I could only leave with my hand-written notes.

Flying to Washington D.C., I had a long list of questions written to force myself to read the report in a detailed way. All of my questions were organized into five broad themes: (1) how much money did RC have to give to his loved ones at the time of his death, (2) how did the electronic payments flow, (3) what is the source and destination of the transactions, (4) why would RC arrange things that way and the biggest question (5) why would the U.S. Government worry about a private citizen moving his money through the world banking systems?

The printed report was three-hundred and seventy-three pages long, although the document I was allowed to view was heavily redacted: only about eighty-seven pages were readable. Redaction is the censorship act of completely inking out and making impossible to read with human eyes, some sentences and words in order to protect Government Secrets. I resented that greatly. I felt like my time was being deliberately wasted.

The executive summary described how RC apparently conceived of and engineered a financial labyrinth of electronic transactions, mostly based upon Satellite to Satellite communications, where the final steps of all of the transactions were digitally beamed down to Earth by encrypted radio signals, first to his headquarters ship and then to his favorite banks and financial institutions that he owned along with his Employees. The task force project team identified and traced the money flow from start to finish for over seventeen-thousand individual electronic transactions. The swirling mass of transactions was designed by RC to culminate into perpetual automatic payments of U.S. Dollars into the bank accounts of RC's loved ones, from RC's bank accounts. It is simply direct deposit money for their entire lifetime. Because it represented payments from a deceased person's Estate, it was all tax free to the beneficiaries. The task force project team concluded that since all transactions that were audited were apparently legal in each country and bank that handled the money and further since the transactions were made with after tax dollars, there was little that the U.S. Government could do except estimate the impact of those transactions upon the U.S. Monetary Supply.

Allowing someone to intervene in that elaborate electronic process so as to exert external control over RC's electronic payments after his death would be impossible. As far as the software, the Satellites and the computer server, it was clear to the special task force team that simply un-plugging the server aboard the headquarters ship in Vanuatu would not shut down the network or interrupt the flow of money. The Q.E.H. Software Program uploaded to all of RC's twelve Satellites, identical mirror copies of itself and all historical transactions up to that point in time. It operated as if it could survive if the main server or any of the mirror copies on the Satellites were to be knocked out or shut off. Given the complexity of RC's code in the program and its dispersed presence, the project team assumed that there were also mirrored image copies of each Satellite's copy of the Q.E.H. Program beamed down to several terrestrial computers too. The master program seemed to exist everywhere, in Heaven and Earth and it updated all of its mirrored ghost-copies hourly. Because the secure network's IP address nodes of each of the copies of the programs were encrypted using "1024 bit double-blind encryption methods and scrambled into a double blind communication connection protocol" it would be mathematically impossible to decipher what the network map routes really are, within the time-span of several human lifetimes. The N.S.A. technicians were envious of such an advanced technology, and did their best to try and appropriate it for U.S. Government use.

Tracing the money flow, the report cited efforts of the project team to conduct several audits of RC's transactions to establish the basis for a description and explanation of recurring patterns and sequences of banking electronic funds transfers that RC had engineered and that were carried out autonomously by the Q.E.H. Program. The pattern was that every morning at 4:30 am Pacific Time, RC signed into the server aboard the ship floating off the coast of Vanuatu, to enter a forty-three character randomized password code into an electronic funds transfer program he designed and it swept and gathered all of his cash from his main corporate account in Delaware U.S.A. and sent it whirling around the globe at the speed of light through a series of currency exchange transactions, hopping over several commercial banks (that RC owned along with his Employee-Owners), banks located in the countries of: Belize, Singapore, Hong Kong, Cayman Islands, Vanuatu and finally from Vanuatu the same amount of money each day was divided equally among all of his beneficiaries and directly deposited into their various individual and personal bank accounts all over the world. Each day, all of RC's electronic funds transactions were remotely monitored by RC's specifically trained Trustees, Lawyers, Bankers and Accountants. Through complex 'power of Attorney' contracts, RC had contractually bound, instructed, and prepaid all of those people to handle all of the taxes that would be due for transactions generated from the Q.E.H. Program: those taxes were paid almost immediately. Those people also handled all the tax reporting and compliance work with each of the Government Taxing Authorities, so that RC's beneficiaries had no paperwork burdens when dealing with the financial gains. The financial gains happened almost in real-time, from those transactions completed during foreign currency conversions and investments from high-speed program trading of stocks on the two major stock exchanges NYSE and NASDAQ, all of buying and selling of stocks were efficiently made and guided by the Q.E.H. Program during the electronic transfers of RC's money, and then those gains were also again moved electronically among banking and investing accounts held in different countries. That flurry of electronically driven financial wizardry resulted in exorbitant amounts of money for all of RC's beneficiaries: on a daily basis, they enjoyed an ever growing amount of tax free money in their bank accounts.

The report's conclusion re-stated its findings (drearily and monotonously) in terse bureaucratic language. "The events that triggered the start of the Extrication Program were baffling, yet the timing was easy to spot. Three weeks after RC was classified as "deceased," curious things happened to his businesses worldwide. All of the businesses were sold 100% to the Employees. The money from the sale of his businesses went into various banks. The money in each of the banks was electronically moved at least once each 24 hours, all movements being made by the

Q.E.H. Program (no one was carrying around suitcases full of cash). Some of the money was invested in currency hedging and currency swap options trading yet then sold rapidly sometime within nineteen hours, but no longer than nineteen hours. There was autonomous program trading and hi-frequency trading from sources no one in the stock exchanges could pinpoint exactly but the agents onboard used U.S. Government decryption technology to discover that the investment orders originated from RC's computer systems. The profits from selling the investments were in turn distributed electronically to RCs beneficiaries. No one in the banks could figure out the source(s) of the money, but there was a great deal of money pouring into his beneficiaries' accounts and into charities worldwide." The report's conclusion had cryptic references to estimates of RC's cash amounts available at the time of his death, how long the payments might continue and forecasts of the impacts of those cash transactions on the U.S. Monetary Supply and the U.S. Economy. The specific numbers were blacked out and thoroughly redacted. I can only take wild guesses at the dollar amounts since none of the beneficiaries or anyone involved with administering the Trusts for the beneficiaries, were willing to speak with me about those numbers. "I have confidentiality agreements that keep me silent, sorry pal."

For several months after the final report of the investigation was given to the President of the United States, there was a top secret and vociferous debate among the President's Staff, since no one could figure out how to shut off the Q.E.H. Program and its electronic funds transactions. Government and private sector experts unanimously concluded that trying to shut it down would be futile. I would not have been surprised if the C.I.A. had a few analysts involved on the project team who wondered aloud whether they should write a memo requesting that a secret request be made to the U.S. Congress to permit one-time use of the prohibited Anti Satellite ("A.S.A.T.") missiles in the U.S.A.F. weapon inventory, to shoot down RC's Satellites, (or possibly get China to do it with their own versions of A.S.A.T. missiles). I could never prove that the use of A.S.A.T. weapons was requested, but I do have my suspicions that it was a viable option brought up in discussions within the Government. Sarcastically, I also thought silently to myself, 'why don't they consider using the same Drone that killed RC to get that thing in the air again to also take out RC's Satellites?'

I found one section that was not redacted, possibly by accident and it was a goldmine for me as an investigative journalist. There was a subsection in the government report titled "Aggressive Humanitarianism" and it involved one of RC's companies headquartered in Vanuatu. The corporation named "RC Aerospace Satellite Systems and Communications Logistics ("R.C.A.S.S.C.L. Inc.") owned twelve Satellites that beamed their data to telemetry Earth stations in the countries of Australia, the Kashmir Region of India, Israel, Greece, Western Brazil, Madagascar, Iceland, Alaska U.S.A. and Nevada U.S.A. Primarily used for RC's commercial businesses, the Satellite Company was also sometimes used by RC to solve the problems of bribery, corruption, crime and illegality regrettably occurring within the third world countries where he operated businesses and humanitarian activities.

The report seemed to be written by an F.B.I. agent and was definitely directed at the N.S.A., as if to telegraph with a tone of sarcasm the unofficial message: "we know you electronic shadowy nerds had access to, and are now using some of RC's exotic technology." One puzzling fragment of the report, which was blacked-out and also thoroughly redacted, was mention of a specific type of super-computer that one of RC's companies had built as a custom project only for RC's use, according to his own original and unique design principles. I couldn't quite make out all of the details, but it hinted at something that my friends who are computer experts guessed might be "a functional equivalent of a quantum-computer," whatever that is.

The report went to great lengths to describe RC's use of his Satellites to eavesdrop on the houses and banking institutions used by tyrants or crime bosses or international terrorists that had crossed his path and attempted to interfere with RC's lawful business activities. In each instance, within twenty-four hours of being informed about the trouble, RC responded by systematically tasking his Satellites in orbit to move to the closest region of the trouble in order to gather enough electronic eavesdropping information to hack into the bank accounts and investments of the alleged trouble-makers. He then beamed all of that data down to Fort Meade in order to share all the info with the C.I.A. and the N.S.A. although he didn't share his info with the F.B.I. and apparently, they didn't like being left out. What RC didn't seem to share with anyone in the U.S. Government were his additional and several stealthily successful private attempts to hack into the bank accounts of those who had stolen from him and his business partners, taking back only the precise amount of money that lawfully belonged to him and then repatriated it back to the specific people and businesses that were harmed. As an act of restorative justice, he put the people and their businesses that had been victimized back into the economic and financial status they were in, before the trouble had started. As a result, the U.S. Government loved the free intelligence information RC passed on. Several third world business leaders found out quickly not to mess with RC or any of his businesses in the neighboring regions. The message and the lesson was simple: stay far away from RC and his business entities or the bad people would very likely find that they had little to no monetary resources left to operate in the real-world, politically or otherwise and that their real-time locations and movements and cell-phone conversations were being transmitted to the relevant law enforcement authorities constantly, so there was nowhere safe to hide anymore. RC preferred that type of non-judicial solution since the particular methods he used were un-traceable and in his mind, those solutions were especially virtuous since they were only used against those who had drawn first blood against him and the best reason was that he avoided escalating a response to the point of bloodshed. RC always preferred to take back only the precise amount of money that lawfully belonged to him in the first place. RC left a lot of left over resources and information to the U.S. Government for them to deal with it as they saw fit.

The other mention of RC's top-secret actions described how RC's private air force jets and cargo planes provided him the resources to carry-out several emergency rescue missions; moving entire villages of oppressed people, people that he knew and protected. RC's unique style of aggressive humanitarianism seemed to include flying his customized jet as the lead aircraft into a problem area, escorted by his private air defense force of five Harrier jets for close air support, in-turn also followed by ten C-17 cargo planes. One example of many in the report, RC and his private air force evacuated an un-named village listed in the U.S. Department of Defense survey maps as village #53947 located at the end of a long 14,000 foot altitude glacial valley at the Eastern-most border of Afghanistan where it meets the border of Northern Pakistan. At the time, it was the home of over 217 people. RC was involved with this village for several years, since one of the village leaders at that time was a college friend of RC. One month before the rescue, RC had provided to the entire village and especially their school, several computers and wireless communications technology, along with new cellphones and Satellite phones. The village leader frantically called RC on a Satellite phone, explaining that a local terrorist group was on their way to the village to steal all of the computer technology. Feeling somewhat responsible for causing the impending trouble by providing technology to the village, RC assured his friend he would help. RC immediately phoned his staff and told them to monitor by Satellite in real-time the troop movements near a hostile area close to his friend's village. RC flew from his private airport eastward to one of his Satellite operations centers. After landing briefly to see the data and broadcast his requests for his private air force to get airborne and help him, he mobilized the rest of the logistics and planning for the rescue mission on his own. Wasting no time at all, RC contacted the U.S. Government, notified all relevant departments of his intentions and immediately shared all of his intelligence information with all of the appropriate agencies. Astonishingly, the report lists a specific 'forewarning' by RC that he was going to use his private technology and Satellites to create an electronic dead-zone-blackout of all communications in the area of the village during his rescue mission and that "you might want to keep all of your military assets on the sidelines for seven hours and out of my way please until I am done there." His goal was to evacuate the entire village and have all of it done before an invasion of hostile forces from an unidentified hostile attack force could overtake the village. The name of the attack force was blacked out, I couldn't read who or what it was. While flying to Afghanistan in mid-air RC negotiated with the United Nations to find a place of sanctuary for the village population, gaining agreement for political asylum for the villagers. Within less than six hours, RC and his private air force and ground troops and logistical operators comprising a collective group of aggressive humanitarians, had completely rescued and evacuated all villagers and their farm animals and belongings, flying the entire village to a United Nations Air Base in Afghanistan. The report did not mention how anything turned out for the villagers after being evacuated. I can only guess that RC would have arranged for lawful immigration to any place in the world that the villagers wished to go. I marveled at the logistical planning that would have been required by RC to coordinate all of the aircraft and people on short notice; how did he synchronize all of the aircraft arrival times for the mission, especially since each different jet has different flight speeds and maximum distances without refueling? How did they find a place to land near the village? I needed to find some way to identify the villagers who were evacuated and to interview them.

After reading the government report it was clear to me that RC had at times operated as his own private economic counter-terrorism financial machine in addition to using his private air force for rescue missions. He acted on his belief of trying to give restorative justice to people he knew around the world who had been oppressed by illegal taking of their money and resources and freedoms. It wasn't necessarily a re-distribution of wealth that RC was worried about, more so than a compassionate and just act of restoring the situation to a fair and just balance. It was also a life of risky but real-world efforts to get people he knew to freedom, economically and otherwise. From those types of extreme missions and from his aggressive humanitarianism, his enemies were many. It did not take too long for anyone with half of a brain to isolate the list of people or entities or governments who had the intelligence, resources, will and motives to carry out successfully such crazy missions. At that moment, I finally understood why it was necessary that RC traveled everywhere with machine-gun carrying bodyguards on the ground and weaponized escort jets in the sky.

Although it was not written anywhere in the parts of the government report that were visible and not blackened-out, I estimated that the one mission of evacuating village #53947 cost RC at least five and a half million dollars. That is my minimum guess at what it cost RC, based upon the assumptions that the shortest flight distance would be from one of RC's private airbases in Alaska straight over the North Pole across Russian airspace down South into Afghanistan, with mid-air refueling for RC's jet, the escort jets, and all of the cargo planes.

If RC was alive and if I showed him my mathematical estimates of what it cost him for that mission, I am certain that his response would be: "who worries about the money ... all human life is sacred and priceless."

## Chapter 5

### Following the Meaning:
*Hopes and dreams discovered from victim's book and personal journals...*

Searching for many answers, I turned to his hand-written journals and the draft of a book he tried to finish before he died. My intent was to find concrete details of what was important to him. What were his hopes and dreams and why was he unfailingly idealistic? Maybe I could breathe a bit more life into the lingering and cherished memories of RC. What I hoped to discover was whether there existed a written plan that RC might have drafted, concisely listing everything he wanted yet to accomplish before he died. I felt compelled to gather clues that would help me to forecast *what might have been*, had he lived longer and accomplished all of his goals.

Each of his ex-wives and his widow, all enthusiastically emailed to me several electronic files of documents they had scanned from what RC had written during their time together. It was a wide variety of material, frustratingly random, because there were useless fragments scattered among gems of truly insightful and helpful information. I felt it was properly respectful that I still had to show my gratitude to them for having received their blessings in a sense, meaning that overall my view was that it likely was better for me to start with too much information instead of too little information.

RC's journals spanned almost forty years of his life beginning when he was eleven years old. It was perpetually frustrating for me to sift through and find some relevance or utility within the content of the documents that the ex-wives and the widow shared with me. I had assumed in good-faith that it would be 'journaling' material. It took me thirteen months of un-yielding effort to sift through all of that stuff: the eye-strain caused three changes to my glasses prescriptions, and caused countless headaches.

In addition to the vast collection of fragmentary journal information, there was also a book that RC was still editing and writing at the time of his death. Thankfully, the book was clear, cogent, creative and convincing. The book was a comprehensive effort of lifelong tinkering, seemingly the result of building the explanation of his theory by dropping one pebble in the ocean each day of his life. RC continued working on a final draft of his book up to the very week before he died. It was an ever-growing and epic-sized tome exceeding 1,600 typewritten single-spaced pages!

His title is: *"A uniquely and collectively exhaustive critical analysis of the strongly competitive form of harsh Capitalism and its consequent harmful and financially diminishing effects upon the populace of several countries by using an historical and an empirical methodology along with a commonsensical taxonomy of suggestions for the pursuit of Humanitarian solutions to fix those problems by practical applications of benevolent technologies that are cost effective and easily accessible and available to all people."* The subtitle was a brief line from one of Wordsworth's poems: "...*getting and spending we lay waste our powers.*"

Looking at the author's name, I laughed out loud in reaction to the very first time I read it: "*Prengalthibarr Mokxshama Vienteubbii, a.k.a. the Renegade Random Capitalist.*" If that was my name, I too would have wanted an acronym instead of trying to get others to pronounce all of that: it sounded like jargon! That was the very first time I had seen his full legal name.

All joking aside, at the moment I read the title and saw the quote from Wordsworth, I thereafter had a sinking feeling like I just ate a rock: my stomach hit the floor. The subtitle hinted to me that this epic-sized book might be an economic critique against consumerism, against industrialization and against over-consumption. Worrying, I expected it would be a book that could be boiled down to a bad recipe that would call upon ingredients from varied sources of liberation theology, Keynesian Economics, a little bit of historical theory from Adam Smith and boat-load of Utilitarianism and that taken in its entirety it would be a smorgasbord of half-baked rants that might end up being subtly Socialist in its subtext, ultimately ending in a train-wreck of altruistic secular humanism. Unexpectedly, it was none of those things.

Once again, I was frustrated with RC mainly because he was completely unpredictable. He never re-cycled or re-used anyone else's theories, philosophies, beliefs, opinions, or real-world experiences. His entire book was written directly from what he thought and felt regarding the most difficult societal problems he encountered during his international travels and entrepreneurial efforts. He actually offered workable and practical solutions that seemed commonsensical and cost effective.

Feeling humbled, I had to admit after his death I was reading his words and becoming increasingly frustrated with RC over the randomness in his mind and soul, as I could detect the Entropy in his soul more clearly through the words in his book. In the past, I gave voice to my frustration by referring to RC sardonically and sarcastically as the *Buckminster Fuller of Capitalism.* When I said that, I was regrettably venting my frustration over my failure to understand how far ahead of me and other people RC truly was intellectually and in how well he efficiently used his intellect to solve real-world problems of unemployment and economic development. His several solutions suggested ways to practically deliver gainful employment, opportunities for as much education as a person wished to pursue, equal economic opportunity for people starting small businesses, access to healthcare, technology development and sharing with all who were interested in benevolent actions, even giving advice for developing new international small-scale markets using the internet. I was frustrated that my simplified phrase "grass-roots capitalism of a kindly form" did not begin to describe what RC was doing in the real-world.

Although the operation of his mind was mysterious to me, his economic and financial proposals aiming toward humanitarian solutions were easily understood and seemed sensible. Unlike any of his contemporaries, RC was not satisfied with merely pointing out and complaining about problems everyone already knew existed; he also expended most of his effort putting forth logical and practical solutions to fix human problems. Most of his writing is spent describing and explaining business transactions and financial solutions to problems faced by real people each day of their lives.

When I outlined the draft of RC's book it showed me his pre-occupations with and being haunted by the guiding themes of trying to find the root-cause of the failure of capitalism that were damaging to individuals and that were signs of recurring systemic failures of capitalism itself. He traced several examples to the disconnection existing between the systemic structural parts of capitalism versus the person participating in the economy, when, according to RC, there should be a positively constructive connection between the two parts of the economy and market. RC described and explained the structural problems within a system where the average citizen's freewill to choose an economy and market to participate in was hobbled by the problem that once in the market as an Employee or owner, there are several forces external to the person, that seek to defeat and diminish and steal the fruits of everyone's labor, including the individual. The result of being oppressed, despite one's best efforts, was apparently caused by overly defined property rights that aimed at concentrating wealth through ever expanding property laws designed to be controlled exclusively by the king in past history and in the present day now the ultra-rich in modern society. Communism and Socialism were also colossal failures as far as economic systems, RC concluded, citing several historical examples where major problems (of power, corruption, greed) are politically identifiable as the causal element in several symptomatic economic problems within those failed economic models. In almost all of his examples, he demonstrated that the property rights of the ultra-rich operate in the real-world as if they outweigh the property rights of the dispossessed and oppressed and insufficiently compensated poor. The disconnection he derived was that the poor and middle class strata of any society have no significant voting power in a business driven economy since they usually do not have property, so the power and influence of property rights are something that they cannot exercise: "if you have no money then you cannot vote with dollars." By "voting with dollars" RC meant that "voting" was something you could do in terms of freely exercising economic choice as a symbolic form of free speech that reflected what is important to an individual during their choice of how to spend their money. Since most modern economies are tending toward consumer spending as the predominant engine that drives them, the poor people are rapidly left behind because they cannot even participate in a market or economy, let alone exercise any significant influence through their spending.

Within RC's chapters devoted to 'solutions' he argued convincingly that the most troublesome structural problems in modern economic systems included, but were not limited to, the Value Added Tax ("V.A.T.") and the Funds Availability Policies of the banks among O.E.C.D. countries. These were merely two of several of the most pernicious problems that functioned as a regressive tax on small businesses who were trying to produce goods and services in the European Union and then the consequence was that monetary supply for the small business in the form of 'working capital' was interrupted by the terrible funds availability policies of several worldwide banks. "It takes a banking institution that is modern and technologically equipped, less than nine minutes to verify the validity of the source of customer deposited funds, yet those same banks and institutional investors will not make the deposited funds of their small business customers available for immediate use: in some shameful and unforgiveable cases the funds are used by the bank for five business days before they are credited to the customer's account for use by the depositing customer. The amount of interest paid by the bank on the depositing customer's account in no way compensates the customer for the opportunity cost and money loss they suffer from not being able to use their own money right away. The solutions required for this situation would be to cut the average V.A.T. in half. As to funds availability solutions, the newly deposited funds should be available one calendar day after deposit into any bank." These were two of several practical examples RC cited as major factors of several economic problems encountered by most people in the world of work. The real-world benefit of these proposals was proven by the financial prosperity that was enjoyed by small businesses in the European Union Countries that did their banking transactions with those banks owned by RC: he used a one-day turn-around funds availability policy and the business owners loved it. By following business practices that were similar to "RC's way of doing business" it was no accident that they became diligent investors and more profitable than their competitors.

For RC, all economic and financial problems in every society around the world he studied were caused by political leaders making decisions arbitrarily in their own self-interest, irrespective of whether any particular decision would have wide-spread negative economic impacts. From RC's perspective, the solution was to require political leaders to deal more directly with the facts of how all of the individual choices people make in a free-market economy are not to be evaluated anymore by the classical economic theories concerning finite resources while ignoring human concerns but instead with a more fundamental humanitarian set of decision making criteria. Using old-school theories leads a person inevitably to view free-market economies as dominated and controlled by the entrenched and powerful ultra-rich by appealing to supply and demand data and examining the 'payoff matrix' as a basis for figuring out economic decision-making, identifying what business opportunities are ripe for picking fruitful profits. RC didn't like economic theory because, as he wrote, "there is no care or concern for the highest and best interests of the people that are behind those transactions." Too often, economic literature spent too much time on how financially successful people accelerate their economic transactions toward "fulfilling a goal of greed, with absolutely no regard for the consequences of their greed and how the impact of what they have done in the business world is oppressive and ruinous on so many people who worked so hard only to survive, striving to pay their bills and still have enough money left over to try and break even and eat real food." RC named that as a cause and effect relationship characterized by "the furiously paced race, with no hesitations, to make others worse-off than you all in order to reduce to ownership the resources of value and profits captured from aggressive transactions and control over valuable resources. By the term worse-off, I mean paying someone less revenue, increasing their expenses, diminishing their assets, increasing their liabilities and decreasing their ownership equity; doing any one of those things or some or all of those things." Worse-off could be a state of being where it also would apply to someone's emotional life, meaning that from RC's perspective, someone could be emotionally worse-off from overwhelmingly negative emotions caused by the work-environment: "don't make people feel overwhelmingly bad or negative things all of the time." Surprisingly, RC was optimistic and hopeful in his solutions. Motivated by a goal of raising the standard of living and delivering prosperity to all humans, intending to eliminate zero-sum games where few win and many lose in an economy and a market, his ultimate solution was to rely on the human spirit's creative drive and curiosity: "ideas are a truly infinite resource, especially when you bring an idea to life through creation and invention; any technology you create for benevolent use in the real-world can be given or sold in a market and that is hopeful as a source to fix economic problems and everyone who thinks can participate directly in either a market-place of ideas or participate in contributing helpful technology to society." RC would have been perfectly happy if everyone on planet Earth was a millionaire.

Throughout the rest of his book, the recurring question that simultaneously preoccupied and tormented him was the philosopher's academic debate regarding humanity's "*economic self always acting rationally but dismally,* versus the *emotional self always pursuing true happiness.*" Why are they at odds and mutually exclusive? Why can't those two selves coexist in true balance? In response to those authors and business people who suggested suppressing the emotional self to accomplish something virtuous in the business world, RC asked, "how is emotionally driven economic behavior good or bad or neutral and why is that so in a free-market capitalist economy?"

Near the end of his book, RC became mathematical, showing in great detail how anyone could quickly calculate and combine the results of empirical analysis of a market by using their own intuition, when trying to understand to what degree any market was fair or corrupt. RC had a special index calculation he called the "*propagation of greed and perverse incentives inefficiency curve*" that could be applied to any business data. The utility of this analysis was allowing you to judge a market's efficiency in common transactions of goods and services among all market participants and how artificially high costs were caused by corruption and illegality. He explained the theoretical curve by saying "look at any market and you realize that a zero sum game approach leads to crashes, several economists have established that fact, but they didn't go far enough - there is always an unofficial market, the cash under the table market, that is the coldest and most corrupt undercurrent of any stream of commerce for the exchange of goods and services; that is what has to be factored into any business dealings, in order to truly know how much trouble you are getting into by using any transaction. Adam Smith was *full-of-it* since he was too anti-humanitarian: he should have gone beyond the empirical approach that has hampered economists since the beginning of time. For proof of these propositions, just look at the failure of econometrics. That academic discipline has failed miserably as proven by its inability to make any forecasts that could have averted human suffering." Pervasive themes throughout his book included that RC believed that Adam Smith had it wrong: the common good is not always served benevolently by the invisible hand of everyone in an economy and market acting exclusively in their own self-interest. Free market competition is good, but the problem is the situation of an unlimited and un-restrained pursuit of self-interest or greed that causes harm by making others' worse-off: that is the main problem resulting from a zero-sum game and there are far more losers than winners in the modern economies of any country. "People don't exist only to slavishly serve corporate interests."

Just the week before he died, RC was adding a chapter in his book on the economic theory of the Nash Equilibrium: he dismissed it entirely as fatally flawed because it was practically unworkable in the real-world since, according to RC, "nothing in an economy or market of any kind is ever functioning at anything similar to a finite point of equilibrium, a way to evaluate a market requires a better model such as the Entropy and random inter-exchange from the example of boiling liquids that start out as frozen ice." It would have been interesting to read the final version of RC's book, had he lived long enough to finish it. He had stopped writing in mid-sentence: the last written words were, "People are not particles in a Physics equation ..."

If RC's book had been published in finished form, I would anticipate that few economists would have taken the time to follow along and understand RC's holistic approach to economics. His writing style shows the intensity and insightfulness of RC's brain-power: the way the book is written follows his seemingly parallel processing work ethic that was way beyond multi-tasking. The views he expressed also gave a glimpse into how his intellect deftly allowed him to get several things done in his life all at once by pursuing several projects simultaneously.

RC once asked me, "Mister Journalist, do you know the definition of an 'economic solipsism' and what the 'fundamental attribution error of profit seeking' really is, in human experiential terms of the difference between what is the product of your thoughts and your feelings when considering what you perceive in the real-world of economics and finance at an individual level?" Before I could answer he posed another question: "now suppose then that you take those two definitions, apply them to any person in any economy of any country and then tell me how frustrated they would be and ask how they would feel, if their decisions about money in their lives are consistently diminished and defeated by the forces from the larger market based economy they participate in, those forces beyond their individual control. Would you agree that they could reasonably feel like too much is taken from them without a just and fair monetary reward? Would it be reasonable then, to believe them when they say that they are asked by those decision-makers who are presently at the leadership level running society, to be asked by them into mindlessly accepting and being passively and predictably content with their conditioned-and-learned-helplessness, no matter how hard their efforts are at doing the right thing and finding financial prosperity in their own individual lives?" I think he was waiting for me to say something relevant and intelligently on-point. An appropriate answer would have been: "yet if you create a business in the real-world, then your ideas are not merely solipsism: it would be something you thought about and then by your efforts it would be created in the real-world. It becomes real when other people interact with it in a market transaction, yet this would be possible only if there were plenty of goods or services to supply and also if there were few or no barriers to entering and using that market, ultimately and provided however, that altogether the first principle is determining whether or if there existed sufficient demand." He would be disgusted though, if I would have given him the flippant summary of that conclusion: "I transact thoughtfully, therefore I am existing in the real-world." RC likely would have lectured me against implying or outright giving any disrespect to Rene' Descartes, along with freely giving me detailed counter-examples of how ill-formed my analogy would have been.

Thankfully, I could never formulate or articulately express those types of answers in his presence: had I been able to, it would have led to hours of tedious debates, for which I never seemed to have as much intellectual energy as he. Reading his book after he died, I remembered RC's questions and manner of conversing with me during our visits in the coffee shop: it was not like a professor and a student setting in a classroom at college, although I always did my best to record our conversations since I quickly found out that scribbling notes was annoying to RC: "... excuse me Mister Journalist, will you please keep up the pace, let's just talk now: you can write later." What was headache-causing for me was that RC asked questions that intellectually challenged one to peer behind the obvious day-to-day mechanics of how to get through basic spending transactions during a typical day. It was some high-speed brain-power on his part that looked beyond what most of us mortals experience as the daily cycle of ongoing futility of traveling to work, working at meaningless jobs, getting paid too little, spending to live, and then continuing on and on in the same cycle, rapidly getting worse-off in every measureable way.

RC often spoke philosophically to me about his views regarding the world of business. "In recent history, the market economy and corporations and businesses were originally designed to help and serve the people. All of that has changed in the modern world, so I ask you, what went wrong and when and why? Why did things get turned inside out and upside down? I had to leave the corporate world entirely: there was a pervasive cowardice, to the point of no one being willing to take any responsibility for anything, except demanding more pay for doing nothing. That behavior he mostly saw from those people in powerful leadership jobs. I hated it and had reached my limit of tolerance with the greed, the specific type of greed that resulted in making others much worse-off ... it was the total indifference to human suffering that bothered me the most. Reptiles, Amphibians, and Sharks behave with indifference: humans should not behave that way. Most people in the corporate world wouldn't commit to giving a truthful answer to any question in order to completely avoid any political risks or to avoid the business risk of imperiling profits. The thing that bothered me was that the majority of people in leadership job roles were completely OK with lying, cheating, stealing and stomping on others in their efforts to advance their own profit interests at the expense of others ... that whole way of doing things was repulsive to me, terrible conduct, horrendous."

What also bothered RC the most, regarding the worlds of for-profit business, was the absurdity of poor decisions made by Chief Executive Officers of multi-national corporations that had devastating consequences on several innocent people; yet those executives would be rewarded financially with handsomely out-sized bonuses even during years when they committed colossal blunders leading to financial losses. RC objected most strenuously to the unjust enrichment of overpaid, over-privileged, corrupt executives, to which RC often also blamed the Board of Directors for insane approvals of outrageous compensation packages for do-nothing executives. RC viewed those so called leaders as cruel and evil, since they used their authority abusively over the property rights of a business entity, to greedily enrich themselves, resulting in unjust enrichment and pathological hoarding of resources. It was easy to spot that problem, because according to RC, it was the root-cause of why other innocent and hard-working people suffer in the process of a business entity acting in a market to make profits. Today in the modern world, too many people working for a business entity have the harshly draconian experience of working long hours, yet if there are layoffs and down-sizing, then through no fault of their own, they could be arbitrarily fired, losing their jobs and their livelihood and then their families begin to suffer. Down-sizing was a cruel thing: it was as RC often described to me "the most cruel and evil game of musical-chairs, ever played."

However RC was OK with capitalism wherever market forces were held in check and where human rights were balanced against property rights: but he abhorred the pathological extremes he often found when doing business in America. "Everywhere I see people working too many hours and getting further behind financially in life. There are fat-cat corpulent corporate people stealing everything from them, using restrictive employment practices to actually extort more than their fair share from those who work for them. A business owner's greed should never create suffering or impose any misery upon those who work with him."

I often thought that someone like RC, with his idealistically humane and generosity demanding world views, should have been in a more helpful profession fueled by idealism, perhaps in a non-profit entity ... and definitely he should not be in an industry where competitive motives driving acquisition of money seemed to dominate everything. One major source of confusion for me as a journalist was that if benevolence and generosity without profit both figured largely in RC's business dealings, then how could RC's capitalism really be called capitalism at all? Should it not instead be termed non-profit charitable giving? Mystified as to why others were bothered by the precedent RC set by giving away too much, RC replied to me: "as long as I am not impoverished, or bankrupt and have something to give, first I will take care of loved ones and then take care of helping as many other people as possible, so why would I let anyone interfere with that right to help others?"

From my professional journalism experience, I thought I understood the way the business world worked: it seemed to me to be that the rules of competition along the lines of kill-or-be-killed and a Darwinian might-makes-it-right were the organizing principles of capitalism as I understood it. That meant to me that the activities of lying, cheating, stealing without getting caught was the way that most billionaire's amassed their fortune; in a phrase, success in the business world meant that you still had to be a robber-baron to make it in life as a rich person. Along the way to success a rich person would give into the expedient weakness of treating people working for them not as human but instead as cannon-fodder in order to reduce them to mere resources and then to exploit those resources for the business owners' exclusive personal gain. I wrote from that perspective in several of my articles, claiming that such a harsh approach to business is what most of the world knew as the dark subculture of capitalist success.

With that mindset I still pondered and mused over what I would have done differently than RC, if I had all of his money. When I was tired and exhausted, the fatigue and low blood sugar would play tricks on my mind, making me sometimes feel despondent: how could 'a guy like RC' get to have everything and I end up with having nothing? If I tried to imitate his way of doing business, I would already be destitute and living on the street. Why could he get away with it so successfully when no one else seems to be able to break-even financially by using similar methods?

To try and quantify what RC meant, throughout his voluminous writing, I had to get something much more concrete, than just my conclusion: "RC seemed to be a humane soul in search of a meaningful life for himself, his loved-ones and for every person throughout the entire world."

I found plenty of concrete proof of what RC's capitalism really was made of, when I summarized his writings. Boiling down thousands of his words, I distilled several recurring archetypal themes and detailed items that RC considered as his "*first principles of a benevolent form of capitalism in the modern technological world.*"

Although RC would scoff at my distillation, here is what I would offer as a concise primer of *doing business RC's way:*

1. Treat every human being with dignity and respect: deal truthfully with all, never resort to violence, always exercise tolerance and support diversity in every form and in every expression of individual thought, action, and freedom of the will.

2. People are more important than anything else, never treat people as less valuable than property or money or other resources.

3. Empathy is more important than efficiency: don't treat people as if they are machines.

4. Never behave or act as if your time is more valuable than anyone else's time. Everyone's time is equally valuable and priceless.

5. Treat everyone very well by respecting what is important to them, even if they have an approach to a value system that is markedly different from yours, provided however that what is considered important is also considered something that is universally humane and benevolent.

6. Everyone's individual freedoms and independence and legal rights should be treated as sacred and inviolable by the business entity.

7. Respect for freedom of Religion and respect for the various Religions of the world must be shown with equal treatment for all persons, in all business activities.

8. People should never be exploited as if they are property or resources and not human beings.

9. Every human being, male or female, should be treated equally well, with equal access to all rights, responsibilities, rewards and freedoms.

10. Work in a way that you feel proud to tell your children that you consistently did the right thing, the humane thing, even though it was not the path of what is easiest and not the path of what was most profitable.

11. Do not let work interfere with family time.

12. Respect each individual's family responsibilities of any kind: cooperate with them and be flexible to accommodate changing work schedules and time-off away from work if needed.

13. Support all Employee-Owners in the pursuit of their education. This includes giving financial support to their families' educational pursuits. Give educational scholarships to each Employee-Owner's family member(s).

14. The business entity should provide free community education classes in the lawful use of computer technology and internet communications for business and educational activities of any kind, provided that it is non-violent in its subject matter.

15. Encourage and support each person's expression of their lawful constitutional rights and human rights and the enjoyment of freedoms, as if they were already American Citizens. Assist anyone who wishes it, to become an American Citizen.

16. The business entity should generously help with time and resources and research and development efforts, to provide affordable electricity, safe drinking water and medicine to as many people as possible.

17. The business entity and its Employee-Owners should strive to help feed as many people as it can each day of the business entity's existence.

18. Your business activities should be conducted in a manner that respects and supports every human being's needs for food, shelter, medical care, education, financial security, peace and lawfulness: once those needs are met, then everyone can spend time pursuing what is important to them; be especially

supportive of those who freely choose to create and develop new and helpful intellectual property and technologies for the benefit of all people.

19. Make sure there are plenty of employment and research and development opportunities within the business entity for artists, philosophers, humanitarians, dreamers and educators. Never kill the dreams of the dreamers.

20. Within the business entity and by following a peaceful and non-harmful business method, completely do away with any system of social class or caste; there should be no artificial barriers for any human being to become what they wish.

21. Use the latest technology to freely connect everyone in your business to everyone else in the world through the internet and through use of the highest quality computers and digital communications devices. Do your best to responsibly use that type of technology with high security encryption and for benevolent purposes at all times.

22. Enjoy exercising your legal rights as a person and as a business entity, provided you do not interfere with other peoples' rights or business's rights or government's rights.

23. Give more than you take from the market economy and the business entity you are working in and the family you are a part of.

24. Live your life by pursing the principle of more generosity and less greed.

25. When doing business activities of any kind, always be careful to do no harm to yourself or others and let no harm be done and do not participate in allowing anything negative to happen by failing to act boldly and truthfully.

26. All Employees of the business must be made significant owners in the business entity. Make it extremely easy and accessible for them to become owners. Never use the 'employment at will' style. Each Employee should be given 100 ownership shares in the business and those shares should carry 100 votes. Everyone should have a vote in the business decisions and operating and investing activities, irrespective of their job title. Everyone should take turns being in leadership roles and executive compensation packages should be given to all Employee-Owners of the business. The business must

be Employee owned from the beginning, or as soon as possible and all pay and benefits should be usable from the first day an Employee-Owner joins the business. Democracy and freedom of expression must be encouraged at all times within the business. Never let the business entity or the Employee-Owners devolve into anything like a Plutocracy.

27. All Employee-Owners must have employment contracts that are negotiated in good-faith and are fair and commercially reasonable: do not use the 'employment at will' model in your business, it is disastrous.

28. Give free legal and accounting and financial planning services to your Employee-Owners and their family members. Emphasize realistic financial planning for retirement and medical care and elderly care for all of the family members of the Employee-Owner.

29. Make available at affordably low costs, home mortgage loans on generous terms and very affordable life insurance and disability insurance policies to all Employee-Owners and all of their family members.

30. Share with the world as many ideas as possible to make everything in life better for all humans on the planet: actively participate in a 'marketplace of ideas' and encourage others to do the same by respecting their freedom of expression.

31. Respect the rule of law within each country where you are transacting business and always respect international laws.

32. Use more cooperation than competition in all transactions and base your cooperative business activities on fair and commercially reasonable contracts that are negotiated in good-faith.

33. In the economies and markets, only compete on the basis of pursuing the merits of truthful benefits for human-kind and through innovative marketplace things of value that maximize consumer choices by offering several different uniquely high quality goods and services; yet be cooperative and respectful to all human beings ... keep everything civil and lawful at all times.

34. When it is time for paydays, consistently and without fail, make the payroll money immediately available for use and pay everyone on a weekly basis. Make sure to use a solidly

reliable financial institution so that the payroll checks are always honored.

35. Pay and compensation should never be based on a salaried model: instead, everyone should be paid fairly for each hour worked, with generous pay for overtime: use the American Legal System definitions of a standard work week and for overtime calculations. Never work people long hours or several days consecutively; allow for plenty of time to rest and to enjoy a healthy lifestyle away from work.

36. Provide generous pay, financial bonuses, benefits and executive compensation packages to each Employee-Owner involved in the business.

37. Keep the internal departments and areas of responsibility of the business entity organized and operating in a manner that is simple and necessary: do not build a bureaucratic or technocratic machine that is unnecessary and certainly never build anything that enslaves people; avoid any social hierarchy that burdens anyone or makes the Employee-Owners feel that they exist only to serve the artificial machine that is the business entity. The business should operate for the benefit of people and not the other way around.

38. Do not use micro-management leadership styles, or cruel or harsh management styles, ever.

39. Rotate and change often, each and every leadership and management roles in the business among all Employee-Owners. Do not let job titles, talent specialization or specialized skills be the cause of any discriminatory or unequal treatment. Especially be careful to avoid using specialization as an excuse for income earning inequality.

40. When evaluating decisions, weigh the consequences carefully: cost versus benefits analysis must also consider humanitarian factors and environmental impact factors. Make sure at all times that the business entity is not just pursuing analyses that focus narrowly on the net present value of monetary profits and financial costs: include in all equations and in all analyses, that all humans are sacred and priceless.

41. Your business should be conducted as if you truly believe that the people running the business entity's activities work as if they have a moral and ethical duty to break-even financially

first, and then if profits are made in the future, that those profits will be meaningfully and substantially given to all who were part of creating those profits and then if there is any money left-over then it should be and will be re-invested in the business. The guiding principle must always be: 'Profits to the people!' Once that step is accomplished, then directly increase the size of the business by diligently and quickly hiring more people in order to help the greatest amount of people possible.

42. Always consider the humane approach to doing anything within the business entity, in terms of empathizing with the emotional consequences of every business decision at an individual human level. Involve all the Employee-Owners in each business decision. Follow a democratically inclusive and equal voting model as the decision-making method for the business entity to carry out all of its functions.

43. Consider carefully any and all unintended consequences of your business decisions and avoid the negative consequences that would harm any human being. Always be prepared to help fix any problems and repair any unintended problems that are created by the business entity: always be truthful and prompt about the responsibility for fixing what you break.

44. Do not let fear paralyze the process of making decisions and do not attempt to get perfect information before making decisions: statistical based decision-making with less than perfect (uncertain) data is OK, that is just part of dealing with the real-world, where business data is mostly messy.

45. Do not reduce everything the business does to an economic analysis of a financial payoff matrix where self-interest is all that matters: that path will lead to several long-term problems for the business and for its Employee-Owners, as well as harming society.

46. Avoid at all times anything to do with bribery or payoffs to government officials, irrespective of whether or if in a particular country that is a customary method of doing business. Avoiding any corruption will be an effort, however small, toward helping eliminate corruption in the country.

47. Never have anything to do with illegal activities of any kind in any country. Define, quantify and measure illegality by how

any business activity is defined by the American Federal and State Legal Systems.

48. Never let the business conduct its operations through any use of lying, cheating, stealing, or any illegal means. The one book that is required reading for anyone who wants to work with me, is "The People of the Lie" by Doctor M. Scott Peck.

49. The business entity must pursue peaceful and non-violent transactions in all cases. Never get involved with any type of weapons technology whatsoever. Figure out how to help and heal people: never harm anyone.

50. Create a meaningful market that delivers something useful and valued and needed in the world. Avoid chasing any popular market trends and avoid copying a business model that someone else already uses: by copying, you are already up against a competitor. Instead, find and focus upon what is unique and creative, and do not worry if you start a new market on a small-scale.

51. Any new markets that the business entity creates must be carefully crafted to allow zero barriers to; market entry, market participation and market exit. Freedom to move in and out of the market(s) created must be maintained at all times for all persons and business entities to use freely.

52. Lobbying activities by the business entity should always be kept at a minimum: instead use a reputable Lawyer and use the existing legal system of each country to petition the government for an improvement in laws that the business must comply with.

53. Minimize your business interactions and communications with politicians and political campaign contribution efforts. Avoid politics whenever possible.

54. It is better to start a small business and keep it privately owned, keep it local, yet use the latest technology for computers and connect your business to the internet so that you can develop real markets world-wide.

55. When choosing the legal structure of business entities, the best one to use is the Private Limited Liability Company. Always consult competent Attorneys and involve them in the creation of the legal form of business, before you start the business entity.

56. Always keep the company privately owned, not publicly owned, to achieve the perpetual goal of reducing pressures toward being stuck with a myopic and short-term time frame horizon. Never let time pressure create desperation that defeats sound decision-making processes.

57. For new business activities, make sure that everyone in the business entity contributes their ideas and questions so that there is an open environment of thorough and complete research of available information, even if it is not perfect information, go ahead and use statistics and probability to fill in the gaps of data. Do your homework before undertaking any business activity: leave nothing to chance. Always make certain that your backup plans also have their own backup plans and failsafe considerations. There are several people who are relying on you for a variety of reasons: don't fail them.

58. To create a meaningful new market that lasts and grows into the future, do not hesitate to hire the best Attorneys, Accountants, Engineers, Scientists and Economic Advisors; ask them to objectively help you spot any potential obstacles before doing any actual transactions in any market. This is a necessary step, even if you are creating a brand new market that has never existed until you created it just now.

59. Set all prices for all of the businesses' goods and services and investments at fair and commercially reasonable cost and price levels that make sense both economically and that also support a humanitarian level of justice and fairness for all people involved in the market.

60. Research and Development should be a significant investment of time and resources for the Employee-Owners of the business entity; especially and necessarily so for a smaller business. Encourage and support each Employee-Owner's creative ideas by offering generously to give them Patent and Copyright protection to their unique ideas and have the business pay a generous licensing-use-fee of money to the individual. Be generous when paying license fees to Employee-Owners for any software or other technology they create and allow the business to use.

61. Avoid debt of any kind, if possible: use cash and equity investments for your business entity in order to pay for and fund its business activities and obligations.

62. All accounting information, money and assets of the business entity must be fully and fairly disclosed to all Employee-Owners often and equally at the same time: no secrets. Encourage frequent and thorough audits.

63. Increase the assets of the business only after the profits have been first invested in returning money to the people who are Employee-Owners.

64. Reduce the liabilities, loans and debts of what the business entity owes, in a way that does not cause suffering and does not make anyone worse-off in any manner whatsoever.

65. Make sure to place the money of the business in different banks among at least four different countries, including the home country where you do business: this is necessary since if there is a war and financial assets are confiscated by the government, it would be catastrophic to have financial resources taken away that are needed by the people.

66. If you have any problems with banks in multiple countries, start your own bank, and do not worry if it may be started on a small scale: that is perfectly fine. Let anyone who has at least one dollar become an owner of your bank or to be eligible with one dollar to use your new bank for their business transactions. Make at least one branch office of your bank be headquartered in America, and fully respect the rules of each U.S. State's banking regulators and also the rules and regulations established by the U.S. Federal Reserve.

67. The business entity should never spend any money wastefully, and never spend money or time or resources of any kind on luxury items or entertainment items; instead, the surplus money should go to all of the people involved in the business.

68. Pay all the taxes that are lawfully valid and applicable, as soon as possible: don't waste time trying to have a complex off-shore tax avoidance scheme. Worldwide tax laws change too often and it is highly likely that the business entity pursuing off-shore tax avoidance will then end-up wasting too much money in the no-win scenario of merely trying to keep avoiding taxes, so ultimately everyone would be made worse

off. Take the direct approach and pay all lawful taxes immediately when due.

69. Do not take part in any business transaction that involves any governmental entity or religious entity that is acting as a market participant. The business entity should pursue a benevolent, peaceful and cooperative form of private enterprise through humane use of free market economic activities.

70. Avoid the pursuit of any policy based upon any growth model that is a copy of a multi-national corporate growth model. Never worry about growing into a colossal sized behemoth: the business entity should be comfortable with its existence and efforts, irrespective of its size. It does not matter if it starts a new market on a small scale at the local level.

71. Enrich yourself only after enriching all others around you and only through transactions that do not harm others in any way: constantly be on guard to avoid use of 'zero sum economic game theory' meaning that no one should lose anything because of your transactions and actions (or your inactions). Do not make anyone worse-off in any manner whatsoever.

72. Never use deceit, deception or anything that could be a half-truth or a lie or anything illegal in any business activities.

73. During difficult economic times, do not force any person or any business entity into involuntary bankruptcy: instead, re-negotiate new contracts to help them out of their financial difficulties in a merciful, dignified and economically sensible manner. Do not try to use vicious competition to destroy competitors.

74. Fair and reasonable competition is good: it provides many choices of goods and services to all people in the world. Respect the freedom of choice of all people and consider that freedom as a sacred and inviolable thing.

75. Pursue business activities and goals that have meaning. Do what means the most to you and is most meaningful to everyone who is an Employee-Owner of the business. You will be perpetually disappointed if all your work efforts are solely expended into the narrow goal of just making a lot of money.

76. In a business entity, when people engage in job roles that require specialization as a good and necessary thing, ensure

that no one loses sight of an holistic approach to the combined cumulative output of what the business is doing; it should have a positive contribution to society and be beneficial to the Employee-Owners in all areas of their lives, and that should be maintained as true, far into the future and beyond the current generation of Employee-Owners.

77. When it is time for you as an individual person to leave the business entity, do so with plenty of advance notice, yet do so quickly and cleanly and at all times consistently do your utmost to leave the business entity in better shape than when you entered it. This is important, since there will often be business members who want to strike out on their own with their unique innovations: kindly support them on their way and treat them well, since it is likely that they may become a trusted and valued trading partner in the future. Overall, it is humane to treat them well, no matter what the circumstances are for their departure.

78. The most important goal for the business entity to achieve is to succeed wonderfully at making each Employee-Owner wealthy and financially independent in the modern technological economy so that they can go anywhere in the world they wish to go and be self-sufficient.

79. Do not let the concept and practice of Mutually Assured Generosity perish from the Earth.

80. On a daily basis, make a soberly objective and realistic assessment about whether or not you are doing more good than harm in the world, in society, in the market, in and through the business entity. If you can see that it is necessary for you to avoid causing harm by exiting a business situation gracefully, then certainly do that quickly and directly. It is most often better for all involved if you then stay out of the way of a business that is going in a direction that is different from what is important and meaningful to you. Be fair to yourself as well as being fair to others.

81. If any country's political climate becomes harmful to the best interests or safety of any Employee-Owner, have ready at all times a legal exit plan to safely get the Employee-Owner and all of their family members out of the country to a safe-haven

of their choosing.  Assist them financially and legally with immigrating to a country of their choosing.

82. Running a business the way I have described is going to be certainly un-popular with other business people and political institutions that are accustomed to taking profits or getting bribes: the best way to handle situations like that is to peacefully avoid those people and institutions altogether. Remember at all times, that the goal of the business is to avoid the pursuit of power or control or hoarding of resources or exploitation of people: instead the goal of any business of mine is to focus on the well-being and wealth of each Employee-Owner and the best interests of their families while at the same time contributing to worldwide society several benevolent technologies, services and intellectual properties.

83. Never formulate any business idea, policy, project or goal in terms of anything that is modeled after the ideas from any writings of Niccolo Machiavelli, Sun Tzu and certainly not Adam Smith.  Those authors were limited by the societal developments of their time: the modern world is much more complex than what they wrote about, and yes, human nature has a different set of challenges now.  Do not let any author from the past do any rational thinking for you.  Do your own thinking.

84. Ideas, creativity, human curiosity: these are the only truly infinite resources in our world: focus all of your business efforts toward encouraging everyone to bring into the real-world their thoughts, ideas, questions, inventions, writings, artwork, technology, and anything that can be considered intellectual property ... make sure that whatever is brought into the real-world is used benevolently and make it available to all people, with no market entry barriers.  If all efforts fail, your contribution would still be judged a success by me if you accomplish at a minimum the construction of an active market-place of ideas, for free.

After I finished distilling the essentials of RC's economic philosophy, my immediate feeling was: "what a tormented, tortured, troubled conscience existed in RC's being!"

Another massive migraine-headache hit me, so I rested for two days to try and recuperate from the barrage of RC's words. Trying to understand RC's mind was taking quite a toll on my life.

RC's repetition and iteration seemed infinite, however RC consistently expressed that he was worried that others knew what he meant by *"treating people well."* To RC that specifically meant that all human beings deserved to be dealt with humanely - that you would never use others for some goal only to fire them from their job or make them go away after they had outlived their economic usefulness. People should not be reduced to dollars in any way and they were not ever to be viewed as *"disposable or expendable non-human things under any circumstances: people are not resources."* RC also took great amounts of time to train everyone who worked with him in business, requiring them to follow his example that a humane leader was never cruel, exploitative or mean: that you never played any games with any person or other entity that would leave them ruined or out in the cold, *"like some evil game of musical chairs. A responsible and humane business person would never ever profit off of someone at their expense and would certainly not push things to the point of destroying someone and their means of financially supporting their family."* RC would never drag someone through a payoff matrix as if they were a rat in a maze and only you the business owner held the cheese: *"get rid of all mazes and games, give everyone cheese!"*

Impossible: it was not possible in the world I knew as real. Those principles seemed a bit trite, old fashioned from another bygone age. Yet RC made what I thought to clichés, into actions with practical benefits, and he further made people in his businesses create profits from those principles: it turned into real money, available for use and enjoyment by real people. I could not believe it. RC showed others how to become financially self-sufficient, helping to feed them in the process, so it was eventually clear to me, from lots of proof and examples, how and why the people working with RC were much better off financially and otherwise, all because of RC's teaching people to pursue a difficult but necessary path of *doing business.*

Looking objectively at the current state of available technology in the world and free access to the internet RC believed that human society should have been more advanced and more benevolent by now, in all countries. RC was pro-technology in all respects, especially encouraging use of the internet for free and open world-wide communications among people everywhere.  He did his best to remove any and all barriers for anyone and everyone to participate in any market that interested them, as long as it was universally lawful, moral, ethical and humane.

Every part of RC's philosophy of benevolent capitalism did not make life easy.  RC felt the constant disapproval and violent opposition to how his capitalist ideals were the perfect opposite of how most business persons behaved and conducted their business activities in the real-world.  Training new Employee-Owners of his to do everything in a more humane way took a lot of extra time and it all made him tired.  He did need sleep, which was the one thing he did not have enough of in his life.  The proliferation of new additional business entities he founded, and the training of new people in the *principled and benevolent approach to capitalism* required so much extra effort and time, that he had to delegate more of the training each year.  It bothered him that he could not be taking more time to be a business leader *in-person*, showing others how to do things by his own examples and actions.  Continually growing demands upon RC from others requesting help with how to best keep the several business entities growing and expanding, started to burn-out RC during the last seven years of his life.  Even though his hair was graying and he showed signs of fatigue, it was for RC however, another chance in his life to live in an unfailingly upbeat, optimistic way, continuing to be ready with helpful solutions.  For health reasons RC resorted to 'taking mini-vacations' of a couple days a month off and away from work, as his remedy to fix burn-out and exhaustion.

Six months before his death, RC invited me along as a journalist to travel to some of his often mentioned mountain meandering spots.  I only made it along with RC on those trips one time.  The trip took forever to drive to from Seattle and the destination was a hiking trail to one of RC's several favorite alpine lakes in Canada.  RC laughed at me when I acted astonished when he roguishly told me that the drive was just the beginning and that the main point of the mini-vacation would be an arduous six-mile-hike.  "What's the matter, don't you want to exercise?"  During the hike, the scenery was breathtaking, but my lungs felt like they were going to explode and my leg muscles were painfully rebelling against my effort to push them to move faster and keep up with RC's rapid walking pace.  "Hurry up!  We are losing daylight!"  What RC enjoyed about the temporary break in his routine was also the same things in the wilderness that I painfully felt as a crushing loss: there were no people, no coffee shops, and no cell phone or

Wi-Fi reception signals and so there I was completely cut off from civilization! Except for the ever-present cadre of RC's bodyguards making every ten minutes a radio-check status call into a helicopter that was hovering five miles away in case RC needed a quick emergency evacuation, nowhere in the mountains did I find anything close to what would be considered as the modern conveniences of civilized society. I was on a beautiful mountain-top alpine lake, yet as a city boy, I felt terrified at the isolation, the feeling of alone-ness and the heavy intrusion of the silence of nature: I do not know how RC could tolerate it at all. For any middle-class person such as myself, the cost of traveling to and from the remote mountains of British Columbia and the Pacific Northwestern United States would quickly empty one's wallet, yet money was not a problem for RC.

RC must have really needed a severe break from the crushing demands on him that he went so far into the mountains, away from city life. According to his journals, RC's flights and drives and walks into the great outdoors were all designed as a small-scale temporary break to get a breath-of-fresh-air, away from the crushing weight of new business proposals; he did not want to anymore deal with meaningless numbers showing the evil shapes and shadows of greed that was painted by those numbers and the tedious treadmill of endless demands upon him and his time, by people who cared nothing for him and certainly cared nothing whether RC would be financially ruined from their endless taking, spending, borrowing from him.

RC spoke fondly of his time wandering in the forests and mountains. What RC gained by spending time in the Rocky Mountains of North America was more than the experience of getting away from the busy world. He sometimes found it refreshing to personally experience at an older age what as a young child he remembered were challenges of being outdoors: sunburn and wind burn, fresh air making your lungs work hard to the point of feeling on fire, physical fatigue from hiking climbing and swimming, mild hypothermia during winter seasons, letting your long-distance vision see panoramic scenery like nowhere else on Earth, enjoying the unique aroma of Alpine Spruce trees, laughing at the psychedelic chimeras seen during high altitude hallucinations, sleeping under a glitteringly clear canopy of stars, RC could go on forever describing those cryptic images and many more examples. RC said that he would commune with nature, preferably by himself, alone in the wilderness, so that he could stay in touch with the memories he had made while growing up in the region.

One time he took twenty minutes to give a detailed explanation to me regarding the finer points and secrets that it took to expertly cook delicious food in a pan over an open fire, most difficult being the Huckleberry pancakes he loved.

The outdoor treks kept alive his traditions, values, philosophies and view of the world. Those were things I guess he also used to fill the void created from not knowing his true parents. What of those things had he tried to pass on to his own children? He would get sounding somewhat nostalgic when describing "Lake Louise and Banff Canada, where my children first learned ski in Winter and then in Summer to fish for and catch Golden Trout ... they enjoyed watching the sunset by a campfire of Alpine Spruce and Tamarack wood, they enjoyed smelling the wood smoke ... I made them Huckleberry pancakes. We also enjoyed sautéed mushrooms. We all liked ending the day by sleeping around a campfire, listening to the wood crackle while watching far overhead the stars and the (Aurora Borealis) Northern Lights. Every couple of hours I would point out what looked like a moving mini-star going towards the northern skyline: look children there is one of my Satellites!"

Another escape from the crushing demands of his business life was to try and find something that made up for and replaced the now empty space in his life formerly held by the Religion of his childhood. RC had a curious way of handling his own experience of Religion. Religion was a touchy and precarious conversational topic I raised with RC several times. RC lost the Religion of his youth, entirely lost it, by choice: he felt it had no meaning for him personally and yet he was guilt-ridden over the conclusion and was heart-broken that his Religion seemed to be another human institution brought down mostly by hypocrisy at its hollow core. The heart-breaking part of his experience was described by him as "though most of the tenets of the Religion were communicated and taught under the guise of the authority and credibility of a faith-based 'revealed' Religion directly handed down from a Western conception of God," RC said "theocratic authority by divine-right as an organizing principle gets its leaders corrupted at the point when commanding and demanding certain things from followers of the Religion are required and non-optional as if mindless conformity to 'divine-right' was all that mattered, absurdly, as if that was a virtue. No one in leadership positions in the Religion of my youth could satisfactorily answer my questions. *"Why does God need money? Why does God always answer my prayers for my friends to find gainful employment with a NO answer? Can you prove to me the basis of your claim that there is a divine-right to make a profit and that somehow I have to give up everything to the religious organization, yet they give me no say in how my donated resources will be used? How is it sanctioned as a virtue by God when a religious entity is participating in business transactions through a free-market capitalist system that allows and actually encourages by rewards of profit-money, the exploitation of poor people for manual labor? Does God not also love the poor people too?"* All I saw during my youth was behavior titled as 'virtuous' by church leaders that in my way of thinking was truly 'mindless conformity to arbitrary authority.' It frightened me that several people followed absurd requests, based on faith, not reason. No one could prove to me that it was necessarily true that the only thing that seemed to matter was sacrificing what you wanted in life to instead work constantly towards fulfilling whatever church leadership commanded to be done. The worst part of it all for me was when the church leadership would say, essentially, that all of your money earned by your own efforts had to be given to them and that fictionally we would be rewarded when we get to Heaven, so now in this life, you should be content with deprivation and suffering in poverty. Those examples of mindless conformity and mindless financial giving were, to me anyway, a very incomplete basis for doing anything in my young life. I much preferred walking the path in life where human beings are capable of rational thought based upon facts and that exercising the freedom of that individual rational thought and action with the use of all the tools of science would help me navigate successfully the real-world, that would be a much better way to go through life, instead of mindlessly following a devoutly religious life."

Ever present, large and looming metaphysical problems causing anguish and worry in RC's life were from his unending colliding conundrums from his sense of guilt and feelings of obligatory generosity. Those two things in his life were inextricably connected somehow and yet intensified as if they fed off of each other. The root-cause of his guilt, deep down at its core, seems to be an unsolvable quandary over how to deal with the impossibility of trying to keep his soul clean after taking profits from some parts of the world and redistributing some of those profits to as many people as possible in the poorer and less developed countries. RC's guilt was apparently a big fire in his soul that consumed his being, and the worry intensified when he pondered making a profit and trying to quantify the true costs of whether the one dollar he kept as profit should also have been given away or not. *"How do I know I am doing the moral, ethical and legally right thing by keeping these profits?"* RC definitely was not naïve about using money for good outcomes. He saw what needed to be fixed in the world and did a great deal to step in and personally fix things for those who needed the most help by assisting them with the starting of small businesses and helping others discover financial freedom and enjoy a better and more meaningful life by pursuing their own educational interests.

With that blend of heavy guilt constantly bedeviling his conscience RC forced himself to still act as if he was optimistic and idealistic, despite all of the economic evidence pointing to ominous trends in his future.

Several times, RC tried to completely give up the world of business. However, sitting on the sidelines was nothing he could tolerate: *"They're not doing it right! Too many people are getting hurt and are financially diminished unnecessarily!"*

Often I have asked myself the question, what would RC have thought of recent developments in the world? I do believe RC would have been a fan of the crowd-funding popular financing trend. As to the Occupy Wall Street Protest Movement, I would guess that RC would have been sympathetic to the sentiments expressed by the movement and he likely would have been a generous financial supporter, (since he would view them as economic orphans seeking redemption of some type), yet he likely would have (if he had lived longer and been asked for advice) suggested that protesting is only the beginning of changing the world for the better and what is also needed in addition to protesting, is the hard work and money and time invested in starting to solve problems in society by first trying out your solutions on a small-scale through use of a small business and then grow slowly and incrementally from there. I also suspect he would have asked the leaders of that protest movement to meet with him and write a detailed list of the problems they saw and what solutions they wanted to try. I can imagine RC leading a discussion along the lines of: *"tell me please in realistically practical and concrete terms, what you will do, if I gave you nine-trillion dollars and you bought every Wall Street entity and owned it outright ... would you immediately destroy it? Would you re-engineer it? Would you build it better? What would you do? How you answer those questions determines your priorities: focus your efforts into what means the most to you. Now after your plans are clear my suggestion for the first step of action is to talk to those people who are already in Wall Street entities and listen to them carefully: get their perspective; they may have already tried the solutions you are proposing."*

RC encouraged doing homework, thoroughly researching as much information as possible and then having the courage to finally talk civilly and directly with those you have disputes with in order to rationally and peacefully work toward a mutually beneficial solution. RC never shied away from anything that was seemingly impossible, so I would have expected he would have been undeterred in that situation. I have to force myself to not dwell too often or too long on what might have been better in the world had RC lived.

Looking at global economies during the past five years after RC's death, I could not help but notice that several things financial began crashing down worldwide very soon after RC was killed. Miraculously, none of the banks RC started and sold to his Employees had the slightest problem during the worldwide economic crisis. I wonder sometimes if that fact is a product of pure coincidence: it is possible that some people studying macro-economics and the American money supply figured out that connection and maybe that is why the U.S. Government wanted to look into RC's finances after he died.

In my opinion the several life-long challenges RC faced, both existentially and empirically, can be traced to the void in his heart and soul that remained after he willingly lost his Religion. Ironically, despite his genuine efforts, he never found another suitable and fulfilling way to express his profoundly mystical and spiritualistic feelings. Spirituality was one area of his life that was unfulfilled and seemed a starkly silent shadow of dark emptiness in his otherwise extraordinary life full of brightly shining accomplishments. RC acknowledged this truth as a vulnerability that he constantly experienced as his own personal *dark-night-of-the-soul.*

Ultimately though, he was never one to get stuck by dwelling passively upon, or spending wasted time by wallowing in or getting stuck in anything negative. During our several interviews before he died, RC would smile triumphantly and calmly, telling me that the loss of meaning in his life from the areas of faith and Religion was *"really no big deal, because I have complete faith in my children."*

## Chapter 6

**Butterfly in my Mind:**
*Afterimages of Spent Transactions, whispers of darkness, nightmares and ghosts...*

Nothing could have prepared me for my last encounter with RC. When RC walked inside the door all I could focus upon was my feeling of shock at seeing his cadaverous appearance. He seemed to have to expend effort to keep open his eyelids. His lower eyelids were now huge puffy bags the size of hard-boiled-eggs, encircled with slightly reddish and purplish skin discolorations. He had a slightly stooped-over-posture that belied either some abdominal pain or spinal injury of some kind, although he was mightily exerting himself to try and forcefully hold himself upright as if all was well. Other visible areas of his skin were colored alternately jaundiced-yellow with a few other patches showing a slightly ashen grayish tint at the top of his forehead. From his overall appearance, I could see painfully and clearly that he had not slept in quite a while. RC was agitated, which was something I had never seen from him during any of our previous encounters. He must have had an intimation of death or some premonition, known only to him, that this would be our last conversation in person.

He was accompanied by his public relations hag and his usual group of bodyguards. The public relations hag sitting beside him looked like she had been crying. Her eyes were red. She tried not to make eye contact with me.

Trying constructively to overcome my feelings of shock and sadness, I attempted a polite gesture of mercy and compassion and started to talk to him. I tried to raise a topic that RC could focus upon without too much effort, so I brought up an article I wrote which had recently been published in a regional newspaper. It was a piece on the worsening economy. "Hey RC, I'm curious what you specifically, I mean in a detailed sense, have a problem with, in my new article?" That would be a first, only, and final time that I really infuriated him ... by my emphasizing, I guess, with a bit too much intonation, when I enunciated the word, 'specifically.'

I had expected the usual RC demeanor: mirthful conversation, subtle displays of a keen intellect and warm irreverence, astute observations

... however all of those emotionally positive displays of his humanity were dormant during our final visit in person. Instead of the usual kindly conversational tone from RC, he tore into me with a verbal barrage I had never heard before in public. His words were like ballistic missiles hitting my skull and launching another severe migraine headache that grew in painful intensity with each new word from him: it was as if the weight of each word was a sledge-hammer hitting spikes into my brain that were three-thousand-degrees burning hot.

His public relations hag handed him an oxygen mask, which he wheezed on and inhaled before straightening up and saying quite angrily the following monologue.

*"Specifically? ... OK, here are the specifics and I am only going to say this once to you during my incredibly short lifetime, so you better listen closely. You use superficial clichés as a crutch for a feigned and faked mental injury so as to try and provoke sympathy from your readers, which would be undeserved. You spend your effort focused on prattling on about transactions – those are sterile, cold and lifeless things, instead of focusing your writing upon meaningful warm human experience of happiness or awe at seeing something beautiful. For example, as a reader of your stuff, the ultimate question I am interested in is how the economy is failing humanity today and what are the best ways to fix it for the benefit of everyone? I am not interested in your obsequious admiration of wealthy people. Most people are wealthy by accident, inheritance, or exploitation, and they rapidly and permanently become cruel from greed. Why can't you write about the solutions to those problems in your articles? Prevarication is the only method you apparently can conceive of in your peppercorn sized brain: presumably that is done in order to coddle your cowardly spine when you try to touch the white-hot temperature of facts that do not agree with your elitist aesthetic viewpoints and those viewpoints you change on a daily basis to try and get imitatively-aligned with and morph into like a chameleon what is trendy in popular culture. That is chasing a bandwagon only to be included in the 'in-crowd' which makes you a prostitute trying to be the center stage spotlight dancer in a harem. You let others define you 100% yet you are hollow because you cannot define yourself without appealing to other's approval. Your political correctitude is attitudinally a betrayal of a deep-seated and ingrained 'approval addiction' which completely hobbles and hog-ties your rationality so as to make more room for your megalomaniacal ego. You are heuristically autistic! You are existentially*

amoral! You can't risk being seen by anyone else as negative or unpopular so you never really convey that you are capable of writing or saying what you really think and truthfully mean. You are pandering to mindless consumerism. You show that quantity over quality is alive and well, or in a phrase that your mental health counselor can interpret for you, that your use of way too many words to make a cowardly point conclusively shows that you are trying to celebrate the populist trend of exhibiting mindless conformity to what is idiotically important to the celebrities of the day and you view that as a virtue, all this is only to make yourself feel safe instead of telling the truth and risking rejection from others. You have all of the ambition of a frozen and hibernating apple-maggot, copying and quoting everyone to make a tapestry of other's ideas and words without citing your sources or giving proper credit and recognition of where the creative sources really are, so that action is clearly theft: you are stealing from others ... you are a petty-thief. You likely wake up and promise to stitch together on this new day a huge pastiche of pretentiousness that could outdo the one you made yesterday, if only to use these two things in comparison to measure the progressive amount of your contribution to society? That half-hearted vain effort is absolutely no contribution at all: you are not producing, you are consuming everything in a slovenly manner only to regurgitate and recycle what you steal, passing it off as your unique creative efforts, as if you were some kind of genius. What you are not seeing directly in front of your face is that out there in the real-world there is economic and social Entropy that is accelerating at a rapid pace, far beyond any acceptable systemic normal rate. To put it in your pretentious vernacular the ghost in the machine is residual greed, it steals away an efficient and fair distribution of wealth to as many people as possible. Today's economic data suggests the beginnings of a high risk of several market collapses that are going to impact millions of people and their families. Why can't you see that? Why can't you warn everyone? Instead of the human story, you are pre-occupied with meaningless things. Mister Journalist, your writing stinks to high Heaven of prideful narcissism and also your sentence structure is vain: do you realize that your average word-count per sentence is over thirty-seven words? Only someone driven by fear and panic can spout such sloppy extemporaneous over-complexification! I am not fooled by any or all of that: you are doing a terrible job of hiding behind a snow-storm-flurry of words. You understand nothing about humanity and you understand nothing about the way the real-world works: it is not all about profits."

---

He placed a fist full of hundred dollar bills on the table in front of me then after taking a breath, continued yelling at me.

*"Why don't you get off your lazy duff, take this money and go feed the homeless people across the street, they are all cold and hungry! That way you at least will not be focused solely on yourself."*

RC pointed to the oft-seen homeless guy that haunted the street corner outside and the sidewalks near the coffee shop every day, and said *"the homeless man, right there, he was the first in his family to go to college: he chose a business degree, became a manager, yet he was a total wash-out because he still operated with the approach of being kind and humane at work, which always got him into trouble in the world of business ... he was kind to all and treated people well ... he didn't like telling people what to do ... he didn't like his bosses asking him to exploit people, he couldn't bring himself to do it ... that's why he lost his job, his career, his finances, his family, his home, everything. That is the person, the one person you should help today; go help him right now – he did the right thing and unjustly paid for it miserably."*

RC moved painfully to get up out of his chair and shouted one last verbal bombastic barrage at me: *"You can't even write in complete sentences and what the hell is the benefit to anyone when they read your other article about romantic love? It was so inexpertly written, that you should have taken that feeble attempt at an insightful article and titled it as 'my fickle pickle.' Albert Camus must have encountered someone like you when he said, 'hell is other people.' From the information you fail to pass onto others clearly, you are failing miserably at being a social semiconductor. So to sum up, have a pleasant day: enjoy your coffee and try not to choke on your own self-serving vanity."*

His public relations hag finally could not contain her emotions any longer: she started crying; and that seemed to be the only thing that would stop RC's rant of rage at me.

RC stopped, looked at the young-lady immobilized by her own tears, then he gasped and gulped air from the oxygen mask she gave to him in an empty gesture of trying to avoid passing out. After four long inhaled breaths, he mustered enough energy to leave, leaning toward the front door of the coffee shop, waving off the several loyal bodyguards trying respectfully to help him. RC feebly, shakily and slowly, shuffled his feet out the door.  His body movements were accomplished more by sheer will-power than by muscular exertion.

The coffee shop crowd he left behind was a crowd suffering in their stunned silence.  No one among the daily regular crowd of patrons that included yuppies, young intellectuals, and the huddled together bohemians lounging in the comfortable couches slurping strong coffee, had ever seen RC behave that way:  RC was their star.  He behaved as if he was a regular customer, even though he was viewed by others as a celebrity. Everything in their past encounters with RC had prepared them to expect a consistently humane version of RC that was smiling, harmlessly aloof and subtly Grandfatherly in his display of genuine kindness; yet today they were wearing facial expressions of confusion.  Most people in the coffee shop seemed to be murmuring about what had happened to the man that just left in a huff.  It didn't seem at all like the same man who used to light up the room by simply smiling.

RC's entourage followed slowly and wearily behind him.  They all seemed to be agitated, sad, looking like they were reluctantly and somberly marching their King to an execution, trying not to let their loyalty be overcome by sadness.  Most of them grabbed their electronic devices; smart-phones, portable computers, tablet computers and each one tried to take some small amount of momentary comfort by sending messages to their social media connections and contacts and friends as they looked down and walked out the door, while quickly clicking away a swarm of symbols into their digital devices ... their despondency signaled the ultimate futility of their cryptic communication efforts.  Their collective lack of energy, non-existent vigilance and obvious exhaustion all told me that they had all been working on little to no sleep and they also knew there was nothing that could save RC from his cancer: the end was near.

After RC's funeral I learned that on that last day I was verbally attacked by RC at the coffee shop, that RC was nearly dead from brain cancer: specifically what was killing him was a butterfly tumor in his Corpus-Calossum.  His doctor later told me during an interview, the tumor was an invasive dendritic growth into both brain hemispheres with a tumor boundary in the shape of a butterfly, known to modern medicine as a "Butterfly Glioma Astrocytoma."   The doctor went on to say, "I have known RC since my first days as a Physician, I met him in Alaska when I worked for the government ... I shouldn't be telling this to you because of HIPAA confidentiality requirements, but when after several detailed tests confirmed my diagnosis, RC considered all of the treatment options and told me: *"hell no to stereotactic radiotherapy. Gamma Knife sounds too medieval, too brutal. I will take care of this myself."* RC did ask if bizarre dream images were symptoms of this type of tumor, I had to say yes. RC told me *"I have a recurring dream that ethereally-silvery-Angels from the Gods are infuriated at me for being an occasional atheist: they decree a punishment which is to have the Angels kill me very slowly. I am convinced that the Gods' favorite method chosen specifically for me is to smite me by commanding the Angels to hurl lightning bolts at the top of my head while I sleep each night, which causes me to feel indescribably terrible pain ... a pain I cannot get away from ... I can never escape from myself to flee the pain inside my head."* RC never told me the voodoo-methods he was likely using for self-medication efforts when trying to take care of it himself. I guess I shouldn't say voodoo-methods, since RC was far too scientific.

It was sadly clear to me that whatever methods he had attempted to use in an effort to cure himself, from the sight of him in the coffee shop during that last encounter, he was losing the battle with cancer quickly.

Recalling the Doctor's story and re-imagining the descriptions of RC's dream-visions, I could imagine vividly the Angels of Death accurately and fatally hurtling an infinite shower of piercing lightning bolts at RC.

However, I could not reconcile that image of death and destruction with any benevolent Deities that would treat RC so tortuously and cruelly. RC's quip about lightning bolts hitting him left me feeling emotionally chilled in a way that hot coffee could not comfort. The description of Angels throwing lightning bolts at RC's skull was a conversation that literally caused me to have nightmares. It is an afterimage that lingers way too long after I wake up in a cold sweat from that nightmare, although it usually is commonplace for journalists to have some dream images relating to things they are working on, RC's descriptions were so vivid and so terrifying it was something that I had to immediately talk to my Psychiatrist about because it bothered me so often and so intensely. Specifically, in my nightmare, I see the Angels attacking RC with a great deal of furious energy and also hurling several lightning bolts of electrified high-voltage blue-white and orange lightning at RC's jet. After their attack is successful, all of the lights and fireworks are followed by deafening sounds of thunder that shakes the entire Earth. The afterimage of RC's jet being blown up is not the worst part of it. In my dream, I also recall that Medical Science claims that in the few minutes after death, the last human sense to shut down is hearing. I wonder if RC had some sense of hearing still functioning as he fell to Earth. What sounds did RC hear as he was dying? What were his final thoughts and feelings?

Those nightmarish and morose questions echo throughout my dreams and haunt my sleep. Questions like that about RC continue to haunt me and it feels like RC's ghost is always by my side, leading me towards the truth but never quite reaching the full and complete answers to my questions. *"Well you have to do your own work, Mr. Lazy Journalist: I cannot do all of the work for you!"* I would often hear RC's ghost say to me in my flights of imagination.

Massive amounts of effort and time have I expended with my Psychologists and Psychiatrists, in order to send RC's ghost away from me and my dreams. Sleeping pills prescribed for me by my most recent Psychiatrist do not begin to help me in any way whatsoever.

Now what do I do?

To prevent my head from exploding from too much information I had to find a way to purge my confusion over the story of RC's life, a confusion that was growing exponentially by the hour. There seemed to be an impossible amount of detective work remaining to be done. I felt the impossibly heavy weight of the task ahead of me. I have to forget what my Therapists say about this story becoming a harmful obsession of mine.

I need to get more money, more funding for this next phase of chasing the truth and of course the most important thing I need are many more facts, much more credible information from reliable sources: I also need motivation fueled by Mojo, Good Karma and more will-power. Those are the fuels I need to make a fire big enough to melt the mountain of information I need to find: it seems now an icy thing of a glacially paced ancient mystery; it is something I need to challenge myself to solve and to prove to myself as much as can be humanly discovered and understood, what really was the true meaning of RC's life and death.

I still need to know why he sacrificed so many profits for benevolent goals and why he helped so many people. I do not understand his motives at all. More confusing still for me is the counterintuitive way

RC's world seemed to work for him successfully. The more money he gave away, the more money he made and that too he just gave away as well – his incredibly successful results did not seem to be the way the rest of the business world functioned.

Critics of RC, after his death, railed hatefully and sarcastically in several public forums: "his generosity was acting-out an insane utopian hallucination spawned from a brain that was taken over by tumors: he was not even measuring-up to our minimum criteria of respecting the first-principles of reducing profits to ownership and holding them properly, which is a failing of his that is too far below standards even for a rookie accidental capitalist."

I did wonder how, and to what degree if any, the brain cancer drove RC's soul and defined RC's character and actions. Was the cancer the driving force in RC's generosity and positive regard for humanity? Was his generosity only caused by the unintended results of pathology? Was the cancer the ultimate reason RC tried to give all of his vast wealth away to other people? Knowing how short his life would be because of brain cancer, was RC using generosity as a bargaining chip with the Gods to grant him a bit more time out of life here on Earth?

My Psychiatrist called me on my new smart-phone. I should have turned on the call-blocking feature, if only I can figure out how to use my new technology. She seems to be 'not so subtle' regarding her descriptions of her worry about my current mental state. For the moment, I have to quit writing and go meet with her for another session. What a nag she is and I'm sure that I will be paying too much money for that kind of treatment!

During the most recent visit to my newest Psychiatrist, I had a flash of insight. While the Psychiatrist bored me with her speaking about how she needed my cooperation to get myself more neatly fitting into a pre-conceived mental health diagnosis category billing code, (which was putting me into a different kind of pain caused by boredom), I let my mind wander to another new reverie of puzzling out the cause of RC's death (for what must have been the ten-thousandth time), to analyze whether I had overlooked something essential, something that would give me a breakthrough insight.

While she was talking about her inconvenience in seeing my during this session, I let my mind fly away from her words, and fixate upon the validity of the data content of several new documents I received, particularly the new information. The new stuff meant new opportunities to discover contradictions in the overall story. New documents from RC's home library were good, however as authentic as they were, I still noticed a few fuzzy things about each documents implications. Incongruities raise my curiosity level, and I have to make sense of it all.

Unlike the documents from RC's personal library, at the opposite end of the spectrum of truth, I did not feel too convinced about the validity of the information I received from the government. It made me laugh with an underlying tone of dismissive suspicion, because the government documents were too neatly tied off, sewn up, solved and put away. I am not paranoid or delusional and I am especially not a conspiracy theorist: yet when the facts of a story don't add up to a clear coherent and consistent picture, I know something is wrong with the information that is available. The opposite extreme also gets me skeptical, when the information received or the data given to me seems way too perfect. The government stuff on RC's life and death was too perfect. Even I know that perfect information is non-existent. The government documents also had me wondering about the information that I needed to fill in the missing pieces of the puzzle but that was still not available to a journalist like me.

My Therapist must have caught me daydreaming, because now she is emphatically telling me where I am going wrong. She claims I am paranoid and imagining all of this stuff about RC and that I must not be taking my medications, which she conjectures quite wrongly as the clinical cause of why I am gravitating toward *only the unsolved parts* of the story of RC's life and death, she says, *"in your grandiloquent attempt to pursue an obsessive pre-occupation of willingly getting lost in a dream-world of theory, instead of dealing directly with something in the real-world that is bothering you."* She can tell that, she claims with a tone of prescient-superiority, because after reading parts of my journalistic documentary of RC, she says my sentences are too long and my thought patterns indicate a pre-occupation with magical *thinking "as if there is something in the real-world that you are avoiding or that you are purposefully delaying the resolution of something that needs to be fixed and put away on a shelf all nice and tidy. Your pervasive problem is that you cannot accept the finality of RC's death."* Like I said, what a nag ... and what a buzz-kill she is: it must be time to change Therapists again.

Getting away from that Therapist, very quickly I spent my way toward confidence. From the expenditure of great amounts of time, energy and money, on my part I felt full of newfound confidence and clear purpose. I concluded that I could successfully make enough progress toward totally solving all of my questions about RC's life and death. I wanted all of my hard work to be published and win some kind of prize. The fame and fortune that would likely follow could be used by me as empirical proof about my abilities in the real-world, (especially giving convincing proof to my Psychiatrist). Miraculously then those rewards would be a fair trade given in-exchange for all of the good and true information I brought to light, for all to see. The happy ending to my story would be that then I could be wealthy and lead a comfortable life free of Psychiatrists, hallucinations, stultifying pain of my headaches, and especially free of debts. Finally, at that outcome of fortunate events in my life, I would truly understand what is meant by reaping the rewards from delivering more than the expected value of perfect information, or near as possible to perfect information.

If someone wonders whether my journalistic motivations have been pure, I am writing RC's story to encourage others to come forward and publish more true facts about a one-of-a-kind person that RC truly was.

The Psychiatrist was wrong about several things.

Although I met and interviewed him before he died, I cannot connect all of the dots from an emerging picture of RC as the real man, and have any resemblance of those connections to the picture in my mind that I have of RC when looking at him through the other documents I have about him. The documents are like a hall of distorted mirrors, images too fragmented to identify what is being reflected in the mirrors. Each document contradicts so many things in other documents and even when all the documents are assembled into a grand puzzle picture, they too fail to capture the real RC.

It was especially perplexing for me when I looked in detail at all of RC's business entities' records archived in his vast library; the records included everything from a Satellite Company to holding companies that invested in development of botanical 'seed-vaults' around the world to preserve bio-diversity of plant life. I could not find a common theme among everything from the business archives ... it was as if RC wanted to have business transactions in 16% of everything on the planet.

Despite the contradictions in the documents, RC was always truthful with me. Confusing it still is to me, the way RC was portrayed at his funeral ... the few facts I can verify from the after-crash investigation reports, my interviews with him before his death and the disparities about facts from those family and friends I interviewed after his death – all those sources of data lead me in mutually exclusive directions.

At this point, I worry that I may have already passed the event-horizon boundary of doing all that I can in researching his story. I have already encountered a lot of fiction from others, too much for my liking.

One thing I have grudgingly realized about myself is that in the case of being confronted by missing information about a news-story I am working on, that my mind will go into high gear and be working on plausible solutions to questions during my sleeping dreams ... during my nightmares. On several occasions in my career, I woke up after nightmares, to images of a precise list of tangible possibilities to investigate further when trying to solve a story's gaps and factual mistakes or misstatements.

What I shared with my Psychiatrist and what helped me make a decision about my "inspirational nightmares" is nothing she wanted to understand; mostly because she already had a billable diagnosis code to charge me money, and wanted to be more efficient about profitably using her time to maximize her wealth. I had the original intent of contacting the Psychiatrist in order to gain helpful insights on how to, in the real-world, sort out both in my life and in my nightmares, what exactly are the real things from what is imaginary and further to identify and distinguish what the lady Psychiatrist merely categorized as my magical thinking delusion, in an attempt of mine to avoid dealing with the painful reality that not everything can be understood by me. What an insult to my intelligence! This Psychiatrist is appearing to my mind's-eye now much more in the shape of her being a particularly unsympathetic wench. Why should I continue to pay someone who is that terrible? At that point in our sessions, she apparently did not seem motivated to try and understand me. I can therefore conclude that she was much more concerned with billable hours and treating me like a transaction that should be maximized for her convenience and benefit, at my expense and loss. She seemed to be steering me toward a situation where I lose: she wins. She understands nothing about me. Exasperated, I decided to stop seeing that Psychiatrist: time to solve things for myself.

I decided to sleep on it and then after waking fully rested, I could make some better decisions about whether to write the final chapter of what is turning into my "Requiem for RC," or should I take more risks and continue to dig further into the facts about what caused his death.

I woke up and the next morning decided to continue the impossible task of digging for the truth. I had to prove to myself that by a preponderance of the evidence, that RC really was dead, that he had not committed a high tech version of suicide, that RC had not engineered his own death to escape a losing battle with brain cancer. RC loved life too much for those possibilities to be true: however miniscule a possibility it may have been, RC would never have had anything at all to do with suicide. The explanation of the causes of RC's death would make somewhat more sense to me if it turned out to be the absolute truth that his death was the result of a master plan of assassination, elaborately orchestrated by an identifiable sinister human force that was so well financed that it operated entirely out of RC's control or awareness, something darkly larger than his bright shining magnanimous self and beyond his command of his unimaginably vast resources. I did have enough anecdotal information to suggest that over thirty-seven governmental intelligence agencies wanted him gone; so, even if I could somehow prove that there was a conspiracy to assassinate RC, then the answers would be simpler for me to explain: everyone killed RC. However, I somehow knew the odds that it was a total waste of time for me to ever assume that it could be provable.

Weighing objectively the likelihood of each theory of the cause of RC's death, I accept as the truth, that his death had *nothing* to do with a spiritual event like the Gods smiting RC by sending Angels to hurl lightning bolts at him or his jet. If there was or is a God, or a Supreme-Being or Being(s), then it was obvious to me that the Omniscient Deity was too indifferent to be noticing or to be interested in intervening at the proper and most crucial moment in order to save RC. I decided that it was more likely, that either a Supreme Being either did not exist, or might have been on vacation or sleeping at the time of RC's death. I get another severe migraine-headache whenever I wonder about those metaphysical things, since the rational portions of my intellect argue conclusively that there is no proof Deities exist, let alone whether they sleep or take vacations or have conjured the reality that Angels could possibly dance on the head of a pin before those same Angels would be dispatched to carry out a metaphysical assassination of RC by hurling lightning bolts at him or his jet.

Disturbed by the images of Angels of Death, I did my best to spend a few moments in the science section of one of my favorite book stores, browsing through a couple paragraphs about Einstein's 'spooky action at a distance' and reading a summary of quantum entanglement: some part of my rational mind took a great amount of reassurance from the conclusion that these two snippets of Physics convinced me that Angels did not exist. So it was then a worry-free trip of getting back to reality again.

"Some chain of cause and effect had cumulatively resulted in the events leading up to RC's bizarre death" ... how many times had I written that sentence on paper during the past five years?

Five years out of my life!

It was now high-time for me to wind-down and completely put away the story of RC's life and death once and for all. I had to summarize neatly and succinctly everything that I had collected and composed up to this point in RC's story, whether the information was complete or not. I had to stop asking myself: "why is it that I cannot find the truthful answers to the question of why RC died?" Yes it is true that I wanted to discover the truth, the whole truth, and it is also true that I gave it my utmost effort, but the truth has proven more elusive to me than I expected: so it is now time to admit that I am done with the story.

Perhaps my mentally intense grinding away at the story, once stopped, will allow the migraine-headaches to stop as well.

At this point in my arduous attempt to discover the story of RC's life and death, I decided to walk home from the book store, past the coffee shop, breathe in fresh air just after sunset, and look high into the sky, straining my eyes to focus by counting the first few glittering stars that appeared in the sky over Seattle. To try and ignore my churning stomach, which had endured far too much acid from multiple cups of coffee during that afternoon, I mused wistfully about some celestial ideas from Quantum Mechanics that I could not precisely recall ... it was one of the theories that, in general, when doing science, you could observe some aspects of atomic particles, yet your presence and the act of observing them had some disruptive impact upon the particles you were trying to study. I also tried very determinedly to remember the details precisely from the one time I heard Richard Feynman give a public lecture about his 'sum-over-histories' theory of Quantum Mechanics ... that thoughtful recollection was disturbing however, since it made me then also wonder why I was seemingly destined to exist with this particular burden of wrestling with an impossible story of RC. Why could I not exist in an alternate reality that would be a much happier experience of a path in life where fate smiles graciously upon me? What had I done wrong to deserve the anguish filled hellish experience of the impossibly incomplete and forever-unfinishable story about RC? I knew I was at the end of my best efforts and the limit of my intellectual abilities to write the story of RC, and realized also that I was now ready to admit defeat ... defeat was clear when I resorted to thinking of God Particles and Quantum Mechanics.

What haunted me that evening was the thought that I couldn't avoid wondering whether my investigational journalism efforts poured into the story of RC's life and death was somehow having a catastrophically disruptive impact somewhere in the Universe.

Is it possible that through provocation, RC caused the development of my newfound empathetic conscience?

# Conclusion

## Exit Strategies:
*More Humane than Profitable...*

An "Exit" sign is what I see now when connecting all of the data points describing the story of RC's life and death, at least in my mind, when I convincingly perform mental contortions of holding up a single unifying theme of RC's existence.

A master-craftsman capably engineering a wide variety of unique *Exit Strategies,* he was that and much more.

Unfortunately, that is the only coherent explanation I can offer after five years of toil and tedium. I say unfortunately, since that grand unifying theory seems too simplistic, too reductionist, too defeatist; there must be a more eloquent and more thorough explanation about RC that eludes me.

During my interviews, several friends of RC suggested that his life story should be written by using different literary styles, because RC can only be understood by looking at his story from several different perspectives. Those suggestions, although encouragingly well-intentioned, struck me as missing something essential that I can emotionally grasp as instinctively necessary and is a crucially important element of the story of RC's time on this Earth, yet that *quintessential something* escapes all concrete words of mine. I cannot figure out how to express it, at least not just yet.

Besides, it would be unattainable to write that way about RC; he was far too complex to be described in a story and stuck into boxes of alternative historical descriptions of his life by appealing to some archetypal psychological patterns. There was nothing in the history of human experience that would show RC was living his life as it had ever been in the past already experienced by any human being before him. There was no historical precedent or pattern that would have predicted an RC.

What am I missing? I have so much data about his life and death yet why can't I find mathematically provable patterns in his life and figure out the meaning? Shouldn't all of the parts of all of the data and my understanding of what RC said about the human equation, shouldn't it all add up to a non-zero number and certainly it should not result in an imaginary number? His death should make sense instead of being an apparent senseless incident.

The parts of our lives where humans interact with each other through social systems of economics and finance and the way the world works, all of my life experience taught me that no one does anything unless it is profitable for them. How did humanity profit from RC's death? Everything related to RC would all make more sense to me, if I could prove that his death was not an assassination resulting from complex goals of greedy enemies of RC. The enemies' cause and crusade against RC is beyond my human understanding. Unexplainably and mysteriously, I feel intensely that it is my duty to explain his death, and it should be provable as something more than *accidental cause-and-effect.* That seems to haunt me: the weight of the dual obligation to both solve the mystery of his apparent murder and also to present the content of RC's life so that it will mean something after he is gone.

Who, if anyone, would really care about RC's story?

Whatever RC's sense of his own mortality was, I truly suspect that by the time he was preparing for his final Christmas Holiday, he already had some intimation that the Universe had already forewarned him by the presence of Brain Cancer, that he was at the end of his precious time alive, and the departure moment to check out of life here on Earth would be a matter of days or hours. My wishful thinking would prefer it as a meaningful end to his story, if I discovered a shred of evidence that he somehow caused or engineered the final events of his final moments on Earth to unfold in such a way so that most everything about those last seconds alive would be transpiring precisely on his own terms and that his way of going out of the world would overcome any catastrophic cascade of human errors that cumulated into a mechanized malfunctioning war-machine that killed him.

Or, if it was true that he was specifically targeted for assassination, then too I mean to say that if he possibly had an intimation of that type of impending death, then I would also prefer it if I could have discovered facts that RC knew about the plot to kill him, and since he was the one person I knew of in the world who could choose to be or not to be 'in the wrong place at the wrong time' then he could have chosen to be somewhere else other than the strike-point of his assassination.

I somehow believe that death had been chasing RC for at least a decade since he was first diagnosed with cancer yet RC had made a deliberate choice to finally allow death only on that final Christmas Holiday to catch up to him.

All of that is wishful thinking on my part. Getting back to reality, I do realize that RC had no superhuman make-believe powers: he was human and obviously subject to the same Laws of Physics that constrain all of us humans to a certain death at some unpredictable moment.

From my personal opinion and sober-minded judgments formed by careful consideration of all the data I possessed and analyzed about him, RC had accomplished much in his life: he provided several times over for all of his loved ones, they were all grown and taken care of, he provided technology and financing and training to so many people among so many business entities, he had accomplished everything he set out to accomplish in life. I wonder if he was just plain bored with life, in addition to being terminal with cancer, and so I wonder if then the only remaining challenge for him may have been to search for his true parents and his true relatives, to introduce them to his new wife and then possibly at least know with certainty that if the relatives were all long gone, then maybe their souls and ghostly vaporous selves were preparing an open place for RC to welcome him into whatever Heaven his family believed in. Perhaps if he had an intimation of impending death he would not be fearful but instead be curious, motivated by scientific principles of discovery of the unknown as if he could empirically test whether there may be anything to that ultimately primitive and medieval notion of "death means walking in the spiritual world." The parts of his soul and mind that I assumed would have been whispering to his conscience about an "archetypal RC viewpoint on the human experience of impending death" would likely have included a scientifically rational analysis of possible alternate universes for him to choose to visit after death. At the moment of his death I would guess that he would have been content that he somehow gained certain and true knowledge that convinced him why death was a necessary part of the human life cycle. His already thorough scientific understanding of Entropy aside, he was too much of an arm-chair scientist to rule out the possibility that the Laws of Physics would show him just how very possible it may be that alternate dimensions in space and time are real destinations in the Universe where your soul goes to, after death, taking with it all of the electrons that were once an active and integral part of his thoughts and feelings, and that it might just be possible after death that he could be zipping around the Universe at the speed of light, enjoying newfound freedoms of interstellar flight.  RC would have most likely preferred that everyone take a moment after his human death to wonder if there is the slightest chance that the dead person's soul is not destroyed and how nice it would be if souls could dwell somewhere positively and happily.

If RC had his way, he would have perhaps liked to persuade me to look beyond my current belief, which is 100% observably true, that when this journalist visits a cemetery I find plenty of proof that when a human dies their body ends up just rotting in a grave or their cremated ashes are absorbed into the Earth.

The shadow of time's arrow lengthened enough to silently hit me today: it is the five year anniversary of RC's death.

Several of RC's friends and family members called me today... they frantically asked me if I knew why RC's Estate Lawyers are only now notifying them that there is a security deposit box with unknown contents that RC willed to them.  I was just as perplexed as they were: however I did believe these people were being honest with me, because I also received a similar phone call early this morning, mentioning something about RC's gift to me of my very own safe deposit box.  When I received a phone call from one of RC's Lawyers, informing me that RC opened a safe deposit box in my name over five years ago and that to claim the key to it, I only need to drop by their law office in downtown Seattle, show my identification credentials, sign a legal waiver and then the key and the box and its contents would become mine.

What could RC possibly be leaving to me?  It felt like a creepy turn of events, since it was really happening after his death ... it was as if the dead hands of RC were moving some levers on some machinery, pushing something from the great beyond towards me. After I signed all of the hold harmless agreements and confidentiality contracts at RC's Estate Lawyer's office, I drove speedily to the bank and presented my identification credentials, quickly opening my newly gifted safe deposit box.  Inside the metal box there was a hand written note from RC to me contained within the length of two pieces of standard parchment paper and a Court Recorded Document of a Trust Funding Declaration and Bequest, involving a Trust Fund at his largest bank in New York.

I sat down on one of the expensive chairs available within the safe deposit vault of the bank, reading and re-reading over and over the letter from RC to me.

*"Dear Mister Journalist: Since the beginning of capitalism in Western Civilizations there have been a few humanitarians from a wide variety of countries, ethnicities, cultural and religious backgrounds, that altogether as a group have systematically traveled the Earth, visiting orphanages, selecting as many children as possible to receive a gift of high quality education and a better life by using our generous financial support for benevolent goals. When they become adults, each one is individually invited to work with us, joining a small group of we humanitarians who care enough about all humankind to work tirelessly to make damn sure that as many poor people as possible receive the benefits of capitalism or whatever system that involves a marketplace and an economy in each country. We humanitarians in this group are made up of normal rational people who wish to voluntarily become Trustees, using prevailing laws and peaceful ways of financing and providing technology to everyone who wishes it, on the condition that they act selflessly and benevolently toward others. Because it was not a secret society, and it truly had benevolent goals and values, I joined that world-wide group, of my own freewill, at age fourteen. Being extremely precocious, I was the youngest of their group of overachievers.*

*After displaying my mathematical gifts and engineering aptitude in several ways that resulted in creating helpful technologies, it led to many investors throwing money my way. I took zealously to creating and developing technology while still enjoying developing my math and computer science skills. I discovered also that I was apparently quite gifted in finance and investment, much to my unanticipated surprise.*

*My most enjoyable experience though, was when my efforts to help people lead more prosperous and meaningful lives became fruitful and were successful, when I could see those efforts last among more than one generation of families. I strived to give back the profits from all money entrusted to me and to continue to invest new money for the continued benefit of others, far into their future.*

*I was able to constantly give away more money than was given to me or that I made on my own. After several years of very hard work on my part, the funds never seemed to go away, no matter how hard I tried to get my life back to the preferred condition and simplicity to the time when I was a poor orphan in the world. The money seemed to stick to me no matter what I did. So to pursue my highest calling, my life's work was to try my utmost to help all of humanity, not just the wealthiest and I certainly was never interested to become wealthy as an end unto itself.*

*Ironic, is it not, that I have tried to live life without hardly any money, giving it away by helping people start their own businesses, yet there was always too much money in my life.*

*Mister Journalist, I am leaving you seventy-seven million dollars ... although it is not to you personally, it is in a Trust: you are the Trustee. If you are thinking about all of the expensive things you can do with the money for yourself, take a breath and stop that line of thought for a moment.*

*The request I have of you is simple: I ask that you don't spend more than 5.7 percent of its total value on yourself during your entire remaining natural life for administration and travel expenses and only do that last: go help others first and search the orphanages of the world for the most humane children and young adults you can find, then locate a loving foster family for them to be adopted into and then watch over their highest and best interests and absolute safety as a benevolent Trustee until they are old enough to decide what they want to do with their lives and finance them in whatever they choose to do, provided that the financing will continue only as long as they don't hurt themselves or hurt others.*

*Respect their free-will always.*

*I ask you to take this money, carefully and diligently channel your vanity and self-centeredness outwards by making it into good energy and use it benevolently in the real-world by competing against other philanthropists with the goal of "donating the most" in terms of money.*

*Do all of that anonymously without drawing any attention to yourself: do not turn this into another one of your ego-maniac circus shows with you in the spotlight. Nothing you do with this money should be about you, or your fame and fortune, ever.*

*Remember my view that you are a terrible journalist. No one wants to read about you because of your confessional and self-absorbed, vain and selfish, elitist writing style. Your entire journalistic record shows that you pick up subjects you know nothing about and use those things as a spring-board only to talk about yourself. Other people in the world today are much more interesting than you: their effort to overcome their individual financial and economic problems in order to lead more meaningful and humane lives is all infinitely more interesting to me than what you have written about, at least thus far in your life.*

*Follow my requests so that you can turn your life toward a better direction and at least make a positive difference in other's lives before you depart the Earth.*

*Mister Journalist, you asked me why I did business a certain way during one of our interviews.*

*My answer is this ... I dreamed of a kindly capitalism, nurturing everyone: the world showed me that kindly capitalism only exists in dreams ... the world I want to leave behind for my children to enjoy is a world where people choose to lead their lives and behave as if all people are much more important than profits.*

*Go forth and genuinely help others in a meaningful and truthful way and do so in a completely non-interfering way.*

*Go to several different countries, not just America.*

*Avoid, at all costs, becoming a member of the 'clan of taking' wherever it exists in the world: create instead of destroying, give instead of taking.*

*Do all of these things for me: otherwise I will haunt you forever."*

Finishing the final sentence of RC's letter, my mind produced an auditory hallucination. I heard clearly the phrase *"all Renegade Random Capitalists go to Heaven: but realize there is only one Renegade Random Capitalist."* I fumbled in my suit coat pockets for my bottles of pain medications, but all were empty. I don't remember walking out of the bank. Stunned to the point of speechlessness, I slowly got in my car and drove away from the bank, feeling as if the passage of time had stopped. Searching for the shortest roadway to my Attorney's office, I needed help, and right away. Driving my car erratically, I was consoled for a few moments by listening to the song "Carnival" by Natalie Merchant.

RC's generosity throws into my life and onto my shoulders a burden of colossal proportions. I cannot find the words to convey how heavy that deed of generosity is. Now on my shoulders is an obligation I did not bargain for. Now my nightmares are infinitely more terrible. I can still hear RC's voice: echoing in my mind, haunting my conscience, pushing me into the darkness. I am asking questions, but only silence answers me. Into the silent darkness ... my fear tells me I cannot go there: I want to stay where everything is warm and safe and near the sunlight ... I need the golden sunlight that shines on the easy things for me to find in life ... at this moment it feels like I am being pulled by RC into the netherworld. I have been named a Trustee: now it seems I must go to work for others' benefit.

What was I supposed to do with an impossible story written by a failed journalist interested in solving the mystery of who killed RC?

It is glaringly apparent to me now that my greatest mistake in life seems to be that I didn't have a pre-planned exit strategy for any phases of my life. It is also clear that I was delusional, in assuming that I would successfully write a compelling biographical story of RC and then move on to my next project after capturing fame and fortune ... nothing even close to that, ever happened ... those dreams are ashes now, washing away in the rain.

Damn Him: there is no way to exit now.

**End Notes -** Honorable Mention of other intellectual property

*... Listed alphabetically ...*

**A-10 Thunderbolt** *- jet*
http://www.af.mil/information/factsheets/factsheet.asp?id=70

**Adam Smith** *- philosopher*
http://en.wikipedia.org/wiki/Adam_Smith

**Andrews A.F.B.** *– U.S. Air Force Base*
http://www.andrews.af.mil/

**Angelina Jolie** *- actress*
http://en.wikipedia.org/wiki/Angelina_Jolie

**A.S.A.T.** *- anti-Satellite weapon*
http://en.wikipedia.org/wiki/Anti-Satellite_weapon

**Asperger syndrome** *– autism related condition*
http://en.wikipedia.org/wiki/Asperger_syndrome

**AWACS** *- Airborne Warning and Control System, jet manufactured by Boeing Co.*
http://www.af.mil/information/factsheets/factsheet.asp?fsID=98

**Baklava** *– Greek and Turkish dessert*
http://en.wikipedia.org/wiki/Baklava

**Brigitte Kahn** *- actress*
http://en.wikipedia.org/wiki/Brigitte_Kahn

**Buckingham Palace** *– main Palace of British Monarchy*
http://en.wikipedia.org/wiki/Buckingham_palace

**Buckminster Fuller** *– engineer and author*
http://en.wikipedia.org/wiki/Buckminster_Fuller

---

**C-17** *– cargo jet*
http://www.af.mil/information/factsheets/factsheet.asp?fsID=86

**CF-18** *- jet*
http://www.rcaf-arc.forces.gc.ca/v2/equip/cf18/index-eng.asp

**Camus** *– Albert Camus, philosopher*
http://en.wikipedia.org/wiki/Albert_Camus

**Carnival** *- song, by Natalie Merchant*
http://en.wikipedia.org/wiki/Carnival_(Natalie_Merchant_song)

**Chevy Nova** *– automobile, Chevrolet, U.S.A.*
http://en.wikipedia.org/wiki/Chevy_Nova

**Chinook Helicopter** *- helicopter*
http://www.army.mil/factfiles/equipment/aircraft/chinook.html

**C.I.A.** *- Central Intelligence Agency, U.S.A.*
https://www.cia.gov/

**CNN** *- Cable News Network, TV News*
http://www.cnn.com/

**Comox Air Base** *- Canadian Airport and Military Base*
http://www.rcaf-arc.forces.gc.ca/19w-19e/index-eng.asp

**Connections** *- TV show, James Burke, BBC*
http://www.shoppbs.org/

**D.E.A.** *- Drug Enforcement Agency, U.S.A.*
http://www.justice.gov/dea/index.shtml

**Descartes, Rene'** *– Philosopher*
http://en.wikipedia.org/wiki/Ren%C3%A9_Descartes

**D.H.S. -** *Department of Homeland Security, U.S.A.*
http://www.dhs.gov/

**D.I.S.A.** – *Defense Information Systems Agency, U.S.A.*
http://www.defense.gov/

**D.O.D.** – *Department of Defense, U.S.A.*
http://www.disa.mil

**E.C.** - *Environment Canada*
http://www.ec.gc.ca/default.asp?lang=en

**Emanuelle Chriqui** - *actress*
http://en.wikipedia.org/wiki/Emmanuelle_Chriqui

**Einstein, Albert** – *Physicist*
http://en.wikipedia.org/wiki/Albert_Einstein

**E.P.A.** – *Environmental Protection Agency, U.S.A.*
http://www.epa.gov/

**E.U.** – *European Union*
http://en.wikipedia.org/wiki/European_Union

**Eva Mendes** - *actress*
http://en.wikipedia.org/wiki/Eva_Mendes

**F.A.A.** – *Federal Aviation Administration, U.S.A.*
http://www.faa.gov

**F.B.I.** – *Federal Bureau of Investigation*
http://www.fbi.gov/

**F-16** - *jet*
http://en.wikipedia.org/wiki/General_Dynamics_F-16_Fighting_Falcon

**F-35** - *jet*
http://www.jsf.mil/f35/

**Fairchild A.F.B.** - *Fairchild Air Force Base, Spokane Washington U.S.A.*
http://www.fairchild.af.mil/

**Fareed Zakaria** - *newscaster*
http://fareedzakaria.com/

**Federal Reserve System, U.S.** – *central banking system U.S.A.*
http://en.wikipedia.org/wiki/Federal_Reserve_System

**Feynman** – *Richard Feynman, Physicist*
http://en.wikipedia.org/wiki/Path_integral_formulation

**Fractal Geometry of Nature** – *book by Benoit Mandelbrot*
http://us.macmillan.com/thefractalgeometryofnature/BenoitMandelbrot

**F.O.I.A.** - *Freedom of Information Act, U.S.A.*
http://en.wikipedia.org/wiki/Freedom_of_Information_Act_(United_States)

**Ford Truck** – *Ford, U.S.A.*
http://www.ford.com

**G.A.O.** – *General Accountability Office, U.S.A.*
http://www.gao.gov/

**Ghengis Khan** – *leader of the Mongolian Empire*
http://en.wikipedia.org/wiki/Genghis_Khan

**Greek Ministry of Defense** – *Greek Military Department of Defense*
http://en.wikipedia.org/wiki/Ministry_of_National_Defence_(Greece)

**Greek Orthodox Church** – *Religion*
http://en.wikipedia.org/wiki/Greek_Orthodox_Church

**Harrier** - *jet*
http://en.wikipedia.org/wiki/Harrier_Jump_Jet

**HIPAA** – *Health Insurance Portability and Accountability Act*
http://en.wikipedia.org/wiki/Health_Insurance_Portability_and_Accountability_Act

**Homeland Security** – *U.S. Department of Homeland Security*
http://www.dhs.gov/

**Icarus** – *mythological character*
http://en.wikipedia.org/wiki/Icarus

**Insight** - *book by Bernard Lonergan*
http://www.bernardlonergan.com/biography.php

**J.A.G. Corps** – *Judge Advocate General, U.S.A. Navy*
http://www.jag.navy.mil/

**James Burke** - *author*
http://en.wikipedia.org/wiki/James_Burke_(science_historian)

**Japan Secret Service** – *secret service agency*
http://en.wikipedia.org/wiki/Kempeitai

**Jewel Kilcher** - *singer, songwriter*
http://www.jeweljk.com/

**Jungian Psychotherapy** – *psychological theory and therapy*
http://en.wikipedia.org/wiki/Carl_Jung

**Kareena Kapoor** - *actress*
http://en.wikipedia.org/wiki/Kareena_Kapoor

**Keynes** - *John Maynard Keynes*
http://en.wikipedia.org/wiki/John_Maynard_Keynes

**K.G.B.** – *Committee for State Security, Russia*
http://en.wikipedia.org/wiki/KGB

**Kryptonite** – *fictional radioactive material from comic book lore*
http://en.wikipedia.org/wiki/Kryptonite

**Learned Helplessness** – *depressive condition*
http://en.wikipedia.org/wiki/Learned_helplessness

**Le Cirque** - *restaurant*
http://en.wikipedia.org/wiki/Le_Cirque

**Liberation Theology** – *religious movement to liberate poor persons*
http://en.wikipedia.org/wiki/Liberation_theology

**LIDAR** – *Light Detection and Ranging*
http://en.wikipedia.org/wiki/LIDAR

**Lonergan** - *author*
http://www.bernardlonergan.com/biography.php

**Machiavelli** – *Niccolo Machiavelli, historian and philosopher*
http://en.wikipedia.org/wiki/Niccol%C3%B2_Machiavelli

**Malthus** - *Thomas Robert Malthus*
http://en.wikipedia.org/wiki/Thomas_Robert_Malthus

**Mandlebrot** - *author*
http://en.wikipedia.org/wiki/Benoit_Mandelbrot

**McChord A.F.B.** - *McChord Air Force Base near Seattle Washington U.S.A.*
http://www.62aw.af.mil/

**Meryl Streep** - *actress*
http://en.wikipedia.org/wiki/Meryl_Streep

**Mincemeat Pie** – *dessert*
http://en.wikipedia.org/wiki/Mince_pie

**Mindy Kaling** - *actress*
http://en.wikipedia.org/wiki/Mindy_Kaling

**Monty Python's Flying Circus** - *Comedy TV series, BBC*
http://en.wikipedia.org/wiki/Monty_Python's_Flying_Circus

**Mossad** – *Israeli Intelligence and Special Operations*
http://en.wikipedia.org/wiki/Mossad

**NASDAQ** - *stock exchange*
http://www.nasdaq.com/

**Nash Equilibrium** – *economic theory of John Nash*
http://en.wikipedia.org/wiki/Nash_equilibrium

**Natalie Merchant** - *singer, songwriter*
http://en.wikipedia.org/wiki/Natalie_Merchant

**N.C.A.** – *National Command Authority, U.S.A.*
http://en.wikipedia.org/wiki/National_Command_Authority

**Nelly Furtado** - *singer, songwriter*
http://www.nellyfurtado.com/default.aspx

**Neuro-linguistic Programming** – *one type of psychotherapy*
http://en.wikipedia.org/wiki/Neuro-linguistic_programming

**New York Times Newspaper** – *Newspaper*
http://www.nytimes.com

**Nia Vardalos** - *actress*
http://en.wikipedia.org/wiki/Nia_Vardalos

**Niccolo Machiavelli** – *historian and philosopher*
http://en.wikipedia.org/wiki/Niccol%C3%B2_Machiavelli

**NORAD** – *North American Air Defense Command*
http://www.norad.mil/

**Nordstrom** – *Retail Store*
http://en.wikipedia.org/wiki/Nordstrom

**N.R.O.** – *National Reconnaissance Office, U.S.A.*
http://en.wikipedia.org/wiki/National_Reconnaissance_Office

**N.S.A.** - *National Security Agency, U.S.A.*
http://www.nsa.gov/

**NYSE** - *New York Stock Exchange*
https://nyse.nyx.com/

**O.E.C.D.** – *Organization for Economic Cooperation & Development*
http://www.oecd.org/

**Office of the Comptroller of the Currency** – *Comptroller of Currency, U.S.A.*
http://en.wikipedia.org/wiki/Office_of_the_Comptroller_of_the_Currency

**O.N.C.I.X.** – *Office of the National Counterintelligence Executive, U.S.A.*
http://en.wikipedia.org/wiki/Office_of_the_National_Counterintelligence_Executive

**Oxford University** – *Collegiate University, United Kingdom*
http://www.ox.ac.uk/

**Parminder Nagra** - *actress*
http://en.wikipedia.org/wiki/Parminder_Nagra

**Pascal's Wager** – *philosophical wager about the existence of God*
http://en.wikipedia.org/wiki/Pascal's_Wager

**Patrick McGoohan** - *actor*
http://en.wikipedia.org/wiki/Patrick_McGoohan

**People of the Lie** – *book, by Doctor M. Scott Peck*
http://en.wikipedia.org/wiki/M._Scott_Peck#People_of_the_Lie

**Pike Street Market** - *Seattle waterfront public market place*
http://pikeplacemarket.org/

**Polya** - *author*
http://en.wikipedia.org/wiki/George_P%C3%B3lya

**Pump-It** - *a song by the band Black Eyed-Peas*
http://en.wikipedia.org/wiki/Pump_It

**Quantum Barrier Tunneling** – *theory of Quantum Mechanics*
http://en.wikipedia.org/wiki/Quantum_tunnelling

**Quantum Entanglement** – *theory of quantum mechanics*
http://en.wikipedia.org/wiki/Quantum_entanglement

**R.C.M.P.** - *Royal Canadian Mounted Police*
http://www.rcmp-grc.gc.ca/index.htm

**Red Barchetta** - *a song by the band Rush*
http://en.wikipedia.org/wiki/Red_Barchetta

**Salma Hyek** - *actress*
http://en.wikipedia.org/wiki/Salma_Hayek

**Sea Stallion** – *Helicopter*
http://en.wikipedia.org/wiki/Sikorsky_CH-53_Sea_Stallion

**Secret Service, U.S.** – *United States Secret Service*
http://www.secretservice.gov/

**SKYPE** - *communications software program*
http://beta.skype.com/en/

**Social Darwinism** – *sociological theory*
http://en.wikipedia.org/wiki/Social_Darwinism

**Spacegrass (demo version)** - *a song by the band Clutch*
http://en.wikipedia.org/wiki/Clutch_(band)

**Spinoza** – *philosopher*
http://en.wikipedia.org/wiki/Baruch_Spinoza

**Spooky Action at a Distance** – *Einstein's critique of Quantum Mechanics*
http://en.wikipedia.org/wiki/Action_at_a_distance_(physics)

**Suburban, Chevrolet** – *sport utility vehicle (truck) U.S.A.*
http://en.wikipedia.org/wiki/Chevrolet_Suburban

**Sun Tzu** – *military strategist*
http://en.wikipedia.org/wiki/Sun_Tzu

**Sven Ole Thorsen** - *actor*
http://en.wikipedia.org/wiki/Sven-Ole_Thorsen

**Tasar** – *non-lethal weapon*
http://en.wikipedia.org/wiki/Taser

**The Day the Universe Changed** - *TV series, James Burke, BBC*
http://www.shoppbs.org/

**The Prisoner** - *TV series, BBC*
http://en.wikipedia.org/wiki/The_Prisoner

**The Sandbaggers** - *TV series, BBC*
http://en.wikipedia.org/wiki/The_Sandbaggers

**Tom Sawyer** - *a song by the band Rush*
http://en.wikipedia.org/wiki/Tom_Sawyer_(song)

**Tufte** - *author*
http://www.edwardtufte.com/tufte/books_vdqi

**U.N.** - *United Nations*
http://en.wikipedia.org/wiki/United_Nations

**U.S.A.F.** - *United States Air Force*
http://www.af.mil

**U.S. Department of State** - *United States Office of the Secretary of State*
http://www.state.gov

**Utilitarianism** – *theory and philosophy of ethics*
http://en.wikipedia.org/wiki/Utilitarianism

**Uzi** – *machine gun pistol weapon*
http://en.wikipedia.org/wiki/Uzi

**V.A.T.** – *value added tax*
http://en.wikipedia.org/wiki/Value_added_tax

**Western Tradition, The** – *WGBH TV Series, presented by Prof. Eugen Weber*
http://www.learner.org/resources/series58.html

**Witch-Hazel** – *medicinal plant*
http://en.wikipedia.org/wiki/Witch-hazel

**Wordsworth** – *Author*
http://en.wikipedia.org/wiki/The_World_Is_Too_Much_with_Us

**Zero Sum Economic Game Theory** – *mathematical theory of economic situations*
http://en.wikipedia.org/wiki/Zero%E2%80%93sum_game

www.ingramcontent.com/pod-product-compliance
Lightning Source LLC
Chambersburg PA
CBHW072236190626

46809CB00018B/2565